Set Among
Princes

The Saga of Claudia Rufina

SHARON L. GRIFFITHS

WINEPRESS WP PUBLISHING

Printed in the United States of America

Packaged by WinePress Publishing, PO Box 428, Enumclaw, WA 98022. The views expressed or implied in this work do not necessarily reflect those of WinePress Publishing. Ultimate design, content, and editorial accuracy of this work are the responsibilities of the author.

Unless otherwise noted all scriptures are taken from the King James Version of the Holy Bible.

ISBN 1-57921-316-2
Library of Congress Catalog Card Number: 00-105600

Part I

"He raiseth up the poor out of the dust . . . to set them among princes, and to make them inherit the throne of glory."

I Samuel 2:8

Chapter 1

"I . . . have heard their cry."
—Exodus 3:7

A.D. 50

Footsteps thudded over the rocky path. Rough hands snatched the infant from my scrawny arms, and lifted the heavy wooden beam that pinned me to the ground. Drifting in and out of consciousness, pulse crashing in my ears, I tried to raise my head, but red-hot pain seared through it. Colorful images flitted through the air, then everything faded into black again.

"It's Glwadus!" That sounded like my friend Rhiannon's voice, muted and hollow-sounding, echoing from some distant planet. "There's so much blood. Is she dead?"

Struggling once more to the surface, blurred faces arched over me, with four pairs of eyes that separated into twelve, then back to four again. Some warm, sticky substance oozed across my cheek, and my mouth was filled with dirt. I wanted to cry out, to let them know I was alive, but the words stuck in my throat.

"She still be breathing!" my cousin Branwyn proclaimed. Her long raven curls and pink hair ribbons drooped in tangled disarray, and her bright plaid tunic was slashed by the flying fragments of metal and wood that hurtled through the air.

Bran, a slightly larger copy of his sister Branwyn, wiped my battered face with his woolly sleeve. "Aye. C'mon you, we gotter carry her to her mum."

Rhiannon sniffed, and dabbed at her swollen eyes, leaving odd black and white streaks on her soot-blackened skin. "Glwadus is the bravest girl I know," she said.

The rescue party grasped my wrists and ankles, as my head fell painfully back like a rag doll, the two skinny, reddish-blond braids dragging the uneven ground. Through a blood-colored haze, my half-opened eyes tried to focus on the fleecy white clouds that floated somewhere overhead, and on the massive stones and sturdy oaken timbers of our hillfort.

The ear-splitting roar of the battle filled the air. Oaths and curses mingled with the crackle of tremendous boulders, the flash of fireballs trailing smoke, and steel ballista bolts screaming out of the sky, launched from Roman catapults, that rained down a storm of death and destruction. Mud-and-wattle houses and outbuildings splintered or burst into flames with the force of the onslaught, and the air hung heavy with an acrid layer of thick smoke. Men like hazy ghosts were running, falling, falling, while horses bellowed in shrill terror. Pale corpses lay scattered on the earth, their dead eyes staring, fixed on silent skies. The wounded groaned piteously, writhing in agony, a leg gone, arms mangled, faces ravaged. Their bloodied hands reached out, clawing at the earth. Ill-omened dread gnawed at my heart, and a pathetic wail burst from my throat.

It all seemed hopeless now.

We had not thought that we could lose the battle. My father was Caractacus, chief of the Catevellauni tribe, the one whom the Romans called the "King of the Britons." His only child, I had tried to live up to his expectations of the valiant warrior son that he had always wished for. *But I am a poor snippet of a warrior, and the agony of this day is more than even the bravest man can bear.*

I was not quite old enough to remember the Roman Invasion of Britain; but Mum had often told me the stories, so I probably knew what happened as well as anyone. Seven winters past, we of the Catevellauni Celts owned fine homes in our royal capital at Camulodunum (Colchester), in eastern Britain. My grandfather, Cunobelinus, strove to maintain friendly relations with the Roman emperors, at times placating them with tribute money, never complaining about the high taxes they levied on imports and exports. But when he died, my Uncle Togodumnus refused to pay a penny more! He even made bold to seize cargo from some of the Roman merchant ships that lay at anchor in our harbors.

The Romans had for many years coveted Britain's natural resources. And they were already angry because our troops often went to aid rebellious Celts on the mainland, making it difficult to keep the peace in northern Gaul. Uncle Togodumnus ridiculed the new Emperor Claudius as a weak cripple. It was said that Claudius dragged one leg when he walked, had a spastic hand, and a severe speech impediment.

But Claudius surprised us when four of his best-trained legions swarmed down upon Britain like a horde of rabid wolves! The old fox Aulus Plautius was in command of the legions that defeated the Catevellauni troops at Camulodunum. They brought monstrous camels and elephants, whose obnoxious odor panicked the fine horses pulling our British chariots, causing them to scatter in all directions!*

Two traitorous villains, Berica, chief of the Atrebates, and Cogidumnus, allies of Rome from the south of Britain, had gone to the Emperor to seek help against the nationalist tribes. The vile turncoats betrayed our country, carrying information concerning each tribe's strengths and weaknesses, which was of great value to the Romans. Uncle Togodumnus was killed in a fierce battle along the River Medway. Then, using the territory of the treacherous Atrebates as a supply base, that hook-nosed rogue Vespasian, who commanded the

---

* Cassius Dio

2nd Legion, carried on a bloody campaign against the Dobunni and the Dumnonians in the south.[*]

The defeated British army escaped, fleeing far to the west, where Mum's father Baran was chief of the Silure tribe in South Wales.[†] Her brother Llyr and many of his warriors joined the cause. But the Roman stalked us wherever we went. A battle with Vespasian's 2nd Legion at the Great Doward, along the River Wye, resulted in much slaughter on both sides. Underneath dark, moonless skies the brave warriors with their wives and children slipped away, refusing to yield to the Roman yoke.

Leading our sheep and cattle, we marched northward, following the loops and whorls of the River Wye. Swollen with the melting snow, the river tumbled in a white foaming torrent over a rocky bed of rapids, flanked by boulders stained green with moss. Emerald pools teemed with bright speckled trout, and red deer frolicked on the summits of the jagged, weather-beaten sandstone cliffs that towered above canopies of ancient gnarled oaks. Tusk marks on the fallen trees that often lay across the path showed evidence of the dangerous wild boars that roamed the forest. At night the yellow eyes of wolves glinted as they circled about our tents at the edge of camp, black figures skulking in the shadows, hoping to ensnare a lamb or calf.

Winter-brown twigs and branches slapped against my cheeks and cut into my flesh, as day after dreary

---

[*] Barry Cunliffe, archeologist "Fishbourne Palace"
[†] Llyfr Baglan

day we hacked our way through the undergrowth, ascending into harsh and isolated mountains lost in clouds, whose bold, saw-tooth peaks and tortured masses of rock frowned above a savage land. Bent down with exhaustion, we followed the string of heavily laden packhorses that inched along narrow paths with frozen, precipitous footing.

Our ragged band tracked the River Wye to its source, then struggled across the uplands of Plynlimon, to find the icy headwaters of the Severn. But near the summit of the sinister granite crag, the skies became suddenly overclouded, and a late winter blizzard attacked us. Only a sprinkle of flurries drifted down at first. The wind rose higher and higher, gusting first from one direction then another, robbing me of my breath. It ravaged the tops of the tall pine trees; the branches cracked and split, and came crashing down.

"Secure the animals!" Daddy's voice was nearly lost in the deafening roar.

A deluge of frosted sparks, driven by the wind, burst from the black, boiling clouds, and cut into my flesh like a thousand needles. While helping to chase the sheep into a corral fashioned from ropes, I slipped on a patch of icy rock, and was jerked off my feet. Terror flashed through my body as I slid down, down over the edge of a precipice. Frantically I clung to a jagged pinnacle, in danger of being swept into the bottom of a steep ravine.

"Mum! Daddy!" I screamed, my hands torn and bleeding, numb with cold.

Mum's strong arms reached out and with a mighty effort, pulled me upward to the rim of the precipice, until my foot gained a firm toe hold. She wrapped me inside her woolen cloak, its wolf-fur lining tickling my nose, as the shadows of night crept up the snowy gorges. Her shoulders heaved while she wept quietly.

"I've lost so many children," she whispered, ". . . not this poor lamb, too." She did not know that I could hear her.

We huddled together while the drifts piled high around us, my eyes closed tightly against the terrors of the darkness. Coughs and wheezes echoed through the camp, for many were plagued with respiratory illnesses.

The dawn came slowly.

Abruptly, the clouds parted and the sky melted into blue. I shaded my eyes to see above the sun's garish reflection, as an astonishing panorama unfolded down the snow-covered valley and all the way to the bright waters of the western sea. Alarmed, I sucked in my breath so sharply that the frigid air stung my throat.

"Ayen't much farther we can go before falling off the edge of the world!"

Cousin Bran stood beside me, his eyes flashing with an angry scowl. He clenched his fists together, reddened by the biting wind. "The Romans want to push us into the ocean, to be eaten by the sea monsters," he said harshly. He blew warm breath onto his hands to bring the circulation back, and shook snow out of his raven-black hair. "They need sacrifices for their god, Neptune."

I shivered, but it was not from the cold.

We pushed onward along the Severn, into the rugged territory of the Ordivices. My father, Uncle Llyr, and the other chieftains chose to settle on Llanymynech Hill,* one of the limestone sentinels that guarded the strategic river valley, which had always been the gateway into north Wales from the east. Its steep craggy face was warped and scarred by deep cracks and fissures.

But a wave of discontent rumbled through the camp. "Mighty strange," a Dobunni warrior, Owain, exclaimed, a mutinous expression distorting his features. "Why would we build a fort here? All our victories against the Romans was in the swamps and forests. Our hillforts be no match for their heavy siege engines!"

Rhiannon's father Rhys lifted his red, bushy eyebrows. "Aye. 'Taint prudent. There's other hills higher than this one. Has Caractacus finally lost his mind?"

"He's gone soft-headed. P'raps we oughtta elect a new Pendragon. Someone wi' a bit o' good sense."

A smile played upon Uncle Llyr's lips. "I can explain. It ayen't so strange as it seems. The Druids

---

* University of Manchester archeology dept. *Several locations have been put forth as to the location of Caractacus' "last stand," but they could not match the account given by Tacitus, whose father-in-law Agricola was an eyewitness to the battle. Llanymynech Hill seems now to be the most plausible site.*

have consecrated this hill as sacred ground. We be nearly surrounded now by the Romans and their allied tribes, and have little chance but to enlist the full power of our gods, to annihilate the Legions in one grand, final showdown."

An Ordivice chieftain regarded us with amusement, his broad ruddy face crinkled. "Ye 'Flatlanders' is always a might bit peculiar,'" he said. "But yet we'll see if we cain't find a field or two where y' can plant your grain. And sure many of our young bucks would be proud to help y' fight against the Romans."

The Druids' temple stood on the massive promontory called the Giant's Head, named for the evil hill-giant Ogwf, whose face was outlined in the rock outcropping. Hard by the temple the warriors constructed our hillfort, with approaches and escape routes carefully planned so as to be advantageous to us and unfavorable to the Romans. Gruesome, decaying skulls of vanquished enemies were mounted atop tall poles, their eyes hollow, their shrunken dried lips pulled back over their teeth in a frightful grimace.

Low mud-and-wattle huts and barns quickly sprouted inside the mighty walls of the hillfort. But ours was a good stone-built house cemented with real Roman mortar, and it had a sturdy slate roof. *A real home at last!* Daddy's bedraggled hound dog Julius Caesar padded back and forth, guarding the entranceway, stopping now and then to scratch his fleas, or the pink scars where he had once been mangled by a wildcat, that ferocious creature the Silures worshipped as one of their gods.

13

Sheep-shearing season brought plenty of bright sunshine. My tenth birthday was the best ever! Bran, Branwyn, Rhiannon and other friends joined us for my favorite treat—steaming wedges of apple dump cake, piled high with fresh whipped cream. There were games and footraces, obstacle races, and sack races, and bags filled with wonderful gifts.

"Oh, look, a doll's house and two new dolls to go with it!" I cried out.

"Uncle Llyr made them from pinewood," Bran's mother, Aunt Penarrdun said. "The dolls have jointed limbs, which allows the arms and legs to move."

Folded next to them was a colorful array of tiny clothes. "I helped me mum sew them," Branwyn said proudly. "We made them out'n scraps of wool and linen. Mum painted the doll's faces. And Bran carved the little wooden horses for them to ride."

"Thank you! What fun we will have playing with them."

Another sack contained several new linen tunics Mum had fashioned for me, embroidered with colorful birds and flowers; and the loveliest red-and-green wool plaid one with its own matching fur-lined cloak. There were warm mittens and stockings knit from yarn. Then Mum took my hand and drew me to the open doorway.

"Come and look outside," she said.

Up the long, treacherous path from the valley floor came my father, grasping the lead rein of a prancing Gallic pony with a rough gray coat and a long mane and tail. Daddy led him up to our doorway, and put the reins in my hands. *My pony*!

Overcome with euphoria, I hugged the pony's thick neck. His ears flickered back and forth, and he nodded his shaggy head. "Thank you, Daddy," I whispered. "He is indeed the best present in the whole world. I will call him 'Tywysog.'"

"A pony is a big responsibility though, *plentyn*," my father said. "Y' must feed and brush him properly each day. Mummy and I won't have time to help you."

Then he turned to Mum, and unwrapped bundle after bundle of salt, spices, a card of brass needles and a pair of shears made of real Austrian steel, trinkets, packets of colorful Syrian-glass beads, a silver hand mirror and ivory combs. Mum squealed and fussed over each item, her eyes sparkling.

Daddy chuckled. "The wool merchants arrived in the valley. They gave me a great deal on our fleeces. It seems the Roman army demands so much wool, they have driven up the prices!"

Leading my pony, my friends and I ventured warily toward the open gate of the hillfort and gazed wistfully upon the green meadows where the sheep and cattle fed on the lush grass, guarded by the herdsmen and their hardworking black-and-white sheepdogs.

"Please, Glwadus, let us ride the pony, too," Rhiannon begged.

"All right. But wouldn't it be grand if we could take him outside the walls."

"Mulehead!" Branwyn crowed. "Don't you know the hill-giants will get you!"

Strange superstitions filled these limestone cliffs, honeycombed with mysterious subterranean caves and passageways, haunted by Ogwf the giant and his band of ogres and ogresses.

"The Ordivices say they've got one great eye in the middle of their ugly foreheads. And with their enormous hands they squeeze children to death or smash them on the rocks and eat them," Bran warned, punctuating his words with dramatic gestures. "And they been known to toss huge boulders down on the farms and villages below."

"But none of us has actually seen one," I argued, digging in the dirt with the toe of my boot. "I won't be a prisoner inside this dull gray place forever! I won't!"

I vaulted onto Tywysog's broad back. I tapped his flank, and digging my heels into his sides, made bold to canter outside the thick stone and timber walls.

"I ayen't scared of no giants!" I shouted over my shoulder with a false bravado, my fiery braids slapping stiffly against my back.

Holding tightly to Tywysog's reins, I sailed as fast as his short legs could run, into the brisk wind that ruffled the meadow grasses. Bran, Branwyn and Rhiannon followed cautiously, protected by Bran's big fluffy dog Sandy. The cliff's great overhanging ledges fell away vertically to the plain hundreds of feet below, which was mottled with infinite shades of green. The sun's rays beamed through the gaps and chinks in the fractured clouds. From above, the rounded tops of the beech, oak and hawthorn trees resembled the backs of woolly sheep.

As pleasant summer days lengthened, my friends and cousins and I splashed under the thin ribbon of water that cascaded over the stone-bedded stream, and spied on the deer and the small woodland animals that paused to drink beside the clear emerald pools. We stretched our necks to get a closer look at the somber buzzards that nested in the crevices, and soared high on blunt-tipped wings; and marveled at the halting flight of the kestrels, whose sharp arrow-eyes swept the ground in search of mice and insects.

Rhiannon's father built a see-saw, then tossed ropes over the low-hanging branches of a tree, knotted them securely, and attached wooden slats to make swings. Rhiannon, Branwyn and I soared high into the air, so high that we could snatch the leaves. Then Bran and I shinnied up the ropes, racing each other to the top.

"From here we can fly across the valley and the whole world!" I shouted down to those on the ground.

Branwyn giggled. "Ye do possess the strangest imagination."

"Bet y' cain't climb the rope!"

"Nor would I care to," Branwyn replied smugly, and stuck out her tongue. "It ayen't ladylike."

That night, a loud banging at the front door woke me from a sound sleep. "It's time," a muffled voice exclaimed.

Mum's footsteps padded across the floor, and the door closed gently behind her. She vanished into the air. The moonlight cast murky shadows on the wall while I lay trembling in the darkness, listening to the shrieks of the night birds, and my father's even snoring.

In the morning Branwyn and I detected strange noises issuing from Rhiannon's house, like the bawling of a kid goat. Wide-eyed, we huddled near the bolted entranceway, curious to see what might happen. The door finally burst open, and Rhiannon beckoned us to come inside. Lying beside their mother's bed-box, was a pair of tiny infants, well wrapped in lambs-wool buntings.

"Look what we got," Rhiannon said proudly, pulling back the fleece to reveal two wrinkled faces. Woolly caps covered golden wisps of hair. "Identical twin girls."

Mum sighed, while she scrubbed her hands in a basin of water. "They're so small. I don't know if they can survive." She wrapped hot stones from the firepit in layers of cloth, and placed them in the baby's beds to warm them.

But within a few weeks the twins were strong and healthy, with chubby pink cheeks. Branwyn and I begged to be allowed to help with their care. We delighted in rocking them to sleep, and soothing them when they cried. We didn't even mind washing their linen nappies, and hanging them out to dry. Their bright eyes took in everything, and they seemed to especially enjoy gazing intently at our faces.

"Look. She's smiling at me!" Rhiannon exclaimed.

"Let's take them for a walk," I said.

We dressed them like dolls, in tiny sacques and bonnets Mum had helped us sew from fine linen, trimmed with colorful embroidered threads, and proudly carried them outside. They giggled at Bran's friendly large dog Sandy, and reached out tiny hands to grasp his velvety ruff. His tail thumping furiously back and forth, Sandy followed us into the meadow, where yellow gorse, wild rock roses and wood anemones claimed possession of any bit of earth, raising their stalwart heads toward the sun. The babies cooed and gurgled at the sounds of the red-throated pipits that cheeped among the bracken, and wood larks that trilled sweet melodies underneath the green beech canopies.

"'Tis a nip of autumn in the air," I said, as we turned back toward the fortress.

In late summer, the hillsides bloomed purple with heather, dotted with patches of yellow ragwort. The harvest was soon with us, and every hand was required to assist with the backbreaking labor. All must be safely gathered in before the winter's storms began. In a hurry of work, we stored quantities of grain in pits, enough to carry us through the long dark months. Sweet-smelling hay was packed tightly into every corner of the barns. The livestock were rounded up, and secured in pens, against the threat of deep winter snows. In the smokehouse, a haunch of venison, and joints of beef and lamb hung from iron hooks. The men cut peat and stacks of firewood.

Mum, Cook and I dried herbs and preserved food. I helped fill large pottery crocks with pickles and relishes, and the root cellar was crammed with bins of turnips, carrots, onions and russet apples. We watched from a respectful distance while my father, enshrouded in layers of cloth, smoked out a hive of bees. The smoke quieted the menacing swarm, and they crawled from their hive long enough for him to scoop up quantities of honey and comb. Cook drained the honey into pottery jars, to be enjoyed with oat-cakes and thin barley bread. The wax honeycomb was melted with the fat of an ox to make candles.

At the end of the harvest we had a grand festival. During the day everyone watched the men and boys competing in uproarious, roughneck games. My friends and I sat perched on a wall, loudly cheering on our favorites. In the evening many guests, scrubbed and wearing their best clothes, arrived at our house for feasting. A black iron cauldron filled with meat and turnips and cabbages, seasoned with herbs and onions, was kept simmering over the great crackling fire-pit in the large banquet hall, and a pig turned on a spit, the wonderful aroma wafting through the house amid a haze of smoke.

Torches were lit, and the guests sat in a circle, atop piles of soft fur-skins scattered about the stone floor. Daddy fastened legs into slats to fashion the low tables on which the food was served, set out in wooden bowls, to be eaten with horn spoons. During the feasting, the chiefs talked of war, and reminisced about Britain's glorious past.

"Our grandfathers twice drove that great and fearsome dragon Julius Caesar from our shores!" one old chieftain exclaimed.

"They saved us from the axes of Roman executioners and the dreadful arena; our wives and children from a life of slavery!" Caractacus said.

The bard, an itinerant storyteller, recited legends of ancient heroes. Though we knew his stories word for word, still we enjoyed hearing them over and over. The bard, who was highly respected in Celtic society, brought news from faraway towns and villages as well. Then he began strumming his fingers over the brass strings of a cithara, and broke into a mournful ballad, tears coursing down his cheeks.

After the feasting, the fur-skins were stacked in corners, and dancers whirled on nimble feet, as far into the night the merry strains of the homemade tin flutes, the hammered dulcimers, citharas and goatskin drums echoed across the wild hills. The men became well-drunken, enthusiastically swigging sour-smelling wheaten beer from a common cup passed about the room, only a mouthful at a time, but they imbibed rather frequently.*

There was a growing murmur of angry voices, and a solid thud of fist on bone, as foolish boasting and an old grudge between two warriors erupted into violence. I cringed in fear, and hid in a corner beneath my sleeping furs, as goaded into fury, one of the men produced a knife from his belt. Spatters of blood dripped onto the floor.

---

* Diodorus Siculus

The hubbub swelled as a group of boisterous, sotted warriors gathered around, stomping and clapping their hands, urging them to "Go at it!"

The firelight fell strongly on my father's face as he leapt to his feet, separating the two adversaries. He grasped the arm of the antagonist and twisted it, forcing the knife from his hand. It gleamed, clattering to the flagstones with a sharp thunk. Uncle Llyr jumped in to seize the other culprit.

"Are y' gone daft?" Caractacus thundered, his eyes blazing. A hush fell over the crowd. "We need all our strength to fight the Romans, not each other. I need every one of you! They say we are easily conquered, because we are a quarrelsome, turbulent people, constantly fighting amongst ourselves over the slightest provocation, unable to agree on anything."

"'Tis a curse on us, I sometimes think," Uncle Llyr murmured.

"Ah, we was just having a bit o' fun," one of the combatants replied in a sullen tone.

The waning sunset of that autumn night stained the sky a crimson hue, and the tall, swaying trees sighed mournfully overhead. By the dim light, I finished brushing Tywysog. No dirt or insects were allowed to remain long on his shaggy coat. When I secured him inside the pen with the other horses, he protested with a disappointed high-low whinny.

He stamped his foot and gave his head a shake, blowing puffs of warm steam from his large nostrils into the frosty air. I pulled an apple from my bag and held it out for him. His soft nose and lips tickled the flat of my palm as he took the apple with his teeth.

"Easy, boy," I said, wrapping his blanket around him. "Go to sleep in your nice warm bed of straw, and tomorrow we will have lots of adventures. I will bring you a special treat." His ears perked up, and he nuzzled my cheek as if he understood.

I scrambled along the rough path toward home, pausing as my gaze swept the craggy precipice outside the open gate of the hillfort, and the wide plain below. The last of October marked the end of the Celtic year. It was the time of reconciliation between our sun god Bel and the Great Earth Mother, when the people gave thanks for the abundant harvest, and prayed for the continued fertility of the crops and herds in the New Year. Huge splendid bonfires rose in the twilight, red flaming beacons dotting the whole countryside round about, to help guide Bel through his dark six-month journey through the land of the dead, and to make sure he would find his way back again in spring.

The following afternoon, after finishing my lessons and chores, I sliced an apple and a carrot, and mixed them into Tywysog's bucket of oats. When Cook's back was turned, I stirred in a generous spoonful of honey, then scurried out to the horse pen and called out my pony's name, expecting to hear his familiar, answering whinny. The air hung heavy with the odor of dung, and from somewhere came the forlorn howl of a dog. The familiar tranquil lowing and stomping of Daisy and Buttercup and the other cattle drifted from the barn, along with the monotonous bleating of the sheep. Daddy was there in the barnyard, but Tywysog and several of his finest horses were missing.

"Where's my pony?" I demanded to know.

My father's face was gray, with a frightening melancholy. "Tywysog is dead," he said. His voice broke off, with an odd choking sound. I could not believe the darkness in his eyes.

"No!"

Caractacus turned away, hoisted a bushel of grain onto his shoulder, and hurried off on the heels of a servant to examine a bloated sheep. Hysterical sobs shook my body. Dropping the bucket, I went banging after him, stumbling over the uneven ground, splashing in and out of the mud puddles. I beat my fists on the wooden rail, and kicked angrily at the small stones and the piles of fallen leaves. A hand pulled me roughly aside, and icy fingers dug into my flesh. I found myself staring into Bran's dark blue eyes, keen as a bird of prey, that burned like coals as he brought them close to my face. He clapped his hand firmly over my mouth.

"Don't y' know anything?" he said hoarsely. "Ye have to keep very quiet. The evil spirits be everywhere this time of year, and they will harm you. The Druids took Tywysog. They took my dog Sandy, too, and your father's best horses. The sun god Bel and the Great Earth Mother require blood sacrifices. This year we must offer many sacrifices to Camulos, the war god as well, to ensure victory over the Romans. We lost the battles with the Romans because we have neglected the blood sacrifices. The gods be angry with us."

White-lipped with anger, I shook myself free of his grasp. "It ayen't true!" I shrieked. "Hush up that talk!"

"The Druids' altars must be piled high with bloody offerings.* My father told me the Druids practice their rituals in enchanted sacred groves of wide-spreading oak trees, hung with ghoulish images."

"Liar! I don't believe you!"

"Yet always we must honor the Druids, for they be the mediators between our people and the gods!"

I doubled my fist, and lashed out blindly, striking Bran full in his freckled face. Caught off guard, he staggered backward, hitting the ground with a heavy thud. Spots of angry color showed in his cheeks as he struggled to his feet, and he reached up to touch the blood that trickled from his nose.

"Whether you like it or not, you red-headed mule," he said through clenched teeth, "you share in the blessings, so you must share in the sacrifices."

I shrank from him, a sense of evil pervading the atmosphere. My knees buckled, and closing my eyes, I sagged to the earth, my shoulder blades pressed

---

* Lucan

against the rugged boards of the cattle pen. The tightness in my throat hurt.

But animal blood alone was not enough to satisfy the gods' terrible appetites.

The following night was much worse, for one of Rhiannon's twin baby sisters disappeared; other households were likewise bereft. Sinister jack-o-lanterns carved from gourds grinned from the front entranceways of the silent homes to signify that they had given the ultimate sacrifice.

Rhiannon and I collapsed in shock as the bitter reality set in, huddled together in the corner of that shadowed home. We turned our cold, dead faces to the wall, enrapt in darkness beyond words. Rhiannon's bright blonde hair drooped about her face, and her eyes were red and hollow. The carefree innocence of our childhood lay scattered in the ashes of those sacrificial fires, and we now shared in the terrible blood-guilt of our kinsmen. Her parents' features shone pale, mask-like, haunted by the spell of unutterable thoughts, but meekly, helplessly submitting to the will of our angry, demanding gods.

"Sure there has to be a better way," I whispered.

But there was nothing to be done. For my people had long been "aliens from the true God, His enemies by our wicked works." Yet still He pursued us in His great love. How He longed to reveal all the riches of His glory, and deliver us from the superstitious fears and pagan enchantments that had so long enslaved us!

Chapter 2

The last of the autumn leaves fell like golden tears, as the windswept hills succumbed to the darkening skies of early winter. I opened the door a crack and stared outside, wondering if there was snow in the looming clouds that rumbled from the west. But even the prospect of building a snowman or streaking down the slopes on my new runner sled could not cheer me. For weeks I had fought the empty, sinking feeling inside, the jagged pieces of my heart tormented by the memory of the horrible blood sacrifices; I found no answer that would give me peace.

"It's time for dinner, *plentyn*," Mum called out, as she helped Cook set out thick wooden dishes heaped with steak and eggs, and turnips drenched in butter. "I must say, Glwadus, I'm getting a might bit weary of your gloom and sullen silence these days. When we make offerings to the gods, we must give them in the proper spirit, without grumbling, lest the gods become angry."

Daddy's expression was grim as he burst through the door and dropped a load of firewood onto the stone hearth. He poured heated water into the copper basin, washed his hands and dried them on a woolen towel. The wonderful blue tattoos on his arms danced and rippled whenever his muscles moved.

"I had hoped the Roman Legions wouldn't find us here," he said. His long drooping mustache twitched. "But we've received word that their new commander, Ostorius Scapula, accuses me of raiding forts along the frontier and of harassing the British tribes allied with Rome. He is determined to hunt us down and exact revenge."

"How dare he say that?" I exclaimed with much indignation. "Ye would never do such a thing!"

Daddy stared down at his wooden bowl. He didn't reply.

"We have lost our protective camouflage of hardwood leaves," Mum said, biting her lip. "The hillfort can now be clearly seen from below."

"We must make ready to defend ourselves," Daddy said, as he swiped up the last of the fried eggs with a flat piece of barley bread. "The powerful Brigante tribe from the north country has promised to send reinforcements."

Amid thin patches of freshly fallen snow and tangles of dead brown bracken, our people prepared for the attack that was sure to come. Branwyn, Rhiannon and I helped the other children carry rocks, which would be used as weapons, and stacked them in great piles near the parapet.

"It seems like a game to the younger ones," I said. Tears sprang into my eyes. "They don't remember the . . . other battles."

Branwyn sighed deeply. "If only the Romans would allow us to live in peace!"

At a safe distance, we paused to watch the village blacksmith who stood at his forge, blowing the fire to white heat with his huge bellows. Taking an iron bar from a mold, he heated it until it was pliable, and hammered it into the shape of a long sword. I jumped back when he plunged the glowing red-hot iron into a cauldron of cold water, where it sizzled in a cloud of steam. With a grate and a whirr, he held it against the grindstone to hone it to a new edge, the bright sparks flying up around his head.

Several warriors stood waiting to have their weapons sharpened, including some of the Ordivices, those tough hill-fighters who always carried their stone-headed battle-axes at their sides. Other warriors sat stringing bows, fixing arrowheads to wooden shafts, and oiling the blades of their swords.

It started out like an ordinary day, the pale December sun but a shadow creeping over the dark and misty mountains in the gray dampness of the dawn. The children and I were writing lessons in our great-room, gathered cross-legged on fur-skins. An enormous log burned in the firepit, flickering off the rough timber walls hung with spears, shields, knives, battle-axes, and twig baskets filled with me-dicinal herbs.

The only sounds were the crackling of the fire on the hearth, and the rhythmic tap-tap-tap of Mum's loom, as the shuttle raced back and forth. She was weaving rolls of linen for bandages, while Aunt Penarrdun and a servant carded tufts of flax and spun them into fine threads. The bandages were packed in a carved wooden chest with medical supplies such as splints, a cauterizing iron, brass probes, a retractor and forceps for removing arrowheads, and the trea-sured pair of steel shears that we were never allowed to touch. Mounds of extra blankets and fur-skins were neatly stacked in every corner of the room.

Mum's proper name was Eurgain, princess of the Silure tribe. Her hair cascaded down her back in a dark copper cloud, nearly black, gleaming even in the poor light. My eyes were ordinary blue, but hers were the indigo color of the sky at twilight, fringed with thick dark lashes. A light sprinkling of freckles danced across her nose. Her gown was embroidered with bright threads, and had delicate puffed sleeves that tapered to the wrist. A belt of brass discs carved with swirling quatrefoils cinched her narrow waist. She wore a gold *torque* around her neck, and armlets studded with British pearls, garnets and black jet, some decorated with snakes' heads.

I'd always hoped I would be beautiful like Mum someday. But growing older, I began to realize, with some envy, that it was my cousin Branwyn who would look like Mum, while I was to be tall and red-blonde and gangly like my father's people, the Catevellauni Celts. *How I hate my red hair.* And such hair! Mum had long ago given up trying to tame its perplexity of tangles and tendrils, and would plait it every morning into two tight braids.

My teacher interrupted my reverie. "Glwadus, I need your report," he said, holding out his hand. "Have you finished?"

My downcast eyes traced the familiar pattern of my red-and-green plaid tunic. "No, sir," I said. Bran snickered beside me.

My teacher Ilid's back rose up stiffly, and his dark eyes flashed disapproval. "I won't have to tell your father that you've been daydreaming again, will I?" He wagged his finger back and forth. "You know that he makes no nonsense about education. We lost the battle at Camulodunum partially due to our own ignorance and superstition. The old days are gone. We must read and write properly if we are to reckon with the Romans. When your report is completed, you will stand and recite."

"Yes, sir." I knew he was right. I bent my head over the surface of my wax slate, a furrow of concentration drawing my brows together, and quickly scratched the letters with my stylus:

Helen and Paris were the cause of the battle, but
    Paris left the fighting
to his brave brother Hector, when the Greek army
    attacked Troy, in order

to retrieve Helen and bring her home. Hector loved
 his wife and his little
son, and it was sad when he was killed below the
 walls of Troy, and dragged
behind a chariot. Achilles the Greek lost his life after his heel was pierced
 by an arrow.

When I finished reciting, Ilid smiled. "Very well. It will do, but there is much room for improvement. Now then, we will work with our numbers on the abacus."

The British called him Ilid, but his real name was Eliab Ben David. He was a runaway slave who had once lived in a village similar to this one, populated with radical Jewish zealots, in the mountains of a far-off land called Israel. They believed that their Messiah, a great Jewish king, would arise and save them from the Roman conquerors. Ilid had been sold as a slave after his village was overrun by the Romans, and was sent to work rowing a galley. Uncle Togodumnus had rescued him years ago from one of the ships in the harbor at Duvrae, and set him free. Ilid had much learning, and taught many of the children in our village how to read and write Latin letters, and a sprinkling of Greek, since we Britons had no written language of our own. The Druids believed it was bad luck to write Brithonic words. They kept only verbal records of our history.

My family possessed a few hand-copied scrolls, purchased from the traders for an exorbitant price.

On gray days I would sometimes creep away to a quiet corner. Borne on the wings of Herodotus, Polybius, or Pytheas the Greek, one could soar above the forest, across perilous oceans and deserts, to explore the pyramids of Egypt, the silver mountains of Tartessos, or the golden palaces of Persia and Ethiopia. I knew the way, for Ilid had drawn us a map of the whole world, writing in the names of the countries and large cities, the mountain ranges, and the courses of the major rivers and highways, from the Pillars of Hercules all the way to China.

I had just started reckoning up sums with the abacus, when the long, ominous wail of the signal horn atop the observation tower reverberated throughout the hillfort, like a loud, discordant minstrel, out of tune.

"The Legions approach!" the frantic cry went up. "Every man to his post!"

All men, women and children were expected to assemble on the parapet. My stomach knotted, my skin prickled, and my legs were blocks of wood that just couldn't move. With trembling fingers Mum fastened my warm plaid cloak tightly about my shoulders, securing it with its jewelled brooch. I stamped my feet down into my boots, and together we scampered up the sweep of the parapet to receive our orders, amid the hysteria and confusion, our blood stirred by the eerie wail of the battle pipes. Daddy hurried past, and bent to kiss Mum firmly on the lips.

"I need you to hurl rocks down on the heads of any of those vile Romans who dare to come within range," he said. He turned about, and placed his large hand on my head. "When you were small I named you 'Glwadus,' for you are destined to become a great patriot. You will rear mighty, stalwart sons who shall forever banish the Enemy from this land!"

But I don't feel like a great patriot. Sadly, Mum and I watched him walk away, with his characteristic swaggering gait. He brushed his hand through his mane of golden hair, swept backward and held in place with lime, in the Celtic fashion, and lifted his iron helmet onto his head. Tall and dashing he was. His eyes, which were often gentle, now glittered with intense blue fire. He wore a hip-length belted riding tunic over plaid breeches that tucked into well-oiled cowhide boots bound up with leather ties. A thick gold *torque* encircled his neck, and a long dagger was thrust into his belt. He carried a brightly polished, double-bladed Roman sword, cast from the highest grade of tempered steel.

He raced from one group of warriors to another, inciting to battle, inflaming them with hope, giving courage to the timid. Legendary for his brave daring, and for his silver-tongued eloquence, he exhorted his troops, mentioning several of their illustrious forefathers by name, and reciting their valiant deeds:

> "Your grandfathers were men of iron, who with
>   mighty valor,

twice defeated Julius Caesar, and won back our freedom,
forcing him to sail back to Rome in failure. We also
have it in our
power to triumph. Let us go against them boldly,
trusting in our gods,
that we may forever possess this land, and recover
our departed glory!
This day decides the fate of Britain, and will be a
struggle to the
death. We must triumph, or else be willing to accept everlasting
servitude. Choose to be free, my brothers!"

These urgings were well applauded, and with
frenzied ardor and a brash spirit of adventure, each
gallant warrior swore by his tribal oath that he would
never surrender.

"If we die, we shall die like brave men!" they all
proclaimed.

The gate was thrown open for the white-robed
Druids from nearby Giant's Head to enter. Their
hoods were pulled closely round their faces, and they
carried flaming torches. Some wore massive bronze
crowns. The shaman wore a huge antler headdress;
he would invoke the spirits of the woodland animals by means of a drug-induced trance. The Druids were accompanied by a host of black-robed
women wreathed in mistletoe, their unkempt hair
flying about in disarray. Eyes wild, reddened by the
drug cannabis, they threw their arms rigid above

their heads, calling upon the gods, and screamed out frightful curses on the Roman Legions.

"All the spoils from the battle must, as usual, be dedicated to the gods!" the high priest declared.

Lots were drawn, and every head turned in the direction of a terrified young man who was brought forth, consecrated that day for sacrifice. I made bold to lift my eyes, frozen in horror at the spectacle, as he was led inside the circle of chanting celebrants. The young man struggled vainly to free his arms from the Druids' iron grip, his fingers clawing at the air. But the Druids bound his wrists with ropes and a libation was poured over him.

The seer brandished a gleaming sword and plunged it deep into the young man's back. The victim's body arched forward, and he cried out as he sank to his knees. His face contorted as the pain washed over him. The seer then read the auguries concerning the upcoming battle, based upon the young man's death spasms and the spurting of his blood, as he writhed in agony upon the cold earth.*

"The gods accept our sacrifice!" the seer proclaimed. "A great victory will be ours this day!"

Excitement tore through the crowd. The Druids and the black-robed women, and all our people danced about with lurid glee. But while the people danced, there was one, my teacher Ilid, who stood aloof, tears trickling down his cheeks. I had never seen Ilid cry, and curious to learn why, I crept closer to him.

---

* Strabo

"Gwladus, you know how I love your people," Ilid said, "for did they not save my life? But in years past, some of my Jewish kinsmen turned their backs on the true God and worshipped that demon Bel, or Baal as we called him. He always requires the sacrifice of human blood, and loves to hear the tortured cries of the innocent. The true God, Jehovah, always punished the Jews severely whenever they worshipped Baal. How I long to tell your people of the true God, but alas, I hardly know Him myself."

The sacrificial victim's lifeless body was placed upon an altar of stones, called a *cairn*. Flammable oil was poured over all, and the body was burned with much ceremony. As the black, billowing smoke and scarlet glow of that unholy bonfire soared upward, the Druids joined hands, forming a circle around it. With voices raised to a frenzied pitch, in a confusion of sounds that resembled no human language, they invoked their powerful magic spells, supposedly made stronger by the young man's blood. They smeared the ashes on themselves, while their eyes rolled backward into their heads. Ilid shuddered and turned sadly away.

A black-robed crone came by, carrying a vat of blue paste prepared from fermented woad leaves, and showed me how to dip my fingers into the mixture and trace odd patterns on my cheeks.

"The blue woad will keep you safe from harm," the crone rasped.

From the dizzying heights of the parapet, several columns of Roman infantry appeared, a dark line of toy soldiers advancing toward us from the fringe of trees on the far bank of the river. The tramp, tramp, tramp of thousands of hobnailed *caligae* were now dimly audible, marching in perfect, steady rhythm. Driven on by a fanatical determination, their commander Ostorious Scapula rode at the head of his men astride a proud-stepping black war-horse. The infantry was flanked by a throng of mounted cavalry. Behind them, the horse-drawn artillery battalion, which included a number of terrifying siege engines, rumbled purposefully along on heavy wheels. Close upon them came the baggage train, and the infantry and cavalry of the rear guard.

The soldiers tested the depths of the swirling river, and discovered a place where they could ford with little difficulty. I shivered with dread as the hulking siege engines splashed across, and were hauled up the bank. The troops halted before the splendid earthworks and the deep trenches our warriors had dug to keep them out of range. But the Romans, noted for their engineering feats, always traveled with ax and shovel. Quickly they filled in the trenches and smoothed out the earthworks.

The standard bearers proudly held aloft the gold imperial eagles, the standards of the 14th and the 20th Legions, and the various standards of the cohorts, in a frightening pageant of cold steel and fluttering banners, scarlet capes and horsetail-crested helmets. Ostorious raised the signal for battle. The officers, who galloped on handsome steeds, brandished their gleaming swords to rally their troops, ordering them forward. In a clamor of drums and war trumpets, the whole line sprang to the colors. All our people shouted out in a loud, blood-curdling Celtic yell, clanging our weapons together in a show of high-spirited defiance.

We hoped our massive walls and the steep cliff would be invincible, but nothing could have prepared us for the onslaught of the Roman catapults. Once within range, they began hurling gigantic stones and ballista bolts hundreds of feet into the air. Flame-throwers launched fiery missiles into the vaulted sky and over the wall, each savage fireball attempting to exceed its predecessor in sheer ferocity. Cousin Bran and his rag-tag battalion of half-grown boys tried to extinguish the fires as best they could, armed only with buckets of water and wet sacks, blankets, and green pine boughs. They drove the cattle and sheep into the scraggy forest to fend for themselves.

The enemy's violent assault did not go unanswered. The crowd of defenders lining the rampart hurled back destruction, raining down a volley of arrows, stones and flaming torches daubed with pitch or tallow, exacting death for death, taking a heavy toll on the advancing Roman line. Grisly corpses began to pile up on both sides of the wall. Yet the enemy came on and on.

Mum and I and some of the other women and children began carrying the injured into the safety of our stout home. Mum worked feverishly, mixing salt into a basin of water. With her small-boned but capable hands, she cleaned the ghastly wounds, removed arrowheads and bits of metal, cauterized oozing blood vessels, and stitched together the ragged edges of the skin.

"Cover each wound with yarrow poultice to stop the bleeding and to prevent them festering," Mum said. She showed me how to tie clean bandages around them.

Burn victims were carried in, many of whom were small children and elderly people who had been trapped inside their mud-and-wattle homes when the fireballs had set them aflame. The burns were red or white or charred black, with sheets of dead gray skin hanging off, like pieces of old shedded snakeskin. There was nothing for the pain, and the heart-rending shrieks, and faces contorted with agony would be forever branded on my mind.

Mum soaked the burns in cool water, then with her shears deftly clipped away the dead skin, the traces of pitch, and bits of smoldering cloth. She spread honey over the burns, and wrapped them loosely with bandages. Some with twisted, blackened bodies, and muscle or bone exposed, were burned so deeply that they no longer felt pain. Death sounds rattled in their chests. Mum sagged wearily against the wall, tears flooding her eyes.

"These will likely all die," she whispered. "There is nothing more we can do."

The terrible stench of burned flesh nauseated me. "Please, Mum, I can't bear it anymore."

I dashed back outside and groped my way through the drifting smoke, ears deadened by the hubbub, reaching Rhiannon's house just in time to pull her tiny brother Morgan from the doorway, which was outlined in orange flames. But an infant's cry froze me in my tracks. In the sudden flash that illuminated the room, my eyes focused in horror on the large basket woven from twigs that rested on the floor beside the hearth. Rhiannon's precious baby sister, the surviving twin, was still inside the house!

Glowing tongues of fire licked the walls, curled around the doorframe, and crept across the ceiling in odd tendrils. Pieces of the burning rafters and thatch from the roof melted, and crashed down from the loft, igniting the sparse furniture in the room. There was no time to be afraid. I took a deep breath and, pulling my cloak over my mouth and nose, plunged headlong into the room, keeping low to the ground, scrambling over and around the obstacle course created by the falling debris.

The thick curtain of smoke nearly blinded me, and seared my lungs and throat. Grasping the baby, swaddled in a cocoon of blankets, I sprinted back out of the doorway, just as the roof and walls gave a final groan and collapsed in a shower of sparks. Something heavy hit me in the back, hurling me to the ground. My forehead struck a jagged rock, and my face was buried in the dirt.

Mum screamed when the children carried me into the house, dripping blood, with dirt and crumbled ash clinging to my face, and my hair singed in odd patches. I tried to hold my breath to slow the pounding inside my skull.

"It's nothing, really," I insisted. By this time one eye was nearly swollen shut.

I flinched and gritted my teeth when Mum cleaned the wound with salted water. The prick of the brass needle stung sharply as she pushed it through the tattered edges of the skin, stitching them together with horsehair thread.

"Poor lamb. Y' gave me an awful fright," she said, while she wrapped a bandage around my head, and sprinkled on a few drops of lavender oil, to help restore the senses. Her eyes wouldn't let me go. "Ya've had a concussion. The wound is deep, and ye must be careful not to open it. It will probably leave a scar. And there may be a black eye for a few days."

Suffering people were stretched out over nearly every inch of the floor. Suddenly the door burst open, and Bran and a friend hurtled into the room, carrying Bran's mother, Penarrdun, between them. They laid her down just a few feet from me, a steel ballista bolt having pierced her chest, causing massive hemorrhage. Bran shook with great convulsions, clutching his stomach. Heaving and wretching, he turned away and vomited outside the door.

"I couldn't make the bleeding stop," he choked. "It just wouldn't stop."

"I can't breathe," Aunt Penarrdun whispered. "Bran . . . I . . ."

Her face was bluish-white, stained by dark pools of blood that dripped from her mouth and gurgled in her throat. She gasped deeply, hungry for air, as death crept in. Mum wept, cradling my aunt's head in her arms. She felt for a pulse, but there was none, for she had already slipped into the great unknown.

Mum gently closed the sightless eyes that had become fixed in their sockets, and shrouded the body with her cloak. Bran, bleeding profusely from a wound on his leg, threw himself down beside the lifeless form, utterly overcome by the loss of a loved one who could never be replaced. There were no words to comfort, no way to undo death.

"The gods have cursed us," Bran said. His voice sounded cracked and hoarse, his face gray as stone.

I curled into a ball, snuggling beneath my sleeping fur, and pulled it tightly like a wall about my ears, trying to shut out the terrible groans of the wounded, and the rattling breaths that grew weaker, weaker. Sure it was all some death-filled nightmare. I would awaken, and everything would be all right again with us. Everyone screamed when a huge boulder struck the roof. Pieces of shattered slate rained down. Ilid sat propped against the wall beside me, his leg encased in bandages. His chin was sunk low against his chest, all the color gone from his face.

"What will they do to us if we are captured?" I asked him, between sobbing breaths.

Ilid would not look at me. "I wish you wouldn't ask me that, child," he said, laboring over the words. The furrows on his brow deepened. "It is the custom of the Romans to sell the women and younger captives into slavery. Women live out their dreary lives doing the most menial tasks, and their children can be sold away. Men are often sent into the arena to fight with gladiators or wild beasts, or are assigned to a slow death in the galleys or the mines. When they find out I am a runaway slave, they will crucify me on a cross, a terrible death reserved for the most unfortunate souls. When my Jewish people were defeated in battle, most of them killed themselves rather than be taken alive."

"But you didn't kill yourself."

"I longed to die with my family, for there seemed no more reason to live. Yet I found no peace in death." He drew from beneath his cloak a flask of yew poison that hung on a leather cord around his neck. He caressed the smooth surface of the flask, and removed the stopper with his teeth. "But oh, to end it all, to have done with everything . . ."

He stared down at the peculiar scar on his hand, where the Romans had long ago branded him as a slave. My hand crept into his. "Ilid, I cain't bear to watch you die. You are the best teacher in the world, and have taught us many things. P'raps your Messiah will come to save you, like you always said He would."

Ilid shrugged, and sighed deeply. His black eyebrows twitched. Slowly he covered the flask, and tucked it back inside his cloak. "Can you fetch me that candle, Glwadus?"

I wrenched the candle from its bracket on the wall, and brought it close to him. Ilid plunged his hand into the flame, and held it there until the flesh was raw and bleeding. His face twisted with pain, but the loathsome slave brand was obliterated. I slathered honey over the burn, tied a bandage around it, and brought him a beaker of chamomile tea.

I stepped across the prostrate forms, and wandered to the doorway to gaze outside. Thousands of ballista bolts had plowed up the ground in rough furrows, and many of the buildings lay in ashes.

"Ostorious Scapula sent scouts to determine the vulnerable points of our position," a warrior said to another as they hurried by. "Many Romans have been slithering like serpents up the slope, and are massed in the adjacent forest."

The thud of axes, the ring of hammer blows, and the crash of timber gave me great uneasiness, as the legions set themselves to constructing assault towers. The Britons sent down a barrage of fiery arrows and flaming canisters of pitch, in a desperate attempt to burn the wretched towers, but they were covered with fire-resistant fresh animal hides, and they would not ignite.

There was a scraping sound of grappling hooks, as the Romans attempted to pull down the ramparts, one stone at a time. Our warriors tried to capture the hooks with heavy ropes. But by now our ranks had been badly decimated, and the men were running out of ammunition. A great battering ram, its end encased in iron, slammed against the crudely built wall. The perpetrators had strapped their rectangular shields onto their backs like turtles to form a protective shell so that our weapons were of little effect.

Far up the slope of the hill, most of our women and children and the Druids streamed toward the escape route that led into one of the subterranean passageways belonging to Ogwf the giant. It would take them into the thick pinewoods, far from the battle site. I thought about joining them, but still felt dizzy and light-headed. And it was already too late for flight.

The assault towers were brought close to the wall, and a barrage of ballista bolts cleared the defenders from the parapet. Drawbridges slammed down, and an avalanche of red-and-silver Roman soldiers swarmed over the wall, in a blur of iron-shod boots and fine steel weapons. At about the same time, the battering ram crashed through the northern wall.

Instantly, hand-to-hand combat broke out at every point. The heavy Roman infantry attacked in close formation, slashing with swords and javelins, battle-axes and pikes. Our poorly armored warriors for a short time stood firm against impossible odds, rushing wildly upon the enemy, heroically sacrificing their lives so that many of the younger men could flee to safety, under cover of the thick smoke, to fight another day.

"Close the gaps!" the chieftains shouted to the warriors still standing.

The battle pipes moaned wearily, still calling to arms, but I no longer heard them. Overpowered by numbers and superior weapons that mowed them down in heaps, the decimated British line staggered and retreated slowly, thrown into confusion, until they finally crumbled. Those who remained alive, all hope gone, fell to their knees and begged for mercy.* A few cast themselves over the brow of the limestone cliff.

I pulled the door shut, and collapsed on the floor like a wilted flower. Mum extinguished the candles, and amid the tortured groans of the wounded, we awaited our sad fate, having gambled and lost all. The Druid seer had lied, and our grim gods who ever demanded sacrifices of the things we'd held dear had proven to be ineffective in a final showdown. There was no more to be said.

A distant tumult rang out, telling us that the soldiers had discovered the treasures of the Druids' temple. It was said to contain finely ornamented gold and silver, huge cauldrons of beaten bronze, pearls and ivory, incense, many coins, precious green-stone and black jet, and ingots of copper, lead and other minerals.[†]

"They will set the sacred groves afire!" one old Briton lamented.

Somehow it didn't matter anymore.

The door sprang open, and a group of Roman soldiers cautiously entered the room, swords drawn, torches held high. They wore plated armor, fastened with leather straps, over red kilted tunics. A burly centurion was in command, recognizable by his broad belt, set with metal-crested plates, and by his

---

* Tacitus
[†] Barry Cunliffe, archeologist, "The Druids"

vine staff, or swagger stick, which he slapped smartly against the palm of his hand. He had the haughty bearing of a career soldier, his features chiseled and hardened by years in the rigorous army camps.

With weary, haunted eyes, Mum turned to face the soldiers, and addressed the centurion in halting Latin. "I am the wife of Caractacus," she said, gentle and bold. "We are here only a few women and children and wounded men."

"On behalf of the Emperor Claudius and the citizens of Rome, we claim all gold and valuables as property of the State," the centurion, Marcus Favonius Facilis, stated. "Then you have permission to carry your wounded down the hill, but quickly."

Mum and the others removed their beautiful gold *torques*, their armlets, brooches and pearls, and placed them in a leather sack. The thieving wretches even opened our root cellar and smokehouse, and plundered all the winter food we had spent so much time preparing.

The Roman medics and our vanquished warriors rushed to gather up the wounded, pulling survivors from the heaps of tangled corpses. Uncle Llyr came and pried Bran from the side of his lifeless mother. Llyr caressed his dead wife's cold cheek, and bent to kiss her forehead, his grimy face tracked with tears. He replaced the cloak over her still form, and resolutely hoisted Bran, his leg wrapped in a bandage, onto his back.

Darkness closed in, and clouds of black smoke and heat enveloped us. I could scarcely breathe or

see ahead, and stumbled several times over the mutilated bodies and the charred timbers and debris
that choked the path. The gullies and mud holes
were stained red with blood.

A barrel-chested Roman medic who carried a
torch scooped me up with one thick, hairy arm. "My
name is Olympas," he said.

He led our weary band down the treacherous
hillside. I might have been afraid of him, but he had
a kind, warm smile, with just a few teeth missing. A
sprinkling of silver shimmered in his tight black
curls, and his dark eyebrows stretched in one continuous line across his forehead. Radiating from his
eyes was a gentle expression of peace that I had never
before encountered. Weary and cold despite the heat
of the flames, my head fell back against his shoulder. We passed by a ravaged grove of trees and
burned and blackened fields, thick with Roman
guards. Olympas sang softly as we trudged along:

> *To Him that stretched out the earth above the wa-
> ters;*
> To Him that made great lights
> The sun to rule by day,
> The moon and stars to rule by night;
> He hath not despised the affliction of the af-
> flicted;
> Neither hath He hid His face from them;
> But when they cried unto Him, He heard.

The enemy camp had been hastily erected inside an earthen and timber breastwork, palisaded with sharp, pointed sticks. At each corner of the fortified square stood a tall wooden watchtower. A few torches were mounted in iron receptacles, illuminating the Praetorian "street." Their tents were made from leather hides, and stretched out in row upon row on either side of the street. Armed sentries patrolled the perimeter of the camp, appearing as ghoulish silhouettes in the shafts of silver moonlight.

"These arrogant, swarthy Roman conquerors reek of garlic and the rancid olive oil they use on their hair," Uncle Llyr said in Brithonic. "And their day's growth of stubbled beard make their jowls appear blue."

The proud Britons, melancholy in defeat, avoided each other's baleful eyes. Triumphant voices filled the night air as the Roman soldiers celebrated our destruction, roasting one of our steers over an open fire-pit, their faces disfigured by the peculiar light. The soldiers gossiped about the plundered treasures, about comrades that had not returned from battle, and argued over which of them had fought most bravely. I could understand most of what they said, with my school Latin, though their lyrical accent sounded strange, and all their words were embellished with hand gestures.

"Most of the British survivors escaped, which means there will be few slaves to sell to the merchants who follow the army," one of them complained.

Ostorious, their commander, received us courteously outside his tent, seated beside a small, lamp-lit table. He was arrayed in full ceremonial regalia, with an insignia that indicated high rank, and an enormous gold military ring on his hand. He had powerful shoulders, and an iron gray shock of hair above a furrowed brow. His black eyes, with weary pouches underneath them, showed neither pity nor cruelty.

"The Emperor Claudius has decreed that Caractacus, his relatives, warriors, freedmen, and servants must appear in Rome," he said. He nervously shuffled a pile of parchment sheets. "But Caractacus has not been found among the living nor the dead, and some are beginning to believe he has escaped again. Until such time as he is apprehended, you must all remain my prisoners at Wroxeter."

He waved one hand, motioning his camp orderlies to give us something to eat.

Mum, Uncle Llyr, Bran and I slumped on the frigid ground, our fingers curled around battered red Samian-ware bowls filled with lukewarm polenta, a thick mush made from wheat, oats, or whatever grain was available. It was said to be nutritious, but its taste was frightfully bland. I choked it down, though hard it was to swallow.

I closed my eyes as a soldier clamped cold iron bands around my ankles, joined together by short chains to prevent escaping. By torchlight, Uncle Llyr and any able-bodied warriors were forced into a labor battalion to dig graves for the many fallen soldiers. The sight of hundreds of Roman corpses laid out in long rows in the moonlight filled me with a savage vengeance that gave some comfort in the midst of my bleak thoughts.

Mum and I were escorted to a large hospital tent, where we cared for our wounded until long into the night. I stuffed straw into mattresses, and shuffled about with buckets of cool water and some thinned polenta in case any were able to take nourishment. But despite our best efforts, many of them died that night.

In the black hours before dawn, I finally surrendered to exhaustion, and swinging my cloak about my shoulders, crept outside the tent to take the air. Yet the stench of death and blood and charred flesh lingered in my nostrils. My thoughts drifted toward Branwyn and Rhiannon and the others. *I hoped they found their way to safety, and were not eaten by the hill-giants.*

The flames still flickered on the craggy cliff-top, a huge funeral pyre that consumed the corpses behind the dark stone battlement. The fire grew smaller and smaller until it twinkled above me like a dying star. I pondered how my old life was vanishing with that light.

The world will collapse, and the skies will fall upon me! But nothing happened.

As I turned to go back inside the tent, my feet became entangled in the leg irons. I tripped on the uneven ground, and pitched forward, giving the wound on my forehead a nasty rap. Reaching up to touch the fresh blood seeping through the bandage, my lip quivered, and I was unable to stop the flood of tears. My head throbbed, as if an Ordivice battle-axe was beating against my eye sockets, and seemed to swell up large enough to fill the whole universe.

The night sky was decorated with a host of twinkling stars. "Sure there is a good and kind God who created them all!"

I couldn't know it then, but the One who made that universe watched over me that night, whispering His love in the stars and in the gentle breezes that crept down from the hills. He knew the number of each oddly singed hair on my head. And He longed to wipe away every tear streaked with blood, blue woad, and black soot, that stained the cheeks of a ten-year-old British girl who stood on the northern fringes of the known world.

Chapter 3

A.D. 51

I can't believe Caractacus has abandoned us," Uncle Llyr said bitterly, narrowing his dark brows. He paced back and forth in our prison cell, chains clanking, the echo reverberating from wall to wall.

"He'll return to rescue us soon," Mum said. "You'll see. He was expecting help from the powerful Brigante tribe. The queen's husband is his good friend, and he was to supply us with reinforcements. They will continue the attack from the north. We shall have our revenge, and all wrongs will be righted."

"I don't know that the whole tribe of Brigantes could capture a garrison this strong," Llyr said, running his fingers nervously through his wavy, blue-black hair.

"We shouldn't have risked a pitched battle," Rhiannon's father, Rhys, said, moaning over and over. "I always said we should've kept to the piney woods. We should've kept to the piney woods."

"Just listen at y' all!" I exclaimed. "Why can't you see that it wasn't Daddy's fault. 'Twas the gods who cursed us! After we sacrificed and did everything they demanded. We tried. We couldn't have tried harder. What good are all the Druids' worthless spells and charms?"

Mum clamped her hand firmly over my mouth.

Our band was held captive at Wroxeter, the capital of the recently conquered Cornivii tribe, in the fortress which was at that time the headquarters of the 14th Legion, built to stand guard over the Welsh borders. Huddled side by side, our cloaks worn thin, we passed the hours in anguish and despair, nauseous with filth, tormented with cold and hunger. Glittering specks of snow blew in at the tiny barred window, as winter days ran together in a series of blizzards and squalls and dreary sleet. Time lost all meaning, and was measured only by each pale sunrise that sprouted above the trees and the ominous, forbidding towers in an endless succession. Blue skies were forgotten, and the hills appeared haggard and defeated.

Spring came, with a deafening crash of thunder and a gray curtain of rain. Amid a flutter of robins' wings, the patches of dirty snow finally melted into the earth. Mum and I agonized over the fate of my father, for we had heard no news of him. Mum's mind, given to extremes of mood, took a dreadful turn, at times shutting out all sights and sounds. Doubled over with grief, she wore a pallid expression, and such a vacant stare. Her silent melancholia intensified my own fears. Jumpy and irritable, I often awoke screaming with nightmares, forced to relive the terror of the battle over and over, as pictures and memories came rushing back.

A clamor of hoof-beats and excited voices drew our eyes to the tiny window. "Something stirrin' outside!" Uncle Llyr exclaimed.

He hoisted me onto his shoulders so that I might see out the bars. "It seems that messengers have arrived from Londonium," I said, gazing carefully about.

The next morning the soldiers loaded us into a *carrus*, a mule-drawn wagon generally used for hauling military baggage. They cursed and mocked us, and prodded us with the points of their spears. With a great deal of whip-cracking and screeching of axles, the heavily guarded cavalcade rumbled along Watling Street, the paved road that led to Londonium. There was no escaping. I died a death, and dared not give a backward look.

The road sliced in a straight line through a broken terrain of ravines cropped with gray boulders and round rolling hills. Skeletons of once-haughty Celtic fortresses now lay in utter ruin. But I was shocked to see acres of wild, forested flatlands newly cleared, giving way to scattered farmsteads with cultivated fields planted with barley and wheat. Thriving under Roman rule, smallholders with their wives and children labored behind the plow, breaking up the heavy earth. Herds of horned black cattle and shaggy, rough-coated sheep grazed peacefully in well-watered meadows. Steadily chewing, they lifted their heads and peered at us curiously over the tops of silvery drystone fences.

"Odd is it, I had thought there could be no Britons left in the tragic land east of the Severn River," I muttered.

Watling Street swept through the prosperous market town of Verulamium (St. Albans), a Catevellauni settlement that had early made peace with the Emperor Claudius. The tree-lined streets were laid out in an orderly grid pattern, similar to the Roman garrison at Wroxeter. There was new construction everywhere. The town's main street was crowded on both sides with rows of narrow timber shops connected by long covered colonnades that extended along the storefronts, to protect customers from the weather.

Farther east, Roman engineers had transformed a low-lying marsh into freshly plowed fields of black-earth islands. Bordered by an extensive network of dark drainage ditches and artificial waterways, they floated in perpetual flatness toward the far horizon, their banks dotted with violets and marsh marigolds. Red-bills and long-legged herons with piercing cry flapped their wings violently, gliding low across the streams.

On the third day we reached Londonium. Before the Roman invasion, the town had been little more than a small trading outpost. But now, with its favorable location, it was quickly becoming a bustling center of commerce and a major supply base for the Roman army stationed in the interior of Britain. Near the long Claudian bridge that spanned the pale-brown Thames, a jumble of ugly, unpainted warehouses loomed above the sturdy oaken quays that lined the busy waterfront. Longshoremen, speaking a babble of languages, transferred cargoes into and out of huge-bellied *corbitas*, or merchant vessels, and mule-drawn wagons.

"It seems the Britons, too, now crave the luxury imported items thought necessary for their new 'civilized' way of life," Ilid said. "Traders have come from all over the world, hoping to earn a quick *denarius*."

Two blocks north of the Thames, we marveled at a grand vaulted building constructed of blocks of smooth quarried stone, held together with mortar. "It is called a 'basilica,' "Ilid explained. "It contains law courts and government offices, the money-changers, and small exclusive shops tucked along the insides of the walls."

"T'was built by giants," I breathed, staring up at its wide portico and rows of columns, and its narrow amber-glass windows.

A cold gray fog rose from the river, drifting across the Forum, an open square paved with large rectangular stones, surrounded by temples, shops and huge statues perched on high pedestals. Wisps of fog rolled over the baker's stall, the boot makers, the confectionary, the fishmongers and the craftsmen's booths, making everything ugly. Pottery shops were stacked high with red Samian-ware bowls and amphorae. Busy shoppers navigated the Forum, some dressed in togas or Roman-style tunics, while others wore British plaids and breeches. But many were arrayed in a curious combination of both styles.

Bran read an inscription carved on the front of one of the temples. "It is dedicated to the Emperor Claudius!" he exclaimed. "These fools be worshipping him as a god!"

Uncle Llyr's head fell, his dark beard resting on his ragged chest. "The Britons have already forgotten what freedom was," he said.

The fog followed us up a low hill overlooking the river, and drifted between the tall houses that leapfrogged up grids of terraced paved streets and muddy trackways. Most were thatch-roofed mud-and-wattle homes, but a few were constructed of brick or stone with red-tiled roofs. The fog invaded the iron gateway of the rather second-rate military camp where my family and our warriors were imprisoned, and even crept in through the barred window.

Quite unexpectedly that evening, the prison guards threw open the great creaking door, and my father was shoved roughly inside the cell, gaunt and sallow- skinned, dragged down with chains. This dirty, unshaven man bore little resemblance to my handsome father. His eyes were troubled, the blue fire vanquished, like a burned-out candle flame.

Mum gave a strangled cry, and rushed into his arms. "My love, I feared ye were dead," she murmured.

His square shoulders shook with sobs as he, dread champion of Britain, clung to her desperately, like a small child. "Many of the Brigantes wanted to help," he said, "but Queen Cartimandua had already made peace with the Romans, and was obliged to surrender me to Ostorious . . . I didn't know . . . if I would ever see you again."

I felt sick to see the ugly scars and bruises where he had been beaten. He flinched when I touched his arm, and a violent cough wracked his chest. The brilliant dash that had once characterized him was gone, perhaps forever. An agonized stare came into his eyes, and drops of perspiration beaded his forehead, as he flashed back over the dreadful memories. I knew he saw once more the grisly corpses on the battlefield, and heard again the terrible cries of the wounded.

"I'm afraid it is all over with us," he said, his voice only a dry whisper. "So many dead . . ."

A thin morning rain drizzled over the curious crowd that gathered on the wharf to watch as Caractacus, King of the Britons, and his followers were hauled aboard a massive vessel called a *corbita*, humiliated and chained like wild beasts, banished from our native land. Many were unsympathetic to our cause, for there had always been rivalry among the British tribes.

One of the onlookers laughed harshly. "It's time indeed that Caractacus finally got his comeuppance!"

"Ayen't been any love lost over the years between the Iceni and the Catevellauni," his hard-faced companion echoed, with a frightening hostility.

"Nay, nor the Atrebates," another said in a mocking tone. "Even with the higher taxes, I say we're better off with the Romans!"

A lightning-flash of anger jolted through me, and my hands curled into tight fists. My father, who had once ruled these waters, was now struck down, a tyrant's slave! A *century* of about one hundred soldiers accompanied us on board ship, and I was glad to see that the kindly Olympas was among them.

"After twenty years of military service, I have finally earned honorable retirement, and am going home to stay," he told me.

The ship rolled from side to side then, causing me to trip over my ankle irons, and sent me sprawling across the slanted deck.

Olympas pulled the centurion Marcus Favonius aside. "Please, sir, I know it's not my place to say it, but the woman and child pose no threat, once we are out to sea. The chains have rubbed raw festering wounds on their ankles, which must be tended to. Could they perhaps be released from their chains?"

"As you wish," Marcus Favonius replied. "But I will hold you personally responsible for them."

"Thank you, sir," Mum said, as the iron shackles fell away with a clinking grate. "We will never forget your kindness."

I reached down to rub my sore, swollen ankles as the ship, leading a small flotilla, sailed down the great muddy Thames, around the rocky headland, then out into an open sea the color of smoke. The screams of the overly friendly seagulls that escorted us drew my eyes upward. Some of them perched, short-necked and serene, in the masts and yardarm, while others circled and wheeled overhead, underneath gray clouds.

The last glimpse of my homeland was the white chalk cliffs of Duvrae. I bit my lip and watched until they were just a blur in the swirling mist, fading away, fading away. Hot tears ran down my cheeks, and mingled with the cold salt-spray of the Channel. Olympas' thick black brows narrowed when he saw my tears, and he attempted to amuse me by pointing out the interesting features of the *corbita*.

I had never traveled on a ship before. In happier times, the cadence of the white-capped waves slapping against the stout wooden hull might have intrigued me. The hull was some 200 feet long, and rose at great arcs at each end, but higher in the lofty stern, where the helmsman steered the craft by means of a huge, spade-shaped rudder. The wooden mainmast creaked and groaned, and the immense square sails billowed under the strain of the northerly breeze that blustered across the deck. The sails were gaily colored, with blue and white stripes, and the Roman eagle symbol was painted in red and black. A bright figurehead in the shape of Neptune, the sea-god, straddled the prow.

"What about the sea monsters, O-lympets?" I asked, suspicion in my eyes, sure that the terrifying creatures were lurking in the briny deep. "They will swallow us, boat and all!"

Words failed him for a moment. "Oh, I don't think they ever swim this far east," he replied, struggling to maintain a serious expression.

The sailors were a surly and quarrelsome lot, with dark, pinched faces and blackened teeth. Some of them knelt on deck, playing dice, cursing and laughing uproariously. They spoke with longing of the waterfront *cauponae* at Boulogne, where a man could get a drink of strong wine. Staggering with the motion of the ship, Olympas and I rambled to the foredeck, past crates full of barking and whining British hunting dogs, which were highly prized in Europe.

The spiny cliffs along the Gallic coast loomed like pallid specters. A lighthouse, visible for miles, was perched high upon a rocky pedestal. "The lighthouse at Boulogne was built about ten years ago," Olympas said, "during the reign of Caligula. Its blazing fire by night, and pillar of smoke during the day, guides the ships into the harbor, and reduces the danger of traveling these treacherous seas. It is modeled after the famous lighthouse in Alexandria, which was called one of the Seven Wonders of the World."

"Yes, I know it from Herodotus," I said, proud to show that I was not a wooden-headed savage.

The fishermen were coming in, and the late afternoon sun was beginning to paint the western skies in a dazzling explosion of flame red, pink, purple, turquoise and orange, streaked with thin cirrus clouds. Along the stout granite quays that jutted far out into the sea, the gently swaying masts and rigging of the large war ships and cargo ships that lay at anchor in the placid harbor appeared as black silhouettes against the sunset. Small native dinghies and hide-covered coracles bobbed about in their moorings, beside the distinctive flat-bottomed ships with leather sails that belonged to the seafaring Venitii Celts of northwest Gaul. Longshoremen and blue-clad sailors stood clustered among the crates and barrels and coils of rope.

I wrinkled my nose at the overwhelming odor of salt-sea and fish that mingled with the smell of tar and pitch. The blue-green waves, marbled by white sea-foam, swept the wide, pebble-strewn beach that was burnished gold in the setting sun. Nets were spread out to dry among the seaweed-covered rocks, or were stretched out like enormous spider webs, hung from the doorways of the weather-beaten cottages. Repairing their nets, red wizened men sat throned on upturned hulls of fishing boats that had been hauled onshore.

A detachment of soldiers rode down from the garrison in the upper town to meet us, followed by mule-drawn wagons, having been alerted by signal from the ship. The Tribune conferred with Marcus Favonius, as we were loaded into the wagons.

"It is well known that Caractacus has many allies in northern Gaul," the Tribune warned, "especially among the fierce Belgaic Celts."

Marcus Favonius sighed. "By this time, surely every Celt west of the Rhine knows why we're here. And my men are in no mood for any more fighting. But the Atlantic route, with its unpredictable winds and storms, poses a greater threat to our safety, in my opinion."

Bran laughed. "Just listen at them. The Romans are cowards," he said, "and prone to seasickness, it is said. The Phoenicians from Carthage traded with our people for hundreds of years, using the Atlantic routes, sailing right up into the Severn estuary. They needed our tin to make their bronze metal."

The Tribune traced his finger along a map, or *itinerari*. "If you take the new Claudian road, traveling through northern Gaul swiftly at night, I can provide you with an escort as far as the fortress at Amiens. I shouldn't think the Celts would attack at night, for fear of injuring their fine horses, especially in the marshy ground."

In a glare of torches, and a jingle of harness straps, the leather-covered *carrus* clattered along the road toward Amiens. Its groaning wheels hit every bump and jolt. Afraid to go to sleep, I lay burrowed in the straw, wrapped in a blanket, gazing out the flap of the wagon, into the strange, yet somehow familiar starlight. The black tips of the lonesome pines stood out dimly against the indigo sky.

In the morning I woke to the rumble of the Imperial hoof-beats echoing across the landscape. Brown-robed, wayfaring peasants who plodded along on wooden feet were forced to scramble to the side of the road as the military cavalcade approached; likewise the rude farm wagons, drawn by teams of sluggish gray-brown oxen, carrying heavy loads of milk and vegetables and lumpy sacks of wool to be sold in the next market town. But our procession was forced to stop when we encountered a slow-moving shepherd and his dog, driving a huge flock of bleating, newly shorn sheep and spring lambs across the road.

Bran snickered. "Silly sheep, the only beings capable of bringing the Emperor's grand army to a halt."

Late that afternoon our wagons approached the Seine, a silvery ribbon that looped around green hills and dark islands overgrown with poplars, oaks and evergreens. The glistening river so mirrored the painted hillsides that the waters themselves appeared to be in leaf. It was dotted with flat-bottomed riverboats and barges, pulled upstream by teams of oxen harnessed to each barge by a tow rope. Led by a bargeman, the oxen, resigned to their arduous lot in life, trudged on a path alongside the river, straining against the current, hauling the heavily laden boats upstream.

On the other side of the river, barges floated downstream, easily with the current, loaded with fine pottery, glassware, casks of wine, and other luxury items from Italy and southern Gaul. Two bargemen stood atop each craft, running from bow to stern, dipping their long poles beneath the flat surface of the water, guiding the boat away from rocks and sandbars.

The Claudian road followed the river for some distance. Whitewashed stone farmhouses presided over reddish-loam fields planted with wheat, rye and millet in patchwork blocks of green and gold sloping gently down toward the river. A plump farm wife paused to wave a cheery greeting, while she deftly tossed grain from a bucket to a throng of geese and chickens scratching about in their untidy pen.

The fiery ball of sun was melting below the horizon, when we finally glimpsed the tiled roofs of Lutetia Parisoreum. The iron-shod wagonwheels rattled along the wooden bridge that led to the stout-walled village, centered about an island in the middle of the Seine. Mauve-gray stone cottages hung with ivy, and trimmed with yellow, green or blue shutters marched along narrow, cobbled lanes. Wisps of blue smoke curled skyward, mingling with the delicious cooking odors that hung over the rooftops and wafted through the arched alleyways.

"Lutetia Parisoreum is home to many of the bargemen," Ilid said.

Filthy and exhausted from the rigors of the marathon journey, we were grateful to make camp inside the thick walls of the fortress of the urban cohort. Envy overcame me, watching the soldiers going to refresh themselves in the steaming bathhouse.

"The soldiers feast on fine fare," I said bitterly, "but our pinched bellies will see now't but polenta again."

Clouds swept across the moon, and a thin rain began to fall, hitting the leather roof of the wagon with a soft swishing. I reached out into the cold raindrops, and rubbed them over my grimy face and arms. Bran sat huddled between Daddy, Mum, Uncle Llyr, and Ilid. Mum gently stroked Bran's dark curls, while he sobbed quietly, missing his mother.

As we neared Lyon, or Lugdunum as the Celts called it, a greater prosperity became apparent. Grand colonnaded villas, painted in white or pastel colors, perched upon every hillside, surrounded by row after row of apple, plum, cherry, apricot and Gallic peach orchards. Grapes hung in unripe clusters, trellised on rectangular frames, flaunting their first scant tinge of purple.

Lugdunum, well situated at the junction of the Saone and Rhone rivers and five major highways, was a bustling trading port, and the most populous city in Gaul. The sun reflected off the white marble temples and tall statues that crowned the acropolis; the nearby theater, its adjacent music hall and the new library. Just across the Saone, a huge new amphitheater was under construction.

Geraniums and begonias brightened every corner, blooming pink, yellow, red and blue, in pots and window boxes, or cascaded over balconies and archways. My stomach groaned as we swept past a *patisserie*, with small honey cakes and sweets stacked on shelves in neat rows. I put my nose to the delectable odor of fresh fried cinnamon pastries cooling on a tray. Nearby stood a green-grocer's shop, its great bins heaped with bunches of carrots, turnips, a pyramid of bright red apples, raisins and chestnuts. There were baskets of figs, enormous golden pomegranates, dates, and almonds from the southland.

A crowd had gathered, blocking traffic as we neared the slave market. Atop a high wooden platform, prisoners of war—or those unfortunate creatures who could not pay their debtors—were poked and prodded, bought and sold like meat. Three men were brought forward, each with an iron collar about his neck, connected together with a chain.

"Sturdy German field workers!" the auctioneer declared. "Who'll start the bidding? How much for the lot?"

Faces sullen, wretched with misery, the three were sold and led away, their chains rhythmically clinking. Then a girl about my own age was dragged onto the slave block, a beautiful child with long golden hair.

"Mama, don't let them take me!" she sobbed in harsh pitiful gulps, her arms outstretched, lifting up wild, suffering eyes.

"It's my name on the account!" the distraught mother cried, reaching out for the child. "Her papa is dead. I done the best I could. Please just take me, and let my baby go free!"

But her creditors had no mercy. "If only people would repay their bills," one of them said, "all would be well. We've heard all the excuses, madame, and waited patiently, I think."

A fat, balding man with a brutal countenance paid money to the agent and, grasping her chain, he led the child away, while the creditors counted their money with glee. The girl's eyes were fixed upon her mother's face until she disappeared from view. The mother was sold to a different buyer.

The scene awakened in me a new wave of melancholy thoughts. I shuddered and averted my eyes, for the slave block would surely be my own fate when we came to the end of our journey. I would probably never see Mum or Daddy again. An icy hand of dread gripped my heart, squeezing the life out of it.

We made camp inside a strong fortress. The army paymaster was handing out small sacks of silver *denarii* to each of the soldiers. Instead of polenta that evening, Olympas brought baskets heaped with chicken delicately browned, loaves of fresh-baked bread with a crock of sweet butter, a wheel of golden cheese, clusters of dates, a sack filled with apples, and *baklava*, a delicious concoction of honey and nuts, folded between thin strips of pastry.

We sat about a small campfire after dinner, underneath a canopy of bright stars. Savoring every crumb, I nibbled my *baklava* slowly, to make it last a long time.

"Are the gods of the Romans greater than our Celtic gods?" Bran asked Olympas, between bites of a rosy apple.

A shocked silence fell over our group. Nevertheless, it was a question that needed answers, for we had all wondered the same thing, but were afraid to put it into words. A strange expression passed over Olympas' face.

"Not everyone believes in the old gods anymore," he said. He drew from his leather pouch an odd little book with copper covers and parchment leaves. It

was written in Greek, but Olympas translated into
Latin as he read along:

> He is despised and rejected of men; a man of
>   sorrows, and acquainted
> with grief: and we hid as it were our faces from
>   him; he was despised,
> and we esteemed him not. Surely He hath borne
>   our griefs, and
> carried our sorrows: yet we did esteem Him
>   stricken, smitten of God . . .

"From the book of Isaiah," Ilid said. "I haven't
heard those beautiful words in years. May I read it?"

Olympas handed him the book, but tears sprang
into Ilid's eyes so that he could not see the words.
He clasped the book tightly against his chest, and
rocked back and forth.

"We Christians believe that the words speak of
Jesus Christ, the promised Messiah, who came into
the world that all men might be saved," Olympas
said. "Our Gentile people once knew the true God,
but we turned our backs on Him because we pre-
ferred to follow our own sins. Men changed the
glory of God into idols, and worshipped the creatures, not the One who created all things. But God's
Son Jesus came into the world to pay the sacrifice
that God required for our sins, the debt that we
could never pay."

"I saw Jesus once," Ilid mused. "He went about
to all the villages of Judea, healing the sick, giving

sight to the blind, and even raising dead men to life. Some thought He was the Messiah. But when He said we should forgive our enemies . . . that's where I lost interest."

Olympas nodded. "But when the Lord Jesus comes to live in our hearts, He helps us to forgive. When I was a young infantry soldier, I was stationed in Jerusalem. I cannot forget that terrible day when we scourged and mocked the Son of God, and placed a crown of thorns upon His head. Then our wicked hands nailed Him to a cross; and sitting down, we watched Him suffer. Yet some of His last words were, 'Father, forgive them, for they know not what they do.' "

Olympas' voice broke, and pain crossed his eyes. He had to turn his face away.

"After He died, our cohort was assigned to watch His tomb," he went on, "since the Jewish priests thought His followers would steal His body and claim that He had risen from the dead. In the night, a great earthquake rumbled beneath our feet, and a white and shining angel appeared. We fell to the ground as dead men, unable to move or draw our swords. When we awoke, Jesus was gone. God had raised Him from the dead."

"It's an interesting story," Ilid said. "I have often searched for the meaning of life. But we Jews had supposed the Messiah would deliver us from our enemies. It is difficult to believe in a martyr God."

"Their hearts were so cold, as in the days of the prophet Jeremiah, that the Jews didn't realize God was displeased with them. When Jesus would have saved them, He was rejected. But His suffering is what makes Him familiar with our own troubles," Olympas said. "He passed through darker days than we could ever know, but with unshaken trust and confidence in His Father God. If we only believe on Him, repent and ask Him to forgive our sins, He will someday take us to live in His beautiful home in Heaven. It was difficult for me to believe at first too, but He has become more real and precious to me than life itself."

I didn't understand it all, but my last thought that night was of a God named Jesus Who cared about all our sufferings. For the first time in a long while I slept peacefully and did not awaken screaming with nightmares.

The captives were loaded into a *corbita* for the journey down the Rhone to the Mediterranean Sea. The prosperous towns along the river bustled with shipwrights, and warehouses for the wealthy textile and timber merchants. The hills and meadows gave way to weatherworn rocks, savage canyons, and black volcanic lava cones petrified into strange and twisted shapes, pointing starkly to the sky.

The ship passed underneath a three-tiered aqueduct towering nearly 2,000 feet above the river, stretching eastward from majestic snow-covered peaks. The aqueduct rose starkly against the clear azure sky, like the massive spine of some monstrous beast. I shrank back in terror, unable to comprehend the principles of engineering that held its enormous arches in place.

"Sure it will topple down on our heads!" I shrieked.

Olympas threw back his head and laughed, then clapped me on the shoulder. "Nothing to worry about. I can assure you that the Pont is quite sturdy."

Nearing Arles, the air became noticeably warmer. Villages sprouted in the midst of almond, cherry, and olive groves, basking in the radiance of the nearer sun. Fields of bright vegetables poked their heads through turned red-brown earth. Farther along, acres of heath and dark clumps of withered pine yielded to salt marshes that stretched into a monotonous expanse of water grasses, and tall swaying reeds with tasseled tops. The murmuring streams resonated with the shrill cries of egrets and brown pelicans, cranes, bitterns, and vivid pink African flamingoes.

I tasted salt on my tongue as, with a huge spread of sail, the ship navigated into the crinkled waters of the Mediterranean, shimmering blue, blue, fairy blue sparked with silvery diamonds. It seemed I stood on the edge of the world. The jagged cliffs along the coast alternated with the curve of white sandy beaches. The *corbita* threaded its way among bleached, craggy pinnacles that rose out of the sea, with blighted scrub bushes that clung miraculously to their sides, their branches gnarled and twisted by the bold westerly winds.

But after several glorious, sunny days on the Mediterranean, the rugged shores of Italy loomed on the eastern horizon. The soldiers gave a loud cheer, but my spirits plummeted.

Olympas shielded his eyes with one hand, and gave a great sigh. "We made good time," he said. "Less than a month, all the way from Londonium."

The *corbita* churned toward the magnificent lighthouse and the granite breakwaters of the new Claudian artificial harbor at Rome's port of Ostia, and slipped through the wide entranceway. A colossal statue of Neptune, poised with his three-pronged trident, stood on a grand pedestal, upreared against the sky. His painted stony eyes seemed to stare directly at me, mocking as we passed him by.

Chapter 4

The foul stench of raw sewage and dank moldiness assaulted me as our band of captives descended the narrow rock-hewn steps that led to the subterranean dungeon, known from ancient times as the Carcer Mamertine. I squeezed Mum's hand tightly as we entered a deathlike, decaying tomb formed from solid volcanic stone. A guard held high a torch, its bold yellow light slicing through the thick, fetid darkness.

Our chains were attached to rings that were fastened into the wall. I shivered as the door's massive iron bolts clanked into place. The guards' footsteps echoed on the stairs, then disappeared. Surrounded by the menacing black ceiling and walls, my throat full of sobs, I clung frantically to my mother. But I could not see her face. Ghostly specters of those who had suffered and died there lingered in the shadows still.

"It feels like being buried alive," I said, expecting to suffocate at any moment. "We will all die."

A low voice emerged from the darkness. "Where you hail from?" one of the prisoners asked my father.

"We are Celts from Britain," he replied.

"Ever heard of Vercingetorix? He was the most famous of the Celtic chiefs from Gaul. He starved to death down here, in the time of Julius Caesar," the prisoner said. "All hostile kings were starved, strangled or beheaded, including Aristobulus, the Maccabee prince from Judea. Jugartha the Numidian king went mad with fear during his conquerors' grand victory parade."

Below us, through a small round opening was another cell; agonized screams and groans ascended through the iron grate. "Down there, the guards say, deranged murderers roam about, awaiting execution," the garrulous man chattered on. "Most are bound for the arena. The Emperor Claudius is an avid attendant at the 'games.' He never gives quarter to an injured gladiator, and delights in flashing the death sign."

"When do the guards bring food?" my father asked.

"Food!" our cellmate hooted. "There is none served in the Carcer Mamertine. Even rats avoid the place! Here your friends are expected to bring you food."

"But we have no friends in Rome," I whimpered. "We will starve."

But Olympas had not forgotten us. Late that afternoon he arrived with three women. "These are some sisters from my church," he said, "Priscilla, Claudia Procula* and Pomponia Graecina Lucina."

My mouth popped open, for I had learned enough about Rome to know by their patrician names and by the wide purple border of their white garments that they were high-born women. Pomponia Graecina "Lucina" (Light-bringer) was the wife of Aulus Plautius, the old general who had led the invasion of Britain.[†] But these gentle invaders were armed with baskets of food, an amphora of water for drinking and washing, blankets, and an oil-filled lantern.

"None of them looks like they could be Olympas' sister," Bran whispered.

"Claudius is planning a public holiday, and a grand victory celebration," Olympas said. "The conquest of Britain was one of his greatest achievements, and he is determined to make the most of it for his own political glory. The name of Caractacus, the infamous 'King of the Britons,' is on every tongue, from the Senate, to the basilicas, to the *cauponae*. Tales of your daring feats have lost nothing in the retelling, I might add."

"Claudius is unpredictable," Pomponia Graecina said, "sometimes kindly, sometimes quick to anger.

---

* *Some believe this Claudia was the sister of Pontius Pilate's wife. Sadly, many early church records were destroyed during the last and worst persecution of Diocletian in 302-313 A.D.*

† Opinion of Giovanni DeRossi, archeologist.

He was crippled by disease as a child, and all his life he has been pushed aside, even by his family, due to his disabilities. He is ridiculed by many who feel that the real power in Rome is held by his wife Agrippina and his freedmen, Pallas and Narcissus."

Priscilla washed my face and brushed the tangles from my matted hair, which reeked of dirt and sweat. She was beautiful, taller than the others, with honey-colored hair pulled back in a simple republican-style chignon. Her tunic was of plain homespun linen. Though she must have been immensely wealthy, she wore no gold or precious jewels, and her dark blue *stola* was fastened at the shoulder with only a plain brass brooch.

"I have a son and daughter about your age," Priscilla murmured. Tears rolled down her cheeks.

"Why do y' come down into this horrid place to help us?" Bran asked curiously, over a plate of turnip greens and roast beef.

She smiled. "It is because we have Jesus in our hearts."

Priscilla and Claudia Procula dabbed at their eyes, while Olympas knelt to pray, his hands clasped in front of him. "Father God, Creator of Heaven and earth, Who delivered Daniel from the jaws of the lions, David from the sword of Goliath, Israel from the Egyptian scourge, hast power to deliver these captives from the hands of Caesar."

I counted every one of those cold stone steps that fateful morning when the guards led us up from that terrible dungeon. I squinted when the sudden sunlight struck my face. Poked and prodded, we were herded into rough open wagons, to be put on display for all to see. Bright-colored banners tied up along the parade route, fluttered in the breeze. Chanting rhythmically, the high priest offered prayers to the pagan gods.

"We worship you, oh gods of Rome!" he declared, sprinkling sweet, cloying incense upon an altar. Clouds of incense would be burned to the gods during the entire parade.

Dancing priests and priestesses accompanied the procession, arrayed in vivid costumes. Military bands played martial music, and the standards of the 14th and 20th Legions were proudly displayed, while Marcus Favonius and his soldiers marched in perfect step. Grand flower-studded floats depicted the storm and attack of the hillfort at Llanymynech.

The haggard British warriors occupied the first of our rude wagons, defeated, frightened, unable to so much as lift their heads. Piled high in the next wagons were the plundered swords and other trophies of the battle, the gold *torques* and gemstones and British pearls, and all the priceless treasures from the Druids' temple. Mum and I, Uncle Llyr, Ilid and Bran followed. Daddy rode in the last wagon alone, standing tall and brave, his head held high, seemingly without fear. The intense fire burned again in his eyes, revealing to everyone in this garish world that he was far from vanquished.

Thousands of jeers and catcalls ascended from the surly spectators, their heads wagging back and forth. They lined both sides of the street, or stood on the steps of the temples, or hung out of windows and balconies, desperate to catch a glimpse of the man who had scorned the power of Rome for eight long years.

"Wild-haired savages!" a woman shrieked. "They *should* be locked in cages!"

A youngster laughed. "Such outlandish clothing. Barbarian breeches! Why don't the men wear proper togas?"

Mum was trying to be brave, but she wore a terrified expression, her cheeks pallid. My heart pounded with smothering violence. Wondering if I might go mad, as Jugartha the Numidian did, I buried my face in Mum's lap, where I couldn't see the cruel faces of the mob. Her arms felt rigid with fear as they tightened about my shoulders.

In the Forum of Augustus, I made bold to raise one eye to peer at the hideous statue of the war god, seated high upon a pedestal in the Temple of Mars. Passing under an arch, the procession reached the Forum of Julius Caesar. The Saepta Julia, an enormous two-storied shopping pavilion, sold an astonishing array of luxury items. Above it all, the grand Temple of Jupiter dominated the Capitoline Hill, its gleaming white marble façade and golden dome standing out in sharp relief against a perfect azure sky.

The rough wagon lumbered through the old Forum, an expansive marble rectangular plaza ornamented with hundreds of statues of gods, emperors, generals and mythical animals. We swept past the Curia, or Senate House. Tall and stately, with its massive bronze doors, it was undoubtedly the most important building in the world. Nearby stood the broad Basilica Aemilia, a courthouse and money exchange.

"Yonder's the Temple of Janus, whose doors are closed only during times of peace," Ilid said. "And a column known as the Golden Milestone marks the spot where all the roads in the Empire converge, and from where all distances are measured."

"'All roads lead to Rome,'" Bran said sarcastically.

"I've had all the heat and glare of the sun-struck buildings I can stand," I said.

Sweat poured down my face and neck. It was a relief when the wagon finally clattered up the Clivo Palatino, which afforded a bit of shade, toward the fabled Imperial Palace. Mounting up in five or six tiers, story by story, it was rich in ornamentation, gardens and gushing fountains. Wide porticoes stretched all along the outside of the palace, supported by massive marble columns.

The odd procession wound through the bleak and narrow lanes of the Suburra, past gray tenements that presented rather a dreary picture. Patrician Street was a curious mix of bakeries, groceries and workshops, intermingled with handsome town-homes belonging to wealthy senators. Their tall facades with few windows faced the street. Statues, bright-painted frescoes and bas-reliefs decorated the elaborately wrought iron-grilled entranceways.

Marcus Favonius led us across a field in front of the camp of the Praetorian Guard, or Castra Praetoria, a strongly fortified garrison with mighty gates and towers, which quartered some ten thousand troops. The open field was the parade ground where the soldiers practiced their military exercises.

Amid a roll of drums and a grand flourish of trumpets, the Praetorian Guard stood to arms, drawn up in formation. The Most Excellent Emperor Tiberius Claudius Drusus Nero Germanicus Caesar Himself, Protector of the People, was seated on a huge platform. Attired in a gold and purple embroidered robe, he held an ivory scepter in his palsied right hand. While sitting down, he appeared to be a dignified man, with protruding ears and a fine head of white hair, not nearly as terrifying as I had always imagined him to be. His wife Agrippina sat at one side, and on the other was his general, Aulus Plautius.

When we passed close to the platform, my father made a courteous bow, and asked permission to speak. The Emperor raised his hand in assent. He seemed surprised that Daddy spoke perfect Latin:

Would that I had come to Rome as a friend and
    ally, as my father
always did. My brother and I vastly underesti-
    mated the power of
the Empire and the wisdom of the great Emperor
    Claudius, a man
more wise and powerful than Julius Caesar him-
    self! But I was lord of

men, horses and lands; what wonder that I parted
  with them reluctantly!
If I had shown myself to be a coward and surrendered without a struggle,
neither my defeat nor your victory could have
  been as glorious! My heart
failed me as I gazed upon your golden palaces
  and your marble temples.
You Romans hold all the wealth and treasures of
  the world in your hands!
Why then do you covet our humble dwellings?*

A bemused expression passed over Claudius'
face. He turned to Aulus Plautius. "What would you
say if I released this brave king?"

Aulus Plautius slowly lifted his thick, bushy eyebrows, which gave him a stern expression, and au-
dibly sucked in his breath. "He has been a worthy
opponent, and fought fairly. I have no objections,
my lord, if that is your will," he said.

Claudius chuckled. "It would certainly violate
all precedent," he said. "The Senate will probably
be furious with me. Obviously, with his great lead-
ership abilities I cannot allow Caractacus to return
home, as he might take up arms again, but we can
keep him here under light guard."

Claudius addressed my father. "You and your
family shall be set free, and may live out your days
at the palace as my honored guests, with full Roman citizenship and a proper pension."

*Tacitus

85

Claudius turned to his aides, calling for a wooden sword. "I shall bestow upon you the wooden sword of peace, the gladiator's symbol of honorable retirement. Your soldiers and freedmen may return home if they wish. Llyr, as prince of the Silure tribe, must work to bring about peace, for that tribe has not yet submitted. He must impress upon his people the folly of resisting so formidable a power as Rome."

Claudius waved one hand toward Bran. "Llyr's son will remain here, as is our policy concerning sons of client kings, as a hostage to ensure his father's good behavior. He will finish his education, and in the course of time, return to Britain. You, Caractacus, and your family must swear an oath never to return to Britain, since it would make me out to be a fool for trusting in you. And, goodness knows, there are enough who already think me a fool!"

As the centurion stepped up to release our chains, a tremendous cheer went up from the crowd. We bowed on our faces in homage to the Emperor, and to his wife, Agrippina. Then Claudius held out his scepter toward me. I was frightened, not knowing what to expect; lifted up with hope, yet afraid to believe our good fortune. The centurion lifted me in his brawny arms, and set me down before the Emperor. Claudius smiled and placed one hand, which trembled a bit, on my head.

"We have a custom, that if we set someone free, and bestow upon them Roman citizenship, then we should also give him our name. From henceforth you shall be called 'Claudia.' You may come to live in my fine palace, and go to school with my little girl, Octavia, who is just about your size."

Dazed, I fell to my knees. My dull gray skies gave way to bright horizons. "Thank you, kind Emperor. It would be a great honor."

I immediately liked the Emperor's daughter, Octavia. She was a year older than I, with friendly dark eyes and soft brown hair framing her little heart-shaped face. The princess took my grimy hand and showed me all about the palace, our voices echoing off the yawning marble walls.

Everywhere I looked was found a new and greater wonder. My bewildered mind could scarcely take it all in. Immense fluted pillars swept majestically toward the frescoed ceiling, ornamented with beaten gold and inlaid with bands of ivory. The highly polished floor was finished in a geometric pattern of black and white marble.

Masses of roses and lilies and ferns erupted from tall Chinese vases. At one end of the magnificent throne room the Emperor's gold and marble chair, overlaid with precious jewels, was mounted on a dais, underneath a purple silk canopy, sparkling in the light of golden candelabrum.

In the sunlit atrium, water in a multi-tiered fountain spewed from the mouths of strange mythical beasts, and cascaded from one marble vessel into another, surrounded by exotic flowers and lush greenery. Octavia and I scampered around it and came face to face with a small band of adolescent boys. Startled, I found myself staring into the most amazing pair of brown eyes, like the eyes of a wild fawn, fringed with absurdly long, dark lashes.

But the beautiful eyes mocked me. "Look at the funny little girl in the barbarian plaid tunic," the boy said. "Whoever heard of wearing plaid?"

"And what is that ugly red scar on her forehead?" one of his companions jeered. He was a stocky boy, with blemished adolescent skin, cold steely eyes, and a bulbous forehead.

My face crumpled like a worn-out autumn leaf. These spoiled rich boys could never understand the suffering my family had endured. My mouth felt dry, as if it was stuffed with wool. Tears sprang into my eyes, but I quickly dried them with the edge of my sleeve, hating for them to see me cry.

Octavia was aghast. She addressed the blemish-skinned boy. "I would expect such cruelty from you, Nero." Then she turned to the pretty brown-eyed boy. "But you, Manlius Acilius Glabrio Pudens, when your father hears about this, he will thrash you within an inch of your life! This happens to be my friend Claudia Glwadus from Britain, who is a real princess of the noble Catevellauni people!"

"I don't care if she's Cleopatra!" Nero shot back. "She's an ugly, skinny little girl. And she needs a bath!"

"Girls!" Pudens grimaced. "They can't ever take a joke."

The boys turned away to find other amusement, and soon busied themselves trying to push each other into the fountain. Octavia and I dashed down a long corridor with room after room leading off to the sides, their doorways framed with deep swags and draperies of red, blue and purple silk brocade fringed with gold.

"Pudens' parents are Manlius and Priscilla," Octavia said. "They belong to the sect of the Christians.* Their family is extremely wealthy, having made a fortune in the salt trade over the centuries, for our people use tons of salt for such things as preserving meat."

Octavia paused beside a fruit bowl set on a sideboard, and handed me an apple and some grapes. "But Manlius and Priscilla give most of their money to the poor, and actually live quite simply. They even freed all their slaves! Can you imagine? The name 'Pudens' is a common nickname, or *cognomen*, that means 'modest' or 'bashful,' which he may have once been when he was younger, but not anymore!"

"Priscilla came to help us when we were in prison," I said. "The Christians are very kind."

"The palace is full of them, including my favorite nannies, Valeria Tryphena and her sister

---

* *Giovanni DeRossi, when excavating the Catacomb of Priscilla in 1889, discovered that Pudens belonged to the wealthy Acilius Glabrio family. According to one of the tombstones, this family "embraced the Gospel when it first arrived in Rome."*

Tryphosa.[*] My real mother, Valeria Messalina, set their family free some years ago."

We passed the music room, where several boys were rehearsing on musical instruments. "My cousin Bran has already found some friends," I said.

"That's my brother Britannicus with him, playing the cithara," Octavia said proudly. "Flavius Titus is the one playing the harp, and Claudia Procula's son Linus,[†] the flute."

Linus had sandy hair, and soulful brown eyes that turned down at the corners, like a British spaniel. Brittanicus was a handsome child, tall and well-developed for his age.

A sad expression flitted over Octavia's face. "Britannicus should be the next emperor," she said, "but my new stepmother Agrippina is determined that her son Nero will be emperor, and she constantly tries to turn our father against us. He is enamored with her, and too gullible to see what she is doing."

Octavia led me to my family's apartments on the fourth floor. My new bedchamber was bathed in sunshine streaming in through the double doors that opened onto a small balcony. The walls, a delicate shade of pale blue, were banded about the top with an ornate golden frieze. The high ceiling was painted with ethereal clouds drifting among a pink and blue sky, so real that they appeared to float from the ceiling. A fresco depicting the verdant hills of Tuscany decorated one wall.

---

[*] Dr. A.F. Gori, archeologist, from inscription found in tombs of Imperial servants.

[†] Junius; and "Liber Pontificalis"

A bed with bronze lion-paw feet, spread with an embroidered coverlet, was piled with tasseled cushions of richly colored silk. The mattress, thickly stuffed with wool, rested on a carved teakwood bed frame interlaced with ropes. My fingers caressed the smooth black and gold lacquered dressing table, inlaid with ivory flowers.

"The traders carried that all the way from China on the Silk Road," Octavia said.

"It's all so beautiful . . . more than I could ever have imagined!"

Everything was fine until I caught my pitiful reflection in the silver mirror hanging on the wall behind the dressing table. Was that hideous creature me? Dark circles ringed my eyes, and my hand rose instinctively to cover the prominent red scar on my forehead.

Moving the silk pillows out of the way, I collapsed on the bed, my eyes downcast. "I look a fright. The boys weren't lying. I am never going to fit in here."

"Nonsense," Octavia said, twisting my hair this way and that. "By the time Tryphena and Tryphosa get finished with you, everyone will know that you are a real princess!"

The apartment had its very own private bath, with a pink marble tub. The freedwoman Tryphena filled it with pure crystal water, which flowed out miraculously from a pipe in the wall. Hot water poured from an ornate copper tank standing in one corner on a platform. The tank had an oil lamp flame burning underneath it. Tryphena sprinkled a generous portion of fragrant rose oil into the bath, then left me alone. Enrapt in fragrant bliss, I scrubbed away several months worth of grime with a rough sponge and washing soda, soaking until the water turned cold, and the palms of my hands were white and wrinkled.

Octavia gave me a lovely white gown to wear, embroidered with bright threads, and belted with a golden sash. "It's made of cool cotton from India," she said. "It's all the rage nowadays, no more scratchy linen."

"But India . . . so far away!"

Octavia laughed. "Since Augustus Caesar took control of the Red Sea some fifty years ago, voyages to India have become quite commonplace."

Tryphena was a dainty, delicate woman, with black ripe-olive eyes, and long dark hair pulled back from her face in a loose knot. Her sister Tryphosa looked much like her, and I wondered, but was too shy to ask, if they were twins. With steel shears, Tryphena trimmed the front of my hair straight across, creating pert bangs to cover the dreadful scar. Then she curled the remaining hair with an odd metal cylinder called a "curling iron" that she heated over a candle flame. She drew all the funny spiral curls up into golden combs, so that they cascaded down my back like a waterfall.

The other servants adorned me like a doll, from sandals decorated with inlaid silver and lapis lazuli, to bracelets that jingled whenever my arm moved.

It was a very different girl who stared out from the mirror. I hugged Tryphena tightly.

My parents had also cleaned up and changed into new clothes. I snickered at my father, who was wearing a white tunic, unaccustomed to seeing his knobbed, freckled knees sticking out. He reached out one hand and would have playfully boxed my ears, had he not been prevented by the barber's straight-edged razor. The man had come to cut his hair and shave him, though Daddy would ever insist on keeping his fine Celtic mustache. But he did allow the barber to trim it a bit. The Emperor's personal physician Xenophon came to bandage his ankles, which were bleeding and ulcerated from the tight chains.

"Claudius gave him back one of his golden *torques*," Mum said, while Daddy fastened the thick collar proudly around his clean-shaven neck.

At dinnertime I followed Octavia into the vaulted banquet hall. Rows of chandeliers glittered overhead, with multifaceted crystals that magnified hundreds of tiny flames into a dazzle of light. My father reclined on a plush couch next to the Emperor Claudius, Agrippina, Aulus Plautius and Vespasian, the ex-slave Narcissus, who was the Secretary of State, and Pallas, the Secretary of the Treasury. Three green marble tables were arranged in a "U" shape, with six banquet couches placed on the three sides. Slaves served them food and drinks from inside the "U."

I wondered how Daddy could eat lying down, propped up on one elbow as he was, but he seemed to be enjoying himself, swapping old war stories and nibbling appetizers of salted prawns, sardines, olives, eggs and almonds, while they waited for the other guests to arrive. Mum sat with the wives, most of them in long-backed chairs, waving in one hand a fan of peacock feathers. Her copper hair, highlighted with henna, was piled high on her head, crowned with a golden tiara set with emeralds.

Octavia and I sat at the children's table. Bran, Titus, Britannicus and Linus entered the banquet hall. But when they passed Nero's chair, the wretch stuck out his foot, causing Britannicus to trip and fall.

"Get up, you miserable epileptic!" Nero croaked. "Don't embarrass your illustrious family."

Titus, who was Vespasian's son, clenched his small fist, and would have slammed it into the older boy's taunting face, had not Linus caught his arm. I held my breath and glanced at the Emperor Claudius, certain that he would come to his son's defense. But he was drinking wine, and seemed not to notice.

"Jupiter help the Empire, Ahenobarbus Nero, if you ever succeed with your abominable schemes!" Titus snarled, his face purple with rage.

Slave boys poured water over our hands to wash them. An army of servants began carrying in huge trays from the outdoor kitchen to the tables. They removed covers from gold and silver platters piled high with roast pork expertly spiced, fried red mullet, duck in a sweet sauce, sheep's stomach, frog's legs, sea perch glistening with butter and green flakes of parsley, boiled crabs and oysters, carrots, beans, mushrooms in a savory sauce, asparagus, stuffed dates, cheesecake, and pastries layered with glazed fruit, or honey and cinnamon—so much of everything! We ate from elaborately sculpted gold plates and goblets set with precious gems.

"Are these made of real gold?" I asked incredulously, holding it up, the jewels glittering in the light's bright reflection.

"Yes," Linus replied, "and very expensive. Not long ago a guest slipped one in his pocket to take home. The Emperor Claudius didn't say anything. But the next time the man came to eat, he found a cheap red Samian-ware bowl and beaker at his place!"

The last part of the meal was enlivened by a military brass band, and a comedic recital by an actor, who related the oft-told story about Claudius' conquest of Camulodunum, the Catevellauni capital, with his mighty circus elephants and camels.

When we rose to go back to our apartments, Pudens, the fawn-eyed boy, passed by me. I shrank from him, but he reached out his hand and caught one of my spiral curls. He pulled it all the way out, and chuckled as it bonged back into place.

"You look pretty tonight, Princess Rufina ('Red')," he said, with the flash of an engaging white smile. "I'm sorry that I made you cry."

Chapter 5

Brass signal horns from the Campus Martius reverberated across the city at the first light of dawn, signalling the first hour of the day. Thinking it was the trumpet used in Wroxeter for the changing of the guard, I opened one eye and peered at the clouds painted on the ceiling, struggling to sort out my thoughts. *Had it all been just a beautiful dream?*

"Come you, Glwadus, it's time to eat!" Mum called out. "You don't want to be late your first day of school."

A slice of pink sunlight fell across the coverlet. I swung my legs over the edge of the bed, my bare toes sinking into the thick Persian rug that warmed the marble floor. I threw open the double doors that led out to the balcony, pinching my fingers in the unfamiliar hardware.

The delicate scent of the night-blooming jasmine still wafted on the cool breeze that drifted in from the Mediterranean. The city glistened proudly in the glow of the sunrise that grew out of the Appenines.

It reflected off the golden dome of the Temple of Jupiter Capitolinus, and the white marble columns and brazen roofs of the tall Temple of Saturn, the Temple of Castor and Pollux, and the many government buildings in the Forum. The spiny aqueducts, with their towering arches, sprawled eastward across the *campagnia*. In the river-mist that hung low over the lazy brown Tiber, the sharp stone prow of the Isola Tiburina appeared as a great hulking ship run aground; but Octavia had said it was really not a ship, but an island.

"I'm feared, Mum," I said at breakfast, dawdling over the platter of fine white bread and honey, apples, stuffed dates, and eggs in pastry hoods the servants had delivered. "I will be so far behind the other children. If the teacher makes me stand and recite, they will all laugh at me."

Bran chuckled, as he reached for another slice of bread. He lived with us now, since Uncle Llyr and the other warriors had returned to Britain.

Mum patted my shoulder. "You will do just fine."

This side of the apartment overlooked the spacious inner courtyard with its long reflecting pool. I stared down at the bright-plumed parrots in gilt-wire cages that chirped to one another through the fragrant rose bushes, the emerald laurels, and the pomegranate trees that bore red fruit streaked with yellow and green. Neatly trimmed boxwood hedges formed an intriguing maze, with a small fountain in its center. *If only I might run in there and hide!*

Octavia appeared at the doorway, holding out a slate and stylus, beautifully ornamented with silver and garnets; and a fine-tooled leather sack with handles. "This is a *capsa,* which children use to carry their supplies to school," she said. "Papa sent these for you, and a set for Bran. Papa said you might be frightened."

The Emperor Claudius' trusted freedman Stachys accompanied us halfway down the hill to the Scola Palatina. Many of the wealthy patrician students rode to school in elegant sedan chairs borne by slaves, outfitted with thick cushions and side curtains which could be drawn against the sun.

On wooden feet, I paused before the door, my knees weak. But there could be no turning back. The *grammatacus*, a young Greek, briefly assessed my educational background. He was an irritable fellow, with a nervous tic in his left cheek that unintentionally invited one's gaze. He grouped me with children about a year younger than myself. I took a seat next to a pretty child with prominent brown eyes and silky honey-brown ringlets.

"What's your name?" the girl wrote on her wax slate.

"Claudia Glwadus, from Britain," I wrote back.

"My name is Acilia. I shall have to call you Claudia, for I can't pronounce 'G-l-w-a-d-u-s.' "

A giggle that rose in my throat was hastily turned into a cough, but nevertheless still drew an icy stare from the *grammatacus*. The walls of the Scola

Palatina were decorated with bas-reliefs depicting scenes from Homer and the classical poems, as well as maps of the whole world, and of the different provinces, and even a map of the stars and constellations. There were statues of poets and writers such as Horace and Virgil and Socrates.

The grammatacus showed me how to write on parchment, using a goose quill pen and a small inkpot. It looked easy, and I enjoyed watching the letters form on the white field. But there was many a black, ugly blot among the whorls and upstrokes that day. The hard benches had no backs, and became more and more uncomfortable as the morning wore on. At one o'clock we were given our homework assignment and dismissed for the day.

Acilia nudged my arm. "Ask your mother if you can go to the Forum after the siesta," she said. "I can get my brother to take us."

My family sat at table with the Emperor's family, then rested briefly in our apartment during the siesta, which lasted for about three hours, during the hottest portion of the day. Sleeping in the afternoon seemed to me a frightful waste of time, when there was so much I wanted to see and do!

Finally Acilia came by for me, with her brother, who, I was surprised to learn, was Acilius Glabrio Pudens, the pretty boy whom I had already met. Octavia, Britannicus, Linus and Titus wanted to go along, too, so we sat down on a low stone wall to wait for them.

Pudens pointed with his chin toward Bran and me. "Why do Britons paint their faces blue?" he asked.

"We only painted our faces during battle," I said, "for the Druids said it would keep us safe from harm. But they lied to us. Hundreds of our friends were killed, including Bran's mother."

"You would probably be surprised to learn that we lived in houses, too, and not in holes in the ground," Bran said in a sarcastic tone.

Octavia scampered up the path, wearing a dark wig, accompanied by the other children and the freedman Amplias. Seeing my puzzled face, Octavia giggled.

"My brother and I have to wear disguises when in public," she said.

The Roman Forum was truly the "center of the world." A throng of pilgrims streamed in and out of the sacred temples, prostrating themselves before the gold-encrusted shrines smothered with flower garlands, and lamps dimly burning. Stalls nearby did a thriving business selling small images of the pagan gods, made of copper, silver, gold or brass.

Senators and businessmen scurried into and out of the various government buildings and banking establishments, pursuing worldly matters. However, we had not come to see these dry, dull edifices. We dashed toward the eastern section of the Via Sacra, the dignified Amplias attempting to keep pace, where the colorful shops and craftsmens' booths stood mushroomed together. Shutters and doors flew open as the siesta was coming to an end. The street suddenly exploded with life.

My new jeweled sandals slapped oddly against the overheated marble pavement amid a jumble of rushing feet. The crowd was forced to give way as a wealthy senator hurried by in a litter borne by arrogant slaves arrayed in fine scarlet livery, who passed the elaborate contraption overhead, bumping rudely against everyone in their way.

The people were a fascinating cross-section of humanity, speaking Latin, Greek, and a babble of other tongues that flowed around me in a din of shrill voices and big gestures. I tried not to stare. There were tall, black-skinned Numidians wearing long white robes; handsome Ethiopians with high, pompous foreheads; and exotic silk merchants from the China road.

Enormous Germans, dressed in fur-skins, wore their hair long, twisted into a knot on the side of their heads, believing it kept the evil spirits out. They hawked amber pendants and earrings from the Alps, along with gaudy enamelled baubles, and wood carvings. Dark-eyed Arabs swathed in odd headdresses sold perfumes and spices from the mysterious East.

Other shops, their facades trimmed with bright red, yellow or green paint, were stacked floor to ceiling with bolts of silk damask and Indian cottons. One stall had an amazing array of children's toys: dolls, hoops, hobby horses, spinning tops, balls and games. In the street, Grecian flute players, tumblers, dwarfs, dancers, mimes and jesters performed for occasional coppers that were thrown their way. Britannicus paid a quadrans to a huckster who carried a talking bird on his shoulder and exhibited a two-headed chicken in a cage.

A Syrian glassblower secured a mass of molten glass on the end of a blowpipe, then held it over a fire-stick. He blew on the pipe till the sides of the glass bulged out into a hollow globe. I sucked in my breath as he attached a blob of glass to each side, and with a grand flourish of his hand, fashioned two delicate handles. The raw molten glass had been transformed into a beautiful drinking goblet!

The alabaster artisan's face was oddly streaked with white, as he labored at his craft. He marked the plain stone, then working with hands and feet, expertly turned it on the revolving lathe, great clouds of dust flying up around him. There was a display of highly polished alabaster vases, urns and figures of elephants and other creatures.

"Look, such a pretty little jewel box," I said, "with tiny blue flowers painted on the lid."

"How much for that?" Pudens inquired of the clerk, and bargained briefly until they agreed upon a price. Pudens reached into his money belt and drew out the necessary coins. Then he handed me the alabaster box.

"The blue is like your . . . eyes," he said with a sly grin.

It was impossible to tell from his expression whether he was paying a compliment or a cruel pun.

But nevertheless I thanked him, running my fingers over the cool, smooth surface of the tiny box, and carefully packed it in my *capsa*.

We sat on a graffiti-covered low stone wall to watch a juggler who had drawn a crowd around him, entertaining them with the trick of balancing swords. He did a fire-eating act, breathing high great plumes of flame. And a magician created illusions most astonishing, snatching objects out of the air.

Suddenly I jumped up with fright, as a small, furry animal rubbed against my ankle. "What is it?" I shrieked. "What is it?"

The children giggled. Pudens scooped up the creature in his hand. "It won't hurt you. It's just a kitty cat," he said, showing me its cute face, with a striped forehead above green eyes, and pointed ears much too large for its head. He dropped it in my lap, where it curled up and began to utter a loud purring sound. "Caesar Augustus brought them here from Egypt about sixty years ago, to solve the rat and mice problem."

"A lot of cats stay down here by the smelly fish market," Octavia said, "hoping for a scrap of food."

I saw more cats now in the background, in an amazing variety of color combinations, stretched out languidly on windowsills and perched among the branches of overhanging trees. They kept watchful eyes on the fishmongers who oversaw tables loaded with silver herring, pike, eel, swordfish, octopus, snails, pink giant shrimp, gray-blue sardines, and piles of hard-shelled oysters. Dark-red crayfish and lobsters moved sluggishly about in stone tanks filled with water. The fishmongers cleaned the fish for customers, tossing the scales into a large pile.

"But who owns the cats?" I asked.

Pudens laughed. "No one would be silly enough to want to own one," he said." The merchants and the neighbors feed them, or they just eat the mice they catch."

As the shadows began to lengthen, several of the fishmongers packed up their wares, gathering the scraps and offal into buckets which were dumped onto the bare earth. Cats who had been politely waiting came bounding now in a desperate confusion of furs, jumping down from their lofty pinnacles, abandoning their snug hiding places.

The next afternoon Acilia visited at the palace with her parents. Her mother Priscilla, Pomponia Graecina, Claudia Procula, and some of the freed-women sat in the summerhouse beneath our window, their heads bent over a work table spread with bolts of colorful cloth. They were cutting out small-sized tunics, one after another.

"Look, Mum, a sewing bee," I said, as we stared down from the balcony.

"They're sewing winter clothes for the two hundred or so children who live at my mother's orphanage in the country," Acilia explained.

Mum could never resist a sewing circle, and she soon bustled down to join them. The other women greeted her warmly. Tryphena was passing around beakers of cold papaya juice.

Pomponia Graecina smiled. "Eurgain, you must show us how to do the ornamental stitching around the neck, like I used to see in Britain."

"I'd be happy to," Mum said.

Mum brought a sack containing bits of wood and a tangle of bright embroidery threads. "Glwadus, perhaps you and the girls can separate some of these threads, and wind each color around a wooden chip."

While they worked, brass needles flying back and forth, the women spoke frequently about their God, and His Son whom they called Jesus. Mum and I stared curiously from one to another. Few modern Roman women had any compassion for the poor and the orphans. Most that we had met at the palace chattered endlessly about the latest scandal, the new fashions, hairstyles, or about herbal and seaweed wraps, mud-packs, or the latest salt treatments to leave their complexions glowing and revitalized. But these Christian women had an unexplainable inner glow, clearly not achieved by mud-packs.

When Acilia, Octavia, and I tired of work, we scampered along the flower-bordered pathways where peacocks preened their jeweled green and blue feathers. Octavia showed us the fishpond, where gold-colored fish darted beneath great pink water lilies. We raced through the courtyard until we were out of breath and beaded with sweat, then flopped down on a stone bench to catch the cool spray of the fountain, beside Acilia's father, the Senator

Manlius Acilius Glabrio. Acilia rested her head in the crook of his bronzed arm.

Manlius was one of the most elegant men I had ever seen, his snow-white toga properly draped at the shoulder, with just the right amount of the wide purple *laticlava* showing, that indicated his senatorial rank. His Umbrian brown hair was wavy and thick, revealing only a few wisps of gray at the temples. He wore no heavy chains of gold like other rich men wore; but there was a glitter of gold tooth when he smiled, of the sort of refined Etruscan dentistry available only to the wealthy.[*]

Manlius was engrossed in conversation with Ilid, who was always looking for intellectual stimulation. ". . . Rome's first dealings with the Jews were actually quite congenial. One of my ancestors, some 250 years ago, commanded a force that defeated the evil Antiochus III."[†]

Quickly warming to the subject, Ilid perched on the edge of his seat; his dark eyes seemed unusually large. "Yes, yes, I know him!"

"Weakened by defeat, Antiochus was forced to surrender his ships and large territories of land, and pay heavy tribute," Manlius went on. "Rome was able to annex the wealthy Greek province of Achaia, and parts of Asia Minor. A few years later the alliance went after one of his successors, Antiochus Epiphanes, who unfortunately turned and vented his anger on Jerusalem."

---

[*] Peter James and Nick Thorpe "Ancient Inventions"
[†] Julius Frontinus, "Stratagems"

"He was the madman whose sacrifices of swine profaned the Temple of God," Ilid said. "He was determined to force my people to worship Zeus," "Then God raised up Judas Maccabeus, who overthrew him. My people still celebrate Hanukkah every year to commemorate the victory and the subsequent rededication of the temple."

"Rome made a pact of friendship with the Jews, though we were still somewhat weak, and weren't able to help them as much as we wanted to. The Jewish people that my ancestor became acquainted with showed them the prophecy concerning the Roman alliance, mentioned in Daniel 11:18,* and later in verse 30, which had been written some 400 years before," Manlius said.

"Amazing!" Ilid said.

"My ancestors were much impressed, and some of them held great respect for the God of the Jews, often visiting in the synagogues. The freedman Amplias, who studies the Scriptures a great deal, says that the book of Daniel also prophesied about events still to happen in the future. But here is Amplias now." Manlius beckoned to the freedman. "He can tell you the rest of the story. Brother, tell my friend Eliab Ben David here how you found the Messiah."

Amplias beamed. "Some men from our fine synagogue traveled to Jerusalem for the Feast of Shauvot, or Pentecost, and were standing near the beautiful Temple when a man named Peter began to preach.

---

* "a prince on his own behalf"

108

He was a poor fisherman, a disciple of Jesus the Nazarene, who had been recently crucified."

Amplias paced back and forth, enthusiasm reddening his cheeks. "As Peter spoke, the men began to look in amazement one to another, realizing that each was hearing the speech in the language with which he was most familiar! They fell to their knees, realizing that this Jesus whom Peter spoke about must have been the Messiah."*

"But when they came home and told what had happened, it caused a terrible schism in the synagogue," Manlius said.

"Those who believed in Jesus were forced to break away and hold our services at the home of our dear friend Aquila the tentmaker and his wife Priscilla," Amplias went on. "But many of the Jews were expelled from Rome last year, because the difficulties between us came to the attention of the Emperor Claudius, who didn't really understand the situation. Being Jews, Aquila and Priscilla had to leave, too. After that, we moved our church services to the town-home of Brother Manlius, on the Via Urbana."

Ilid shook his head in wonder. "I see that many strange events have transpired since I was in Britain," he said quietly.

"If you are in need of employment, my wife is always looking for a man of letters to teach the children at our orphanage," Manlius said. "We can't pay a great deal, but you would have your own cottage,

---

* Holy Bible, Acts 2:10

and meals provided. The orphanage is located on the Via Salaria, about two miles outside the city."

"Yes," Ilid said. "I think that position would be quite suitable."

Britannicus and his friends raced by. "Come and see my new toy!" Britannicus called out to us. "The governor of Egypt sent it. It's *awesome!*"

Octavia, Acilia and I followed them to the playroom to behold a miniature theater, created by the Egyptian inventor, Heron, which was powered by weights and gears. It had tiny doors that opened and closed, and human figures that whirled about on a little stage. Squads of horsemen, chariots, and wagons went dashing by. Tiny ships sailed from a busy harbor, and dolphins leapt up and down in the rolling waves; then there was a storm, complete with flashes of lightning, swaying palm trees and sound effects.* We sat and watched it over and over.

"I don't think I should ever get tired of it," I vowed.

Octavia showed us her extraordinary collection of dolls too, with painted faces of wax, ivory or terra cotta, and tiny wigs made from real hair. All wore elaborate tunics, decorated with silk ribbons and flowers, gems and pearls. Doll's houses were furnished with tiny tables, chairs, lamps, and even miniature pots and pans in the kitchen.

"My mother gave me most of them, before she . . . died," Octavia said.

---

*Peter James and Nick Thorpe, "Ancient Inventions"

Titus' older sister Domitilla came by, looking for him. "It's time to go home now," she said. "And Mama is sick, so don't be a pest." She carried an infant in her arms, and drew back the blanket to show us his tiny face. "This is our new brother, Domitian, only two weeks old."

"Oh, I love babies!" I exclaimed. "May I hold him?"

"Sit down in the chair," Domitilla said as she passed him to me. "Be careful of his neck, though. He can't hold his head up yet."

With his dark hair already beginning to curl, and his round and ruddy face, he already resembled the other Flavians. I held him up to my shoulder, rocked and cuddled him, and kissed his soft downy head.

Chapter 6

A.D. 54

Y ou're both growing so tall!" Octavia exclaimed.
"Mum says I have sprouted up five inches," I
replied. "And Acilia is not far behind."

Octavia, Acilia, and I sat in the palace courtyard,
finishing our homework. By the time three years
had passed, I was doing well at school, and could
now speak Latin without a trace of a foreign accent,
could trill my "Rs," and knew all the current slang.
Though not much for mathematics, I had mastered
Greek, the language of the educated class; and
learned history from Xerxes to Alexander the Great
to Hannibal and back again. I knew Socrates and
Plato, all the adventures of Odysseus and Ulysses,
and had struggled through Horace's eccentric works.

I had finally become accustomed to being called
"Claudia," though many of my friends nicknamed
me "Rufina," because of my reddish-blonde hair.
Acilia sometimes tried to talk to me about Jesus, or
invited me to church, but I was too enamored by

life in the magical city to consider serious things. It was easy to become oblivious to everything outside of Rome with all its amusements, even to forget what happened in your old life.

"Help me study my lines for the poetry recital on the last day of school," I begged. "Our class is doing Virgil's *Aenid*."

Octavia sighed as took the paper from my hand. "I can't believe I'm graduating this year," she said. "I will soon be fourteen. An old lady."

"Now don't make me laugh, or I shall forget my lines."

> What though the radiance which was once so bright
> Be now forever taken from my sight,
> Though nothing can . . . bring back the hour
> Of splendor in the grass, of glory in the flower;
> We will . . . grieve not . . . rather find
> Strength in what remains behind.

The clouds overhead had thickened into a canopy of gray, and large raindrops began pouring down. We hastily gathered our books and dashed for shelter in the nearby palace gymnasium, where the older boys from the *collegio* were competing in an uproarious game.

Acilia purchased nuts, sausages, rolls, and fruit drinks from the restaurant boys who peddled snacks. Then we wandered up through the rows of stone benches until we found seats. The boys were kicking around a leather-covered bladder ball. Deafening cheers and applause rose from the enthusiastic mob that watched from the sidelines. Someone shouted out the score, while others argued briefly.*

"It is a rough game adapted from the Chinese 'T'su Chu,' "Octavia said. "They are allowed to touch the ball with their feet or body, but not with their hands."†

Tall and muscular, Pudens was the star athlete, the one who could always run faster, kick the ball farther, and win every game or competition. He was handsome and popular, always laughing, always reckless. Everyone hoped to win his favor, especially the haughty-eyed girls from wealthy families, who constantly followed him around. Graceful and beautiful, they were the sort of girls who always made me feel like a clumsy barbarian giant. They minced along on tiny gilded sandals. I smoothed the folds of my rumpled gown, and tucked my rather large feet farther underneath the bench.

Roman girls accented their eyes with black kohl liner, with dark ash on eyelids and brows, powdered their milky white complexions with chalk dust, and painted their cheeks and pouty lips bright with ochre. Perfume swirled around them, from the fragrant unguents they applied to their skin. Complicated hair arrangements were ornamented with jewels and pearls, or broided with gold threads. Arrogant and self-assured, the girls provided a whole cheering section, screaming madly for Pudens with shrill and strident voices.

---

* Seneca
† Peter James

Acilia grimaced, as she chewed on a handful of almonds. "My mother is just sick at heart about these pagan girls who chase my brother around. She prays every day he won't marry one of them."

Nothing can go wrong today! The sun's early rays slanted across the sky in a pink and golden aura. It was the end of June, and school was finally dismissed for the summer. Most of my friends were planning trips to their country homes, for Rome could be frightfully hot in summer. Linus had already departed for his father's estates in Tuscany, and Titus to his grandmother's at Cosa. I was filled with excitement, for my family had been invited to accompany the Emperor's family for several weeks at their summer palace at Lake Albano.

I picked up my embroidery and wandered out to the boxwood maze in the courtyard, searching for a bit of solitude beside the fountain. But the Princess Octavia already occupied the little bench in the center of the maze. Her thin shoulders heaved with great sobbing breaths.

"Dear Octavia, whatever is the matter?" I asked in alarm.

"Oh, curse the goddess Venus, who ever brings sorrow to Papa's house! When I was a small child, my father chose a husband for me, Lucius Junias Silanus. We were betrothed, as is the custom. Though quite a bit older than myself, he was always kind to me, and very handsome. Perhaps I could have grown to love him in time."

Her voice trembled, so that she could hardly speak. "But Agrippina was afraid that Lucius would someday rival Nero for the throne. She brought false charges against him, and forced him to commit suicide. She has now persuaded my father that I must marry Nero, whom I loathe and despise!"

Aghast, my arm went around her thin shoulder, unable to think of any words of comfort. How could Claudius allow such a thing? The same Emperor who had been incredibly kind to my family seemed to care so little about his own children. Now dear Octavia would be sacrificed to Agrippina's ruthless ambition. Burrus, one of Agrippina's allies, was now in firm command of the Praetorian Guard. Nero already led the Praetorian troops during parades, and his portrait had begun to appear on coins. Agrippina had made distributions of money in his name to the soldiers and to the populace.

"How can I marry anyone so detestable?" Octavia whispered.

"We'll run away," I said fiercely. "I have friends and cousins in Britain who still have not submitted to Rome."

"But everyone in the whole world knows who I am," she sighed. "They would only track me with hounds and bring me back."

The wedding day came too soon, carefully chosen among days thought to bring good fortune, according to the calculations of the stars. I was to be one of Octavia's young women attendants. She stood in her chambers, frightened and still like a delicate fawn, her dark eyes clouded with unspeakable agony.

The young maid Paezuza parted Octavia's hair into six plaits with the ceremonial iron spear, an ancient Roman symbol of the violence of marriage by the capture of the Sabine women. The plaits were wound around and held in place with strips of wool, in the sort of odd hairstyle worn by the Vestal Virgins. Octavia was clad in a lustrous white tunic studded with pearls, with a woolen girdle about her waist, fastened with the ritual knot of Hercules.

Tryphena and Tryphosa, tears coursing down their cheeks, placed over this the golden collar, and the brilliant saffron-colored cloak. We covered her head and the upper portion of her body with the fine orange silk nuptial veil, known as the *flameum*, and she was crowned with a wreath woven from verbena and marjoram. There were saffron-colored sandals for her tiny feet.

It came time for Octavia to bid farewell to her childhood toys, her kites and hoops and puzzles, and her wonderful mechanical toys, for they were now to be presented to the household gods. I had to turn my face away as her fingers caressed each one of her beautiful dolls.

"You must walk up to the altar with me, Claudia," Octavia murmured.

The merry voices of the guests could now be heard outside in the hallway. We emerged from her chambers, amid the loud greetings and congratulations that arose from the crowd. It seemed that everyone in Rome had turned out for the wretched occasion. We minced slowly down to the grand atrium, where the marriage gifts had been put on display. Swags of gaily-colored ribbons, banners and elaborate garlands of flowers adorned the palace walls, and hung suspended between the grand fluted columns. Nero appeared, surrounded by his entourage. Octavia managed a weak smile to welcome her bridegroom. How brave she was!

On leaden feet, we trudged toward the altar, which the priests of Jupiter had erected and decorated with a profusion of flowers and burning candles. The innocent beribboned ewe lamb was brought in. The high priest of Jupiter then sacrificed it in a horrifying, bloody ritual, and opened its entrails to read the auguries.

"Perhaps the auguries will be poor," I whispered. "Then they will be forced to stop the wedding." It was her only chance. She squeezed my hand hopefully.

"The auguries portend to good!" the high priest proclaimed triumphantly. "I see a guarantee of many happy children and a joyous old age!"

Our hearts sank. The necessary marriage contracts were signed before ten witnesses, who then affixed their seals to them. In front of the sacrificial altar, the young couple then cut the small, coarse cake of *spelt* in half, and placed it upon the altar, offering prayers to Jupiter. They ate a small piece each, to signify the communion between the new-lyweds, and their religious connection to the gods.

Octavia spat out the ancient words, which blended their lives together: *"Ubi tu Gaius, ego Gaia"* (where you are master, I am mistress).

Trembling, and with great loathing, I grasped the hands of Nero and Octavia, and united them, as was the custom. Thereupon, the guests applauded heartily and cried, *"Felicitor*, may happiness wait upon you!"

After the ceremony, everyone sat down to the lavish, sixteen-course banquet, one of the most elaborate ever, for Claudius and Agrippina had spared no expense. The tables were set with the finest gold utensils, antique candlesticks and flowers carefully arranged in Chinese vases. Their fragrance, and that of the flowing wine and the roasting meats perfumed the air with a sickening aura that added to the churning in my stomach.

In the center of the feast, a whole roast pig dominated the table, crowned with sausages, and was served with blood pudding. Servants carried in steaming platters of chitterlings; chicken livers with mushrooms; roast peacock; and anchovies on a bed of eggs. There were shrimps; African snails; pigeons drenched in white sauce; artichoke hearts with vinegar and oil; sow's udders; boiled blackbird breasts; and stuffed mice with their fancy coating of honey and poppy-seed. For dessert there were damson plums, red pomegranates, sugar apples, marzipan, and the beautifully decorated wedding cake.

"You've hardly eaten a nibble of the delicious food," Mum said as the plates were being cleared away.

"I seem to have lost my appetite," I murmured.

When the evening star arose, Nero pretended, as was the custom, to seize his bride from the arms of her "mother" Agrippina. The guests, festive at all costs, hooted with glee, most of them by this time well-drunken from the huge-bellied amphorae of strong wine which flowed unendingly. It seemed their very souls were sodden with wine.

A procession formed, led by boys carrying torches of hawthorn, and flute players. Friends followed, reciting a bawdy poem created for the occasion, and threw nuts and sweets into the crowd. When they reached Nero's suites, Octavia paused to attach woolen strips to the heavy door, and placed a small amount of oil on the lintel.

The young men attendants lifted her up and carried her over the threshold, which was spread with a white carpet and luxuriant greenery. Female attendants presented Octavia with a distaff and spindle, the ancient symbols of virtue and domestic diligence. Nero handed her a blazing torch, and Octavia lit a fire on the hearth. She prayed to the gods for a happy marriage.

Her wedding day, which should have been the happiest day of her life, seemed to me like a funeral, in a house that contained only mourning. I retired alone to the summerhouse in the courtyard, underneath a savage sky, overcome with horror and madness. The myrtle trees made tortured sounds as the ill wind whipped them about. A gentle hand touched my shoulder. Tryphena and Tryphosa stood there. No words passed between us. We clung to each other and wept until long into the blurred black night.

Scarcely had we dried our tears, when another tragedy intruded upon our lives. My father fell ill from a severe case of pneumonia. He drifted in and out of consciousness, spiked a high fever and had great difficulty breathing. His handsome face lost its brightness, and his strong form withered, seeming to fade into the thick mattress. His body was wracked with fits of coughing and he sometimes brought up streaks of blood. Burning hot, he screamed with delirium, and went into convulsions.

Mum stayed by his side night and day, sometimes relieved by Pomponia Graecina or Claudia Procula. They attempted to bring the fever down with cool compresses and willow bark tea. They pestled laserpicum root in a mortar to make a poultice which they applied to his chest, and gave him doses of elderberry extract four times a day. They made him breathe an aromatic inhalation of balsam, and forced sips of ephedra tea and Egyptian horehound syrup between his fevered lips to clear his lungs.

On the fifth day his fever broke in a deluge of perspiration. His skin felt cool and he no longer coughed up blood. He smiled at me weakly and was able to take some chicken broth and thinned polenta, which I fed him with a spoon. But in the afternoon he was visited by Xenophon, the Emperor's personal physician, carrying his bag of potions and ointments, dessicated insects, animal parts, strange herbs, and instruments. With a scalpel he opened my father's veins and let a great deal of blood run out into a basin.

"It seems that a sick person would need all his blood in order to fight the disease," I whispered to Mum, who stood nervously by wringing her hands, while my father's face grew ghost-white.

"Impudent child," the haughty Xenophon snapped. "This is exactly the remedy he needs, the very latest in medical technology!"

Toward evening, surrounded by a huddled group of mourners, my father's pulse grew weak. A dusky bluish color appeared about his lips and fingertips. He struggled for every breath, but they became shallower and farther apart, until there was only silence.

"I love you, Daddy," I whispered a hundred times. But the strong hands I had always clung to grew cold and limp. Darkness shrouded my soul as the servants carried him away.

Weak and trembling, Mum collapsed into a black mood, and for days she closed herself inside a dark and shuttered room, refusing to take food. It seemed that the gods' evil curse again held us in its hand. Mum began to lose weight, her cheeks sunken and hollow like an old, old woman.

"Mum, please, you must eat something!" I begged and pleaded from outside the locked door. "I can't bear to lose you, too."

"Would that I had died myself," she said, her eyes red and swollen from crying. "I dwell in continuous night, my heart forever buried in his grave."

One terrible afternoon, when Bran and I returned from school, we found her crouched in a corner, holding a knife in her hand. She raised her face to me, her skin strangely pale and wax-like, and stared with vacant eyes, as if no one was alive inside her. The veins on her wrists were lacerated, and blood dripped down in rivulets onto the floor.

"No more of the . . . agony," she whispered. "In madness I now pray for death, abandoned by the gods and perishing . . . nothing beyond, nothing beyond. Drowning in a terrible pit, sliding down . . . down . . . into blackness . . . cruel, bitter Fate."

Fear gripped me. My head pounding like a hammer, I tore through the hallway in a blur, screaming for Tryphena and Tryphosa. They came running, and Tryphena quickly bandaged Mum's wrists with a tight pressure bandage, while Tryphosa knelt beside her, crying out to their God. Servants carried Mum to her bed. I pressed her chilled hand to my cheek. But her mind had drifted off, far beyond my reach.

"We can only hope that she hasn't lost enough blood to cause death or permanent brain damage," Tryphena said.

Pomponia Graecina Lucina, Claudia Procula, Tryphena and Tryphosa kept vigil by her bedside, feeding her spinach and calves' liver, pureed like a baby's food, and dandelion tea, to restore the blood, until she was able to walk again.

The young servant Paezuza whispered the latest gossip, while she curled my hair a few weeks later. "The short-sighted Emperor Claudius, grown weak with illness, has finally begun to realize that his marriage to Agrippina and his adoption of Nero was a mistake. Claudius thinks the freedman Pallas and Agrippina are plotting against him. Claudius freed that despicable slave many years ago, and set him over the Treasury of the whole Empire. His ex-slave brother Felix was appointed governor of Judea, and has even married a Herodian queen, Drusilla."

"Perhaps Pallas fancies marrying Agrippina!" I exclaimed.

Paezuza giggled. "Both brothers *are* terribly good-looking."

In the afternoon, Acilia and I wandered through the palace with Bran, Britannicus and Linus. The Emperor Claudius, as he tottered through the hallway on his old crippled limbs, caught Britannicus in his arms, and embraced him with the utmost affection. I could smell the strong odor of wine on Claudius' breath even from where I stood.

"You must be the next Emperor, my boy, and a fine one you will be. The Empire must have a legitimate Caesar!" he stammered, his head very shaky. He stretched out his hand to the heavens, as if imploring the gods, then to the boy. "You must grow up quickly, my son, and cast out all my enemies."

"He has been drinking too much recently, instead of trying to solve his problems with a clear head," Bran whispered.

"He doesn't realize that his lips are becoming too loose and careless for his own good," Linus said.

A shadow flitted across a curtained doorway, and for a moment we caught sight of the freedman Pallas. Bran and Linus exchanged uneasy glances.

"That wretched Pallas heard every word," Linus said. The muscles on his neck stood out prominently. "It is a perilous situation, but there isn't much we can do to assist him. Vespasian is away on a military campaign; my Uncle Longinus would help, but he is far away in Illyria."

"And Claudius' loyal Chief Secretary Narcissus has gone to Sinuessa to 'take the waters'," Bran added.

"The Praetorian Guard is already firmly in the grasp of Agrippina," Linus said quietly.

Agrippina realized that the time had come to act. As we sat at banquet that evening, Claudius was, as usual, drinking wine to excess. A savory plate of mushrooms, of which he was especially fond, was brought to him, after having been first sampled by his official food taster. Agrippina ate from the same plate, but she ate around the side. The deadly poison she had prepared for him had apparently been hidden in an uncommonly large mushroom placed in the center of the dish. Because Claudius had been drunken and bleary-eyed, no one at first noticed that he had become unconscious.

Octavia screamed. She stumbled toward him, and collapsed on the edge of his banquet couch. "Papa's skin is turning blue!" she exclaimed. "Something is dreadfully wrong. Call for Xenophon the physician!"

I jumped up so quickly that my chair clattered backward onto the floor behind me, and ran to Octavia's side. Xenophon rushed into the room, and poked a feather down Claudius' throat to make him spew out the poison. But he only seemed the worse for it. I stood terrified, numb as a statue, while the life of the Emperor faded away.

Britannicus' face lost all its color. "Papa!" he sobbed, as he bent over his father and shook him, attempting to awaken him. But there was no sound, only the terrible silence.

Claudius' skin was becoming very dark from the poison. Agippina ordered the servants to carry him to his quarters. She feigned grief, but her eyes were dispassionate as ice. She embraced Britannicus as if broken-hearted.

"Poor, poor child," she said. "You are so like your father!"

Then she herded him and Octavia into Claudius' sickroom with the dead body of their father, where they were held as virtual prisoners.

Agrippina led the public to believe that Claudius was still alive, until all the arrangements had been made for Nero to succeed to the throne. The following day Burrus, Agrippina's handpicked Praetorian Prefect, presented Nero to the Praetorian Guard.

"Where is Britannicus?" some of the soldiers asked.

Since he could not be found, they resolved that Nero should be declared the new Emperor. Nero expressed profound gratitude, and distributed gifts with a lavish hand. Immense honors were heaped upon him. All the people raised their arms and proclaimed him as their new emperor.

"Hail, Caesar!" the cry went up from thousands of voices. "Hail, Caesar!"

"I promise to rule the Empire wisely, as Augustus did!" Nero exclaimed in his grand speech to the crowd.

The Emperor Claudius was given a splendid funeral, and enrolled among the gods. Nero delivered a most reverent eulogy, written by his tutor Seneca, the Stoic philosopher. Then the foolish people thronged the pagan temples, giving thanks to the gods on behalf of Claudius' evil murderers.

I woke in the morning with a headache, a weight lying heavy on my chest. *The nightmares are coming back, just like when we were in prison, dead men walking through my dreams, mutilated, reaching out . . .* I stumbled into the next room, where Tryphosa was delivering a tray of juice and honeyed eggs.

My eyes were drawn to the window, where heavenly voices, sweet-sounding melodies in some for-

eign tongue, drifted upward from the inner courtyard. Armed with pruning shears, rakes, pails and
buckets, a battalion of black-skinned slaves labored
with amazing fervor, keeping up their steady pace in
time to their songs. Some pulled weeds, while others
trimmed the boxwood hedges into wondrous animal
shapes. Tryphosa came to stand beside me at the window, and we listened with delight. Though I couldn't
understand the words, they somehow cheered me.

"Those slaves must be new here."

"Nero has slain Claudius' loyal freedman Narcissus," Tryphosa explained sadly. "Nero seized his
vast estate, which included all his slaves. Most of
the Narcissiani are black-skinned Mauretanians.*
Some were brought to live in the palace. I know
them, for they go to our church.†"

A young slave Narcissus Maurus was assigned to
the children's table at dinner, helping to carve the
meat, and wipe the sticky chins. We watched, fasci-
nated while, brandishing a small knife, Maurus lopped
off the head of a fish, and lifted out its backbone with
a single stroke. When a child asked him for a drink
of water, Maurus, with shining face and a wide white
grin, produced it with a grand flourish and a song.

Bran laughed. "You seem as if you are an actor
in some elaborate theater production, rather than a
poor slave in Nero's banquet hall," he said to Narcissus Maurus. "How can you be so happy in such
grim circumstances?"

---

* Quintus Curtius.
† Romans 16:11.

"It is because I have Jesus in my heart."

In December, during the feast of Saturnalia, Nero and a number of his courtiers were playing a game in which lots were drawn, wherein those present were expected to perform certain feats.

"Britannicus, dear brother, be a good laddie and go to the front of the banquet hall and sing a song for us," Nero ordered.

Britannicus shot him a withering gaze.

"Watch and see how foolish he makes himself look," Nero cackled to his throng of drunken friends.

Bran provided the accompaniment, drawing a horsehair bow across the brass strings of a cithara, in the sort of haunting melody beloved by the Celtic bards. Britannicus, possessed of a harmonious voice, crooned a mournful ballad telling the sad tale of the loss of his inheritance and his father's throne.

Silence descended over the erstwhile merry crowd. There were few dry eyes in the room. When the song was finished, everyone applauded heartily except for Nero, who was visibly upset, his lip curled back in a look of utter loathing.

"Perhaps he is more jealous of Britannicus' exceptional singing voice than angered by his words," Linus whispered. "For Nero fancies himself to be a fine singer and actor."

"Now see what you've accomplished! Are you insane?" Agrippina scolded Nero under her breath. "Everyone in the crowd sympathizes with

Britannicus. After all I've done for you, it seems you could learn to use some wisdom in these matters."

"I am the Emperor, Mother, not a child, and I will rule exactly as I please," Nero said, flinging his empty wine goblet from him. "And I must say I am getting a bit tired of your constant nagging!"

"Don't be impudent with me! For it is I who set you on that golden throne, and don't ever forget it," Agrippina replied in a threatening voice. "I can take you down, and just as easily put Britannicus in your place!"

February 12th, A.D. 55

The morning dawned with a gloomy sullenness, the ancient Appenines shrouded in gray mist. I scampered down the stairs to the banquet hall, where Octavia, Tryphena, Tryphosa and others bustled about, decorating the walls with greenery and colored ribbons, to observe Britannicus' "coming-of-age" celebration, when he would assume the *toga virilis.*

After a grand feast, Bran and I joined the procession that marched through the Forum to the *Tabularium*, where his name would be enrolled among the citizens of Rome. The parade route was filled with a throng of well wishers, singing and scattering flowers before Britannicus.

"It seems everyone loves him," Bran said.

Britannicus reached the base of the Temple of Jupiter Capitolinus, and Bran and I followed him and the surging crowd up the endless flight of stone steps. With loud monotonous chanting and contrite supplications, middle-aged senators, matrons in splendid costume, freedmen, slaves and beggars, all crawled up the steps together on their knees.

"It looks as though they are competing in some extraordinary sack race," I whispered to Bran, with an ill attempt to suppress a giggle.

By the time we reached the top of the stairs our knees were raw and bleeding, cut by the rough stones. Agrippina was waiting to greet Britannicus. Inside the massive gold-domed temple, hundreds of candles flickered in glass holders of red, green and blue, giving out rainbow-colored light. Britannicus uttered a prayer to the god Jupiter, and poured out a libation. An unblemished white bull was brought forth, its horns gilded, its neck encircled with a garland of flowers. I cringed as the high priest slit the throat in a bloody ritual, accompanied by the music of the pipes; the gory carcass was laid upon the flaming altar in front of the temple. The acrid smoke curled high into the air.

In the evening Britannicus donned his white adult tunic, and his boy's clothing was dedicated to the household gods. In the banquet hall, we shared the children's table with Britannicus for the last time.

"Tomorrow he will be moving across to the adult's table," Narcissus Maurus said.

Slaves carried Nero into the hall on a litter, accompanied by six Grecian flute-players. Nero was dressed in a gaudy flowered silk tunic and silk slippers trimmed with gold. His hair had been dyed blond, and arranged in tiers of curls.

"Isn't he the fine dandy!" Linus snickered.

During the meal, the servant who was Britannicus' official "food taster" presented him with a drink which had been prepared deliberately too hot.

"I can't drink it," Britannicus said.

Immediately, as planned, the servant poured in a portion of cold water, which contained a most lethal poison. Without thinking, Britannicus drank deeply of the concoction. The poison overtook him so quickly that he went into severe convulsions; his breathing and speech failed instantly, and his mouth fell open in a silent scream.

"No!" I shrieked.

I sprinkled cold water on his face. Bran fell to his knees and tried to blow air into Britannicus' mouth to revive him. But it was too late. There was neither a breath nor a pulse. Dimly I saw Octavia making her way toward us, her face pale. She stood watching in mute horror, her shoulders wracked with sobs, eyes flooded with tears. Several of the children seated at the table rushed from the room in terror, and some of the servants scattered. Everyone stared accusingly at Nero, who reclined languidly upon his banquet couch picking at his teeth, as if nothing had happened.

"Nothing to worry about," Nero assured us. A gleam lighted his pale gray eyes. "It's just an epileptic seizure. His family is prone to them."

But Britannicus did not move, though Xenophon hastened to assist him. Titus, in despair at the death of his best friend, seized the offending drink, taking a tiny sip himself. He too fell on the floor, severely ill.

"It *is* poison!" he shouted. He did not die, but was quickly carried off to the infirmary.

A frightened stare passed between the despicable Pallas and Agrippina. For once they had not been involved in the murder.

"Do they realize that in Nero they have created a madman?" Bran muttered.

Tryphena and Tryphosa came, and I followed them as they led Octavia to her chambers, for she was in danger of going into shock. Xenophon administered a sedative, and we wrapped her in warm blankets.

"If such things can be done, what hope of life remains for me?" Octavia whispered. Her little white hand felt icy cold as she squeezed mine. "Oh, gods, let me not suffer . . ."

The following afternoon Bran, Linus, Acilia and I wandered down to the Forum. Few words passed between us. We sat on a low stone wall, overcome with dejection and a sense of terrible injustice.

"I suppose we always knew this would happen," Acilia said wearily.

"Instead of an honorable funeral, Britannicus was hastily cremated," Bran told us, "before the public could see his body, which had darkened from the poison. His ashes were interred like a common beggar."

"Nero 'celebrated' the murder by distributing gifts of money to much of the populace, and he also lowered taxes." Linus said. "He's sponsoring a magnificent array of entertainments at the Circus Maximus, with tightrope walkers, clowns, jugglers, Asian acrobats and chariot races. Nero himself drove the chariot for the Green team. But I know what evil lurks beneath his great generosity, and I for one am not deceived."

"I sure miss Britannicus, and no one knows yet if Titus will recover," Bran murmured.

"It was for the good of the Empire," we overheard someone in the crowd say. "It was inevitable that the two brothers would one day do battle. Did not Romulus kill his own brother Remus? Better that one should die, than for Rome to be torn apart by civil war."

"Yes, remember how many died during the civil wars of Pompey and Marc Antony and Augustus," another chimed in. "Romans killing Romans—such a dreadful thing to see."

"Many are offering sacrifices to the gods, thanking them for preventing a war of succession. Perhaps we are entering a Golden Age. See what fine gifts Nero gives!"

"Our poor dear Nero is now a fatherless child, and deprived of a brother's help as well. All proclaim him the great Giver of Peace to the human race, the Father of our Country, who rules the world in clemency and hope! Pray the gods he will forever keep this name, while Rome commits her citizens to his benevolent hand!"

The same depraved mob that had cheered Britannicus' coming-of-age celebration and ascended the steps of Jupiter with him, now applauded his vile murderer! Crushed with sorrow, my head fell to my chest. *I have finally come to see Rome for what it really is . . . what I thought in the beginning. Not a glamorous utopia, but an evil empire, populated with a brutal and idolatrous people concerned only with money and foolish pleasures.*

We trudged back up the Palatine Hill. The sun was going down in a fiery red ball. We stood on the balcony, the rich voices of Narcissus Maurus and his cousin Simon resonating back and forth in the courtyard below, as they moved about, lighting the lamps. Their dark faces glowed like angels, caught in the radiance of the soft light.

"I wonder what the words mean that they are singing?" I asked.

"I know the words," Acilia said. "'*The Lord is my light and my salvation; whom shall I fear? The Lord is the strength of my life; of whom shall I be afraid?*'" She squeezed my hand as we parted company. "Will you come to church with me tomorrow?"

"Yes, I will come."

Part II

"The people that walked in darkness have seen a great Light: they that dwell in the land of the shadow of death, upon them hath the Light shined."

Isaiah 9:2

Chapter 7

"I was found of them that sought Me not."
—Romans 10:20

I dreaded bringing up the subject to Mum the next morning, knowing how deeply she had revered the old Celtic gods. "It is the first day of the week. I don't want to go to school today, for I promised Acilia I would go to the church of the Christians with her."

Bran looked thoughtful as he finished cutting the top from his hard-boiled egg. "The Christians seem to have something we don't have."

"Peace and joy in Jesus Christ," Mum replied. "That is what they have."

I glanced up, wondering if I'd heard correctly. "Begging your pardon?"

Mum smiled. "It was the Christian women who pulled me through those dark days after your daddy died. They showed me that there is a God who loves His children, and will sustain them even in the most difficult trials."

It was true. She was no longer plagued by bleak, suicidal moods. "I never thought you'd give up the old religion," I said.

Mum drained the last sip of her pomegranate juice and set the beaker down on the table. "I have long suspected that there is nothing in the pagan gods we have always served. The more I longed for truth and peace in our old religion, the less I found. We will all go to the Christian church today!"

The services were held at the townhome of the Acilian Glabriones on the Via Urbana.* Walking with Tryphena, Tryphosa, Amplias, Stachys, and Narcissus Maurus and his kinsmen, we passed through a brick archway set with massive wooden doors, into the grand atrium, its lofty roof supported by two rows of tall pillars, into the grand atrium. It contained no statues or lewd frescoes; instead the walls were decorated with Scripture verses painted with bright borders. The pleasant courtyard with its splashing fountain set with blue tiles, was visible beyond a window of expensive clear glass panes that let in plenty of sunshine.

"Yours is surely the only house in Rome without statues," I said to Acilia.

"The Jewish Christians who first brought us the Gospel warned us sternly about fashioning graven

---

* Inscription on the 4th century Church of St. Pudentiana: states that it is built over the site of "the house-church of St. Pudens, the senator, and the home of the holy apostles." Excavated in the 1920's by archeologist Rodolfo Lanciano, it is believed to be the earliest known place of worship of the western church.

images," she said, "because people can easily fall into worshipping them. Image worship, in every case, the Lord abhors."

We already knew many of the people, such as Pomponia Graecina Lucina, Linus and his mother Claudia Procula. Acilia introduced me to the Jewish preacher Apelles Aristobulus, the dark-skinned Rufus, and his kindly old mother.

The amiable nut-brown woman smiled sweetly. "So nice to have you with us, dear," she said, while pressing a neatly bound parchment volume of the Gospel of Matthew into my hand. "This wonderful little book will tell you the story of Jesus' life. We Christians always use modern codice books, for they are compact, and easy to refer to."*

"Oh, thank you," I said, staring down at the copper-covered script.

"The service is always conducted in Greek, but there is a Latin interpreter for some like your mother, who do not understand Greek," Acilia said.

A marble-topped table was spread with a loaf of bread and a silver chalice filled with wine. The congregation sang psalms, and a man stood up to pray. Then Brother Rufus read from his copy of Matthew, a man who had been a disciple of Jesus:

> . . . And sitting down, they watched Him there; and set up over His head
> his accusation written, THIS IS JESUS THE KING OF THE JEWS. Then

---

* T.C. Skeat, *Early Christian Book Production.*

were two thieves crucified with Him . . . and they
that passed by reviled
Him, wagging their heads. Now from the sixth hour
until the ninth hour
there was darkness over all the land until the ninth
hour.
And about the ninth hour Jesus cried with a loud
voice, saying,
"Eli, Eli, lama sabachthani? My God, My God, why
hast Thou forsaken me?"
And straightway one of them ran, and took a sponge
and filled it with vinegar,
and gave Him to drink. Jesus, when He had cried
again with a loud
voice, yielded up the ghost . . . and the earth did
quake and the rocks
rent. When the centurion and they that were with
Him watching Jesus,
saw the things that were done, they feared greatly,
saying, 'Truly this
was the Son of God.'

Brother Rufus read about how Jesus had been buried
three days, then He rose from the dead. Then Apelles
Aristobulus read these words from the Last Supper feast,
which Jesus ate with His disciples just before He died:

He took bread, and gave thanks, and brake it and
gave to them, saying,
This is My body which is given for you; this do in
remembrance of me.
Likewise also the cup after supper, saying, 'This cup
is the new
testament in my blood, which is shed for you.'

A lengthy prayer was offered up, of praise and glory to the Father God, in the name of the Son, giving thanks to be counted worthy to receive the offering. And the congregation said "amen." The deacons passed the bread and the wine around to the Christian believers. A collection was taken, from those same believers, which would later be distributed to those in need.* After the service was finished, they all greeted one another with what they called the "kiss of peace."

"A number of them are slaves or freedmen who have responsibilities to their masters, and are required to return to their places of employment," Acilia said. "But those who can, stay for dinner. This is called an *agape* feast. Everyone brings baskets of simple fare, enough for their own families and a little extra for the poor and strangers, so that none are left out. The food is put together and spread out on a table."

After dinner, while Acilia and I were clearing the tables, we felt something stinging our backs. "Oh, no, Pudens is teaching our little cousins how to shoot peas at us through a papyrus tube!" Acilia exclaimed. She grimaced at her brother, and laughing, we dashed into the kitchen to find refuge with Priscilla and the other ladies.

"My brother still hasn't received Jesus into his heart," Acilia said, while we helped wash the plates

---

* Justin Martyr

143

and beakers. "He always says his friends at school will make fun of him. We pray for him every day."

At the evening service, Apelles Aristobulus preached about a shepherd who had lost a sheep, and searched diligently until he had found it. Bran understood it first. He knew all about lost sheep, having at times helped tend his father's flocks in Britain.

"I am that lost sheep," he whispered. "I cannot save myself."

Mum's fingers ran unconsciously over the ugly red scars on her wrist. They stayed behind that evening, engrossed in conversation with Brother Rufus, Apelles Aristobulus and Manlius.

"I won't go back to that evil palace without the Lord," Mum said, wiping her tears. "I am a poor sinner. I must accept Christ as my Saviour and make my peace with God! *He* can give us life and eternal happiness!"

Mum and Bran knelt together with the men, and with deep thanksgiving, praised the God of all grace for His Gift of such a wonderful Saviour. God's great love and forgiveness dawned upon their souls with a dazzling Light, sweeping clean the dark corners of their hearts. Folded in Jesus' arms, like the lost sheep in the story, the pain in their eyes was replaced by a deep heavenly peace and joy.

Can it be so simple? Steeped as I was in idol worship, and the appeasement of grim heathen gods, surely I must work hard to please this new God before He would accept me.

Chapter 8

"As many as received Him, to them gave He
power to become the sons of God."
—John 1:12

A.D. 56

What will you do after graduation?" Acilia asked
me.

"I am already sixteen years old, and you are almost fifteen. Most of the girls our age are married
or betrothed by now."

Acilia and I browsed through the splendid
shops in the Saepta Julia's two-storied pavilion, re-
marking over all the latest fashions, exotic silks
and cottons, and golden jewelry set with emeralds,
pearls and jacinth. Antique shops bulged with
pricey teak and ivory furniture, Etruscan statuary,
crystal vases and faded Babylonian tapestries. Hundreds of Rome's wealthiest citizens thronged the
Saepta's elegant marble pavement, including many
elderly people walking briskly, enjoying their daily

constitutional,* protected from the hot sun by the vaulted roof supported by rows of tall pillars.

"My parents refuse to arrange a marriage for me right now," Acilia said. "They have always been opposed to these early marriages, pointing out the numbers of immature mothers who die in childbirth."

"Did you hear that Titus' pretty sister Domitilla died that way just a few days ago? Paezuza said she had a baby girl that they named after her."

"Oh, that's so sad! But it doesn't surprise me," Acilia said. "Her father Vespasian has always been a bit of a skinflint, and was happy to marry her off quickly to a rich husband."

"And poor little Octavia. She hardly had time to be a child. I surely do miss her," I said. "As wife of the Emperor, it seems she is always burdened down with official duties, or traveling somewhere." The storekeeper held up a silk shawl glimmering with golden threads, and I draped it about my shoulders. "How does this look on me?"

"No, the color isn't right," Acilia said. "Try the green one."

"Anyway, it's terribly expensive." I laid it back down on the marble countertop.

We stopped to buy a hot *calzone*, a pastry filled with pork and cheese and black olives, and sat down to eat on a stone bench near the fountain.

"Yecch, they put anchovies in mine," Acilia said. She carefully picked them out. "Don't you just hate

---

* Xenophon

anchovies! We will be leaving for our orphan's home in the *campagnia* next week. I wish you and your mother and Bran could come with us. Mama is always looking for volunteers to help out. Your old teacher, Eliab Ben David, works there full-time, and Olympas, whom you know."

"I'd love to go. I should be lonely as a ghost here in the city without you."

"I'm not inviting you for a leisurely vacation, though. It's some of the hardest work you will ever do. Some of the orphans were former street beggars, and can be quite a handful. The babies are mainly those who were abandoned by their parents, who leave them to die by exposure on the side of the road."

"That is a hideous custom."

"Yes. Papa has gone back into his law practice, and he and Mama have adopted many of the orphans out into loving homes. Some are blind or crippled, or otherwise disabled, and often don't live long. But Mama says that they were all created by God, with worth and dignity in His eyes, and if they die they should be in the company of those who care about them."

I threw a few coppers to a silly mime and a troupe of jugglers. "It's so sad that people would abandon their own babies like that."

"Some are from poor families, who can't face bringing more children into that hard life. But many are the children of the rich. By our law, when a man dies, his inheritance must be divided equally among all his sons. The more sons he has, the less money will go to each heir, and the family fortune will dwindle. And girls are nothing but an expense."

In the dark hours of the morning our family set off in Manlius' and Priscilla's luxurious enclosed vehicle called a *carruca dormitoria*, drawn by a team of four stout Reate mules. The *carruca* had seats inside, cushioned with plush bolsters, that could be folded down at night and made into beds. A thick rug carpeted the floor. A cupboard stored foodstuffs, a small brazier, and cooking utensils.

"This is beautiful!" I exclaimed, running my fingers over the soft cushions and the highly polished brass fittings.

"Sorry, there's not much room to sit," Acilia said. The *carruca* was stacked with new tunics, and crates of toys and dolls for the orphans. "Everyone in the house-church likes to donate items."

"It's all right," I said. "Bran and I will ride above with Patrobas. We like to watch the scenery, since we don't own a *car*, and can't get out to the *campagnia* often. Though we are allowed to live in luxury at the palace, my father's pension is actually quite small."

"A law forbids wheeled vehicles in the city after daybreak,"* the freedman Patrobas explained, as the *carruca* lurched through the murky streets, amid a jumble of carts and wagons and long droves of mules that struggled to get out of the city before dawn. The sun was just peeping over the mountaintops as

---

*Juvenal

we passed through the tall Roman gate known as the Porta Salaria.

The Via Salaria was the old salt-carrying road that led into the Sabine Hills. It swung across a flatland, between clouds of umbrella pine, dark cypress, palms; and groves of olive trees with crippled trunks twisting in all directions. Their gray-green leaves quivered in the early morning breeze. Magnificent well-kept villas, painted gleaming white or pastel colors, were set back from the road among elegant gardens and vineyards heavily laden with clusters of grapes, some drying on racks in the sun. Garden walls of rough basalt were festooned with trailing ivy.

The roadside was thickly sown with marble slabs, curious tombs and sepulchral monuments. With their endless gloomy epigrams full of hopeless sentiments, they were inscribed with the names of Rome's wealthiest patricians, some nearly eaten away by centuries of wind and rain.

Patrobas followed my inquiring eyes. "We have a law in Rome that the dead must be buried outside the city walls," he said. "Tombs line most all of the roads leading out of Rome. Pagans believe that the hereafter is a place of vast emptiness, where no one knows each other, and that people must proudly exhibit their names on these splendid tombstones in order to be remembered somehow. Very sad. As Christians, we know that we may be unknown on earth, yet well known in Heaven. Mankind once knew the true God, but gave Him up to serve their own vile lusts."

Two miles outside the city, Patrobas jumped down to throw open an iron gate, and the *carruca* jolted along a lane bordered with peach, almond and glossy pear trees, and sweetly fragrant pomegranates and figs. Beyond the trees sprawled the ancestral mansion, its yellow stucco face crumbling in places, revealing the ancient brick framework underneath. One blue shutter sagged on rusted hinges.

Patrobas chuckled. "It's not very glamorous now, though in years past, when the Acilian Glabriones owned many slaves, it was a grand palace with beautiful gardens. But now it is a real working farm, supplying food to feed all the children who live here."

More than a hundred tousle-haired youngsters rolled in the green grass. As we jumped down from the wagons, a pack of the little brown moppets, some with scabbed knees, others trundling hoops or clutching stuffed dolls, swarmed over us, spreading sunshine with bright smiles and sticky kisses. Several flung their arms around my waist and held on tightly. One small boy had his hair shaved off due to head lice. Another had only one arm, and a girl hobbled about on crutches, her leg in a brace. But nothing could slow them down.

Shallow steps led up to the wide stone-flagged entranceway. The carved old doors creaked open, and Olympas and Ilid, whom everyone now called "Eliab," rushed out to meet us.

"It's so good to see you all!" he cried. "And I must tell you that I have found the Messiah, our Lord Jesus Christ."

"And I, too," Mum replied. "Praise be to God!"

"Manlius and Priscilla have been so kind," Ilid said, "They also helped me settle things with my former Roman slave–master."

It was evident that the house had once been a fine showplace. But it now had a decidedly lived-in look, the elegant marble floors scuffed from the traffic of many little running feet. The white-washed walls, begrimed with fingerprints, were hung with parchment verses from the Scriptures, many of them obviously decorated by the orphaned children. One of them read, "When my father and mother forsake me, then the Lord will take me up" (Psalm 27:10). Next to it was another verse, "Yea, they may forget, but I will not forget thee. Behold, I have graven thee on the palms of my hands" (Isaiah 49:15).

Near the atrium stood a bright, happy room, flooded with beams of sunlight, filled with healthy, chubby infants who clamored for attention. In an adjoining room severely handicapped children of various ages lay in cribs hung with colorful toys. Some had breathing problems, or were blind, deaf or crippled. Others had difficulty swallowing due to malformed faces and lips. Though it was well into the morning, the overworked caregiver was still struggling to feed them their breakfast.

"It takes a long time for them to eat," the caregiver explained, brushing a strand of blond hair away from her eyes. "You have to be very patient."

"We came to give you two pairs of extra hands, Morag Julia," Acilia said. "This is my friend, Claudia Rufina, from Britain."

Morag Julia turned about, her emerald eyes sparkling with interest. "Oh, I come from northern Gaul!" she exclaimed. "My dear husband was a Roman Tribune, but he was killed in battle just this year. Many of the workers here are widows, some with small children of their own. Widows have a very poor time in the Empire because there are few jobs. Many have been forced into slavery. So we are very grateful to have steady work and a place to live!"

After breakfast, Morag Julia allowed the handicapped children to play on a thick carpet on the floor, with balls and toys. A blind child practiced music on a lyre, while another began weaving a lovely basket. Later Morag read them a story from the Scriptures and sang songs with them. Many of them sang heartily along with her. She showed them large red letters mounted on sheets of papyrus, and a few proudly recited each letter.

"We hope to teach some of them to read, and acquire skills according to their abilities," Morag said, "so that they can learn a suitable trade, and become valuable members of society."

After lunch, Morag Julia, Acilia and I laid them in cribs for their naps. Morag showed us how to exercise contracted arms and legs, while rubbing fragrant unguents on them. While the children rested, we laundered mountains of soiled clothing, linens and nappies in a huge stone tub in the sun-dappled courtyard.

"You must be exhausted doing this day after day," I said to Morag, while she and I were hanging out the laundry on ropes to dry.

A sad expression clouded her face. She lapsed into the Gallic speech of the Belgaic Celts, which I understood well. "Many winters ago, my husband and I lived in Rome for a time, and I gave birth to a beautiful baby boy. But he had several webbed toes and a large heart-shaped birthmark on the back of his right shoulder."

She paused to wipe her eyes. "The foolish mid-wives who attended me convinced me that he was an evil omen, and would bring sorrow to my husband's house. They persuaded me to abandon him outside the city walls. Later, I sent a servant to fetch him back, but he was already gone without a trace, probably eaten by wild beasts. Such aches it put in my heart!"

"'Twas not against the law," I said.

"Yet I knew it was a grievous sin. Later a friend invited me to the home of some Jewish Christians, where a young man named Aquila preached about a God who could forgive sins. What a healing medicine it was to my tormented soul! But until the day I die, I will stare at faces in crowds, wondering if one of them could be my son."

Morag stared off into space, then went on. "The Lord never blessed me with any more children. But He has placed these special lambs in my care, and it gives me great joy to serve them, that the light of Heaven might shine on their little faces. So I try never to complain."

In the evening Morag, Acilia and I donned voluminous sailcloth garments, and helped the children with their baths in the large pool in the *balineum*, the private bathhouse. We dressed them in clean tunics and nappies, then met with the others around a roaring campfire, for prayers and the singing of psalms, which played a primary role in the daily routine of the orphanage.

Mingled with the smell of the wood smoke was the sweet and pungent odor of Asian citronella grass, which warded off gnats and mosquitoes. I looked from one to another of the Christian workers gathered around the firelight, and thought how their faces seemed to shine, peace radiating from every pair of eyes.

In the morning Olympas said, "I need some strong young people to help me carry supplies to the leper colony. Anyone interested?"

"I don't . . . know," I muttered, grimacing behind his back.

I had seen lepers before walking in the road, limbs ravaged, faces grossly disfigured, the flesh eaten off. If a stranger approached, they would draw their cloaks tightly about them, and cry "unclean, unclean," from their eroded lips. Shunned by society, no longer allowed to venture into the cities and towns, they were banished to the caves and dens of the earth.

But Acilia was delighted. "It's very pretty up there, in the Sabine foothills. Don't worry. Despite what they say, leprosy is not easily spread to healthy people."

After devotions and a hearty breakfast, our party set out. Bran and Pudens rode along with us. The heavily loaded wagon lumbered along the narrow, gravel-sprinkled trackway that bordered the property line, half-shaded by olive trees and orchards planted beside golden fields of wheat. Yellow dust rose in clouds behind us. Herds of long-horned white Tuscan cattle grazed in a sunny meadow dotted with bright lavender and pink clover. A weeping willow dropped its mournful tendrils down beside a lazy brook that babbled through the pasture.

The twisting, rutted road narrowed as it wound up and up into the foothills, where the air became noticeably cooler. Trees thronged one side of the road, and to our left, the sun's rays slanted down the pine-clad valley. As the wagon neared the gleaming, whitewashed village, I wrinkled my nose as an obnoxious rotten-egg odor replaced the fragrant scent of the pines.

Pudens grinned. "There are a number of warm sulphur springs in the area," he said.

"The ancient Sabines have always believed that sulphur water was soothing to the skin. When Mama and Papa became Christians, they wanted to help the many lepers that roamed the land," Acilia explained. "Also, vegetables and grain raised in this sulphurus soil are very nutritious for the lepers. In this village, their healthy spouses and children may come for visits, and some even decide to stay. They are careful to keep the latrines and baths and eating utensils separate, so the disease rarely spreads."

The village consisted of six dormitories, a few cabins, and various barns and outbuildings. Fat brown, white, or gray-speckled chickens strutted about the tranquil grounds, running in and out of doorways, and pecking among the rocks. With clucks and squawks, and a flutter of wings, the pompous creatures regarded us with curious, critical eyes, heads nodding here and there.

A few bearded goats, tethered to small stakes in the ground, nibbled at patches of trampled grass, their lower jaws chewing monotonously. Outside the clearing sprawled a fertile garden with neat rows of cabbage and asparagus, broccoli, spinach and eggplant, and clusters of beans climbing over poles. Peach and cherry trees surrounded the garden, their boughs hung low with ripening fruit. Through the trees, a graveyard marked with hundreds of simple headstones, was tucked within a flowery glade.

We ducked our heads inside an outbuilding containing a weaving room that bustled with industry. Women and older children were carding and spinning wool and flax fibers into threads, and winding them into large skeins. Others were occupied at the dye vats, preparing brilliant dyes from flowers and berries. The skeins were plunged into the boiling vats for several minutes, then rinsed and hung outside on the stone wall to dry. The shuttlecocks on the huge looms flew back and forth through the warp, and gaudy rugs and blankets slowly emerged from the jumble of wool. Flax threads were woven into narrow widths, which could be sewn together to make bed sheets, or used for garments and bandages.

"They all work very hard to make the colony nearly self-supporting," Acilia said.

"After we launder the rugs in hot water and ash, we lay them out to dry in the hot sun. Then they can be sold in the city," one woman said. She was a handsome woman, with no apparent symptoms of leprosy.

"Do you stay up here all the time?" I asked curiously.

She smiled. "My husband is a leper. I loved him, so no one could persuade me not to come. But we found the Lord Jesus here, and we are happier now than we have ever been."

The flame-red sun went down slowly, lingering among the tall pines. Faces rapt, the odd group made the Sabine hills ring with gladness that evening around the campfire as, with husky voices, they heartily sang psalms, despite their hideous lesions, noses and ears missing, eyes filmed over, and the indescribable stench of rotting flesh. Some with whole hands eaten off, had only little nubs left at the end of the wrist. Others had a different form of leprosy, with great bubble-like sores that distorted the face.

My heart was deeply touched as they sang:

He was wounded for our transgressions,
He was bruised for our iniquities;
The chastisement of our peace was upon Him
And with His stripes we are healed.

A man stood up to speak. He said his name was Brother Philologus. His face was grotesquely deformed, eyes white and unseeing, his nose decayed.

"I didn't think much about the tiny spot that first appeared on my skin," the old leper said. "I tried to hide it, but within a year the spots had spread all over my body. The doctors at the Isola Tiburina and their sacred snakes could not cure me. I was quickly thrown out of the hospital, and cast out of the city as well. But when I came here, I learned that I had a disease much worse than that of leprosy; and that disease was called 'sin!' We are all born as sinners. 'There is none righteous, no not one.' But God is holy, and will not allow even one sin into His presence."

He leaned heavily against a tree stump, for his missing toes and atrophied bones made it difficult to stand.

"All our efforts to heal our sins and clean ourselves up can avail nothing, for the Scripture says in the book of Isaiah, that 'we are all as an unclean thing, and all our righteousnesses are as filthy rags.' But God's Son, the Lord Jesus, loved us and saw us in our great need. He came to earth to die in our place, and bore God's punishment for our sins. We only have to ask Him to come into our poor, sinful hearts, and to forgive us."

Suddenly it was made startlingly clear to me that my good works could never appease this God, nor get me into Heaven; that Jesus had died to pay the debt that I could never pay.

"The leprosy has invaded my throat," Brother Philologus went on, "and I cannot speak further. Soon this wasted body will depart this life, and join the others in yonder graveyard. But my soul will enter His bright gates with joy, and I will someday receive a glorious new body, without spot or wrinkle!"

"Amen!" the fervent cry went up from the group.

When the service came to a close, I went to speak with Brother Philologus. "My name is Claudia. I would like to be saved."

Together we prayed, and I asked the Lord Jesus to forgive my sins.

The following day I asked Brother Philologus if he might baptize me. All the brethren assembled beside the visitors' pool.

"Who is it being baptized?" a blind leper whispered loudly to another.

"It is the British princess, Claudia," was the husky reply.

"Praise be!"

Brother Philologus sat beside the pool, placing his leprous stump of hand on my head. "Do you believe in God, the Father Almighty?" he asked.

"Yes, I believe."

"Do you believe in Christ Jesus, the Son of God, who was crucified, and rose again the third day? Have you trusted Him to forgive your sins, and do you believe in the Holy Spirit and the Resurrection of the body?"

"Yes, I believe."

"Then I baptize you in the name of the Father, the Son, and the Holy Spirit."

In that decaying world, I had found a new life; made clean and bright, spotless in the eyes of a holy God, fit for His beautiful Home above. And I understood too, that Christians did good deeds, not to appease God, but out of love for Him.

"We have a new volunteer today," Morag Julia said. "Her name is Sergia Paula." She was a lovely child of about thirteen, with masses of glossy black curls that framed her ruddy cheeks, and extraordinary violet eyes.

"I recently moved here from Cyprus, where my grandfather Sergius Paulus was Proconsul,"* Sergia Paula said. "We have started a church and school in our house in the thirteenth district."†

"Since we got done so early today, with the extra help, perhaps you girls would like to take two or three of the children out for a walk, in the nice push-cart that Olympas built for us," Morag Julia said.

---

* Acts 13:7

† From a group of inscriptions discovered in Rome.

The August morning was awash in sunlight as Acilia, Sergia Paula and I ventured out along the Via Salaria, with three of the handicapped children. They delighted in the songs of the larks and finches that perched in the tall cedars and umbrella pines. And in the speckled butterflies and the tiny green hummingbirds that pirouetted above the blood-red poppies, yellow buttercups, brown-eyed susans, and pink clover.

We sat down to rest on a cool, grassy bank that overlooked the river, with the blue and purple grandeur of the Sabine Mountains in the background. An assembly of wide-eyed toads blinked at us from the muddy flats, while they croaked out a loud symphony. The children squealed as a harmless black snake slithered across the grass, and disappeared in some long swaying reeds at the water's edge.

I leaned back against a stump. "This is a beautiful spot. I could stay here forever," I said.

Suddenly Acilia became deathly quiet. "Sh-sh-sh, I think I hear a baby crying," she said.

We searched among the boulders covered with sphagnum moss and lichen. Then my eyes focused on a small white object. It looked like an abandoned doll, but it had a lusty cry, and wildly flailing limbs. Though Acilia had told me about such unwanted babies, I had not expected to see one on such a fine morning.

"Hurry, we must take him to Mama," Acilia said.

We started toward him, when I gazed in alarm at a pack of feral dogs emerging from a grove of trees. They had apparently caught the baby's scent.

"Take the children back to the house quickly!"
I commanded.

Acilia and Sergia Paula propelled the pushcart back along the Via Salaria. I picked up a broken tree branch, and tore the leaves and twigs off, to use as a weapon. Noses quivering, ears pricked, the feral dogs bared their teeth, and their cold eyes glittered as they crept closer to the helpless infant, their bellies low to the ground. Shouting and screeching like a madwoman, I picked up handfuls of pebbles and pelted them, and waved my heavy stick. A few turned and ran, tails tucked between their legs, but several of the larger ones stood their ground belligerently, daring me to advance.

As I maneuvered closer to the baby, the dogs began to circle around us. Horrified, I watched their stealthy approach. My foot caught in some coarse vines, and I fell backward against sharp rocks and bramble-bushes. Intense pain shot through me, but I gathered all my strength to pull up into a sitting position. Snatching the infant from the ground, I headed for a nearby poplar tree to climb. He ceased his crying and nestled his soft downy head into my shoulder contentedly.

One of the hostile creatures, his black mottled fur bristling, sprang at me, a fierce growl escaping from his throat. I felt his hot and fetid breath even before his jagged yellow fangs bit into my flesh, tearing a chunk from my leg. All courage gone, I edged higher into the tree. But it was small, and the branches could barely support us. The dog's jaws dripped red with my blood, his lips pulled back in a snarl. One of the poplar branches cracked beneath my weight, but I was able to grasp the one above it.

A Scripture verse came to mind: "Call upon Me in the day of trouble."

"Dear Lord," I prayed, "the day of trouble surely is now!"

"Stay back!" a voice commanded.

Suddenly, as the black monster was jumping high, trying to snap at my feet, an arrow whizzed by, and caught the dog's chest with such force that the feathered end vibrated like the wings of a hummingbird. With a pitiful yowl, the ugly brute collapsed to the earth in a bloody heap. Another creature fell, then another. Glancing down through the leaves, I saw Pudens standing with his bow and arrows. He expertly dispatched four of the snarling dogs, and the rest slunk away into the trees.

Pudens held out his arms and I handed the baby to him. Then he helped me climb down from the tree, blood spurting from the bite on my leg. He wrapped one arm around me, and I fell against him, choking and sobbing. Pudens pressed my head tight against his wildly beating heart, and murmured soft comforting words. He brushed back my hair, which had by this time fallen out of its clips, and cascaded down my back in a tangle of dead leaves and pine needles.

"You could have been killed, princess," he whispered, his breath coming in ragged gasps.

"God sent you. I prayed, and there you were, just like an angel! You saved my life."

Pudens chuckled. "Actually, Acilia sent me," he said. The warmth of his supporting arms, and his deep, gentle voice calmed me. "The danger is gone. I'm here now, and I won't let anything hurt you again. But we have to get you back to the house quickly. You are losing much blood. The dog's bite must have severed an artery."

"I think I can walk a little." But I was beginning to feel faint, and groaned with each painful step.

Priscilla and Mum came running from the house, and took the infant, quickly wrapping him in a blanket. Olympas and Athro brought a litter to carry me, and I gratefully settled back against the soft cushions.

Pudens shook his head. "Of all the girls I know, you are the only one crazy enough to do what you did," he said.

I didn't reply.

Mum laid me on one of the shabby couches in the atrium. She tended to my wound and mixed up a poultice. "Now we shall have to wonder if the dog that bit you was afflicted with hydrophobia," she said. "There has been a recent outbreak among the wild animals."

That was a possibility I hadn't pondered. "How long before we know?" I asked. Hydrophobia caused a hideous death, too terrible to contemplate.

"Several weeks," she replied tersely.

Priscilla bathed the baby boy in a copper basin of warm water, and wrapped him in cotton cloth. Acilia brought goat's milk in an odd firkin, which was designed especially for feeding babies. It was usually a sloppy, painstaking procedure, but the little fellow was so hungry, he gulped it down quickly. When his eyes began to droop, Acilia laid him beside me to sleep.

"I wish I could keep him myself," I said, stroking his soft hair. "But he needs a real mother and father."

"A dear Christian couple was in here today, from Sergius Paulus' new house-church, hoping to adopt a baby boy," Priscilla said. "But I only had little girls available. They said they would stop back at the end of the week. He is a beautiful baby. I should think they would be thrilled to take him."

Ilid and Olympas carried my couch out by the campfire that evening for devotions, underneath the moon-laced trees and a sky that glittered with stars. Olympas prayed, thanking the Lord for preserving my life.

Pudens' brown eyes fastened on me from across the campfire. They seemed to increase in size, and glowed with a warm light that I had never seen before, as the fire's golden reflection danced across his face. My heart raced, and I quickly lowered my head, swallowing a tear that caught in my throat; grateful for the dim shadows, for no one could see the bright spots of pink that colored my cheeks.

For several weeks I was pampered and petted, and the story of the wild dogs was oft retold and embellished. Every tiny ache or pain caused me to imagine that I had contracted hydrophobia. But the fear gradually subsided as each day went by.

The harvest was soon with us. Singing merrily, Acilia, Sergia Paula helped pick olives from the heavily laden trees. Then we stood alongside the other women, holding the edges of a great cloth. The men shook the branches that could not be reached from the ground or from ladders, and beat the olives down with long poles until the cloth was filled with the round black fruits.

Haymakers, bright scythes glistening, swished and cut hay all week in the far pasture. The hay was tossed this way and that with hand rakes, until it dried in the hot sun. The women helped gather the hay into bundles.

In a stupor of exhaustion near the end of the day, I was happy to rest in the back of the farm wagon, as Olympas drove another load of hay to the barn. Pudens jumped into the wagon beside me. I tried not to notice how the glint of the afternoon sun sent dashes of golden light through the tips of his Umbrian brown hair that perfectly matched the light in his eyes.

His steady gaze made me squirm uncomfortably, and I quickly looked away. I felt tongue-tied and shy. After working all day in the crushing heat of the sun, I was an unsightly mass of grime. I drew my sleeve wearily across the ugly beads of perspiration that chased each other down my forehead in a most unladylike way, and ran into my eyes, making them sting.

Despite a protective wide-brimmed hat and the oozing mass of zinc oxide, my skin had gradually burned
unfashionably brown over the summer, studded of
course with a profusion of Celtic freckles. With the
pieces of hay in my oddly sun-bleached hair, I must
surely resemble a barbarian field servant!

Well, no matter, I thought. I was a sensible girl,
not one silly enough with romantic notions, to be
turned aside by a handsome face with beautifully
sculpted lips and an engaging white smile; nor even
a pair of soft brown eyes with ridiculously long lashes.

The late afternoon sun dipped behind a woolly
cloud, and a cool, refreshing breeze rustled among
the pines. The old wagon wheel struck a rut, and
jolted suddenly. I made a wild grab for the side of
the wagon to steady myself. Pudens' hand brushed
mine, and his fingers entwined around it. He pressed
my calloused hand to his lips, and rubbed it softly
against his cheek.

"*Bellissima*, you are the most beautiful girl I have
ever seen," he murmured in his deep, lilting voice,
a look of longing in his great velvet eyes.

My thoughts scattered, like the wary cicadas
with quivering wings that danced in every direction
as our wagon rumbled along the path. I could only
manage a tiny, cracked giggle.

"You say that to all your girlfriends."

"Please don't laugh at me, Rufina." His voice
broke. "I love you. It frightened me so much when
the dogs attacked you. I knew that I couldn't live without you. I have to go back to law school in the city

tomorrow. But I'm going to ask our parents to arrange a marriage for us. Please say you love me, *Bellisima*."

Dazed, I felt the blood drain from my face. I tried to speak, but the words choked in my throat. My eyes misted, as I gazed deeply into his. But there was no need for words. He already knew that I loved him. That I had always loved him.

"You two all right back there?" Olympas strained to see around the bales of hay.

"Yes, we're fine, sir," Pudens replied, with a wide grin. He gripped both my hands and steadied me as we climbed down from the wagon, to help stack the hay in the barn. A chorus of finches called out in the dense thorn-bush, and hundreds of dusky cicadas chattered about us in a frenzied rhapsody of approval.

Chapter 9

"Set your affections on things above."
—Colossians 3:2

Mum and I met with Manlius and Priscilla and Pudens at their townhome on the Via Urbana for our betrothal ceremony. Papers had been drawn up, with the marriage settlements written down in full detail. Friends and relatives attended, some of whom acted as witnesses, while others came just to wish us well. Refreshments were served, and Manlius and Priscilla lavished Mum and I with costly betrothal gifts, as was the custom. A wave of joy enveloped me when Pudens slipped a delicately carved gold ring on the third finger of my left hand, over the *vena amoris* that was said to connect directly to the heart.

Sure no sorrow could ever cloud my world again!

But Mum didn't have much to say later as we sat on the balcony in our apartment, sipping chamomile tea. Night was coming on, and the shadows grew long and jagged as the sun disappeared over the high ridges above the city. Thousands of lamps twinkled on one by one in the plazas and the court-yards below, and a full moon arose.

"It worries me that Pudens doesn't profess to follow the Lord," she said slowly. "We haven't been Christians very long, and I don't know much, but I think it would be a mistake to marry an unbeliever."

In my state of euphoria, I was surprised to learn that Mum did not share my enthusiasm. "I'm sure he'll change in time," I said. "We can't get married for two or three years yet anyway, till he's finished with law school. Brother Manlius and Priscilla don't seem to see anything wrong with it."

"I'm afraid his parents want so much for him to be a Christian, they may not be seeing things clearly. They don't want him marrying one of those hea-then girls. But unfortunately, a child cannot get to Heaven by holding onto his parents' toga; each per-son has to come to the Lord for himself. I want you to be happy, not having to spend your life compro-mising your Christian principles. I'm afraid I am going to have to pray that the Lord will put a stop to this if it's not His will."

I kissed the top of her dark-copper head, now sprinkled with gray. She was an extremely determined little person. "He makes me so happy, Mum. After we are married, I will help him to overcome his faults. Everything will turn out all right. You'll see."

Priscilla stopped me after church the following day. "The Lord has opened the way for us to start a free school for the poor children who live in the tenements not far from our townhome," she said. "I wondered if you might like to work here as a teacher."

"Yes, I'd be thrilled to!"

"We have been praying about reaching out with the Gospel to those suffering souls. A free school may be the fastest way to win their confidence."

The children trickled in slowly at first, but once word got around the neighborhood, I was swamped by a class of forty to fifty enthusiastic seven-year-olds. I was to teach them to read and write Latin, and to get them started in geography and arithmetic. When Priscilla passed out a new slate and stylus to each of them, their huge dark eyes sparkled, and they looked in amazement one to another.

The little urchins would arrive at the crack of dawn, barefoot and dirty, torn and patched oversized tunics hanging loosely from their shoulders, clutching their precious wax slates to their ragged bosoms. Everyone assembled in the atrium to start the day with psalms, prayers and Scripture reading. It delighted our hearts to tell them of our Lord Jesus Christ, who loved each one, and had died to set us free from the pagan chains that once held us.

"Miss Claudia, Miss Claudia, come quick!" One of my students, a child named Marcia, rushed into the courtyard sobbing, just as we were finishing classes for the day. "It's my Mama. She says she's dying, and she don't know how to die. She has to see you!"

Marcia reached for my hand, and I called out for the freedman Patrobas to accompany us. We dashed through the busy, dirty streets, then underneath a low arch, and through the bleak passageway leading to her tenement home, strewn inches deep with trash and shards of broken amphorae. Drops of water spattered across my face from scraps of ragged laundry hanging high overhead. In the blighted, bare-earth courtyard, groups of idle, tough-looking men regarded us briefly with bold and hostile eyes. They were laying wagers, standing clustered about a pair of angry fighting cocks struggling to their death.

Crumbling walls of dark and ancient brickwork were scrawled with graffiti, decrying the unsanitary conditions in which the occupants were forced to live: the constant plague of rats and roaches, and inadequate kitchen and toilet facilities.

"Rents are exorbitant in these low, crushed *insulae,*" Patrobas said. "Thus, as many people as possible are crammed into any available space."

We entered a cave-like labyrinth, and climbed five narrow flights of wooden stairs, worn hollow in the center by the constant tread of feet. The overcrowded tenement clamored with crying babies, flies buzzing about garbage, and loud, quarrelsome voices. The odor of garlic and other cooking smells mingled with the stench of refuse, damp mold and stale wine.

The tiny room was nearly bare, except for a thin straw pallet on the floor. The light was so dim I could scarcely see the thin, pale woman lying there. I pushed open the shutter, letting in a sliver of sunlight, then recoiled as a battalion of cockroaches scuttled across the floor and vanished into the dark corners.

The dingy yellow-gray walls, hung with sooty cobwebs, were brightened by two Scripture verses Marcia had painted in school. One said: "Prepare to meet thy God" (Amos 4:12), and the other, "Look unto Me, and be ye saved, all the ends of the earth: for I am God, and there is none else" (Isaiah 45:22).

A bit gingerly I knelt on the floor beside the woman, who had been coughing into a filthy scrap of cloth held tightly to her mouth to contain the poison vapors. Flushed with fever, she fought for every breath.

"My name is Penelope," she said. "I think I'm dying. My daughter tells me that your God can forgive sins. I have a lot of sins."

Patrobas withdrew from his cloak a well-worn copy of the Gospel of Matthew, and flipped it open. He read to her the wonderful story of Jesus' death and Resurrection, and told her about God's beautiful home called Heaven.

"What can I do?" Penelope whispered.

"You must believe in your heart that Jesus is the Son of the true and living God, who created all things," I told her, "and that Jesus died and rose again. Then you may pray and ask Him to forgive your sins."

Penelope's eyes glistened with tears as she breathed a simple prayer. It was the first time I had helped lead a soul to Christ, and I realized that there is no greater thrill on earth. None of Rome's tawdry amusements could ever come close.

She closed her eyes, overcome with weariness. Patrobas brought a litter and we carried Penelope to Manlius' and Priscilla's house, where she was lovingly restored to health.

Penelope became a missionary to the residents of her tenement, to the poor, the elderly, the downtrodden. Mum, Priscilla, Pomponia, Claudia Procula, Acilia and I, and other teams of volunteers often followed her as she made her rounds, winding through narrow, tortuous hallways to find sick and lonely people. Trapped in the few menial jobs that were available to them, their meager wages barely covered the cost of the high rents.

Constantly praying for God's guidance in every situation, we brought food and medicine; changed bandages, helped care for children, picked out head lice, assisted with laundry; filled lamps with oil, scrubbed floors, or carried water up from the public fountains to those who were no longer able to do it. Mum was often called upon to deliver babies. Few objected then, if we sat down to read the Scriptures and to pray with them.

The house-church expanded and outgrew Manlius and Priscilla's grand atrium, as many from the tenements turned to God from idols, and emerged from sin and darkness to become devoted followers of Christ. They were received into fellowship as brothers and sisters.

"The church is running out of space," I said to Priscilla one Lord's Day, as we watched the crowds pouring in. "What will we do?"

"Praise God!" Priscilla said. "The Lord has blessed our feeble efforts more than anyone could have imagined. Now we will have to pray about more places to put them all!"

Our prayers were quickly answered. Patrobas swung open the door, admitting one more couple. Priscilla shrieked, and ran into the arms of a beloved long-lost friend.

"This is dear Priscilla, and her husband Aquila," she said. "All the way from Corinth."

Aquila explained. "In the years following the death of Claudius, the exiled Jews began to trickle back into Rome. We finally moved back from Corinth, and have taken up residence in our old house on the Aventine Hill."

"We have been praying about having church services in our home, as we had in former times," his wife Priscilla said.

Thus, some from our congregation then began attending their house-church. Mum, Bran and I lived nearly halfway between, so we sometimes visited there.

"Today we must attend the Theater of Pompey," Pudens said enthusiastically one sunny afternoon.

"The King of Persia is visiting. Nero has had the stage, seats and balconies gilded in his honor. I should love to see it!"

I shot him a puzzled look. Christians did not generally attend the theaters. Roman theaters had a difficult time competing with the blood-sports of the arena, or the exciting chariot races. For this reason they had "progressed" from the mild Greek tragedies and comedies to lewd, pornographic productions, which they hoped would draw a packed house.

The whole city was decorated in honor of the King of Persia's visit, ablaze with lights and garlands, and reeking of incense. The ornate Porticus of Pompey teemed with hawkers and hucksters and assorted vagabonds.

The tiers of stone seats curved downward in a horseshoe shape, toward a central stage, gleaming golden in the subdued sunlight that filtered through the billowing canopies above our heads. The canopies, supported by masts and crossbeams, were fashioned of purple gauze, dotted with gold stars, and a gold image of the Emperor. The theater's ornate gilded rear wall provided a backdrop for dozens of colorful stage-sets that could be quickly moved into place.

A fine mist of water, scented with perfume, cooled the silly spectators who jostled each other for the best seats. With a flourish of trumpets, the tyrant Nero was carried in on a flower-covered sedan chair. He offered incense to the gods at the theater's shrine on the upper tier, then floated down through the crowd, while all sat in reverent silence.

But the resplendent long-haired King of Persia outshone even Nero himself. A leopard-skin mantle was slung across his brown shoulders. The light trembled in a thousand sparkling rays over the regal collar studded with precious rubies and gold and emeralds that ornamented his neck. His girdle was likewise stiff with precious stones. On his wrists he wore bands of gold set with gems. Gold rings mounted with pearls and sapphires dangled from his ears.

An orchestra in front of the stage provided music to accompany the drama. The characters, arrayed in rich and outlandish costumes, acted out the necessary portrayals of sadness or fear: the head hanging low, the hoarse voice, the tormented eyes. The spectators clapped and hissed, laughed and cried pathetically as the obscene play unfolded. The women in the audience hung on every word, tears coursing down their cheeks, their charcoal eye make-up streaking their chalk-white skin.

We'd dragged poor Bran along with us as a chaperone, for no unmarried Roman girls of good family were permitted to accompany a young man on a date without a chaperone. I glanced anxiously at Bran. His head was bent down and his eyes were closed; I knew that he was praying. Pudens, on the other hand, seemed to be thoroughly enjoying the bawdy spectacle. My heart felt suddenly hollow, plagued with foreboding.

When Bran and I arrived back at our apartments that evening, his face was grave. "I didn't want to be the one to have to tell you, Glwadus, but Pudens has got in with some strange new friends at law school, a bunch of weird poets and would-be fresco artists."

Bran's voice broke. "They indulge in absinthe, thinking that it expands their minds, and makes them more creative. But they're so depraved, they don't even realize how crude their art and poetry really is. I'm very worried about Pudens. Linus and I have tried to reason with him, to encourage him to give up these new friends, but he just won't listen. He needs a lot of prayer."

Chapter 10

"... Comforted of God."
—II Corinthians 1:4

A.D. 58

My students have done splendid work!" I finished grading exams, while Pudens sat beside me in the courtyard.

A white mantle of snow glazed the summits of the Apennines, and a crisp westerly breeze stirred up a whirlwind of dead brown leaves. I quickly gathered up the papyrus sheets as they began to scatter in the wind. Bare, low-spreading tree limbs moaned, and scraped against the rough stucco walls. The pale sun slid behind an ominous cloud.

"Tomorrow starts the festival of Saturnalia," Pudens said, drumming his fingers on the arm of his chair. "I want you to go with me to the arena."

A long silence fell between us. "Why can't we go to the Pincian Gardens?" I asked, without looking up.

"I have a new friend who is coming with us, and I don't want him to be bored," Pudens said. "He just moved here, and he wants to go to the arena."

Something died in me. "I love you dearly, but please don't ask me to go to that horrid place."

A sarcastic smile distorted his features. "What harm can there be? If you love me, you would try to do some of the things I like to do."

I gazed at him steadily for a moment, before answering. "I am a child of God. I don't belong in a place like that."

His brown eyes frowned with displeasure, something evil reflected in their dark depths. He reached out and touched my cheek with the back of his hand.

"You need to stop being such a backward provincial," he murmured in his most charming velvet voice that closed around me like a trap. "Is it so bad to want to show you off to my friends? Life is full of many pleasures, why not enjoy them all? And besides, there are plenty of girls who would be happy to go with me."

The words cut deeply.

The door from the atrium burst open, and Patrobas admitted a rough-haired creature, one of Pudens' new poet friends from law school. He had a bristling black beard, an insolent, self-confident air and an extremely foul mouth. And I didn't like the way he leered at me with brutal, mocking eyes.

I struggled all that night with my conscience, so afraid of losing Pudens, or making him angry. The dawn came too quickly. I dragged myself to the breakfast table, eyes pouched and gloomy, unable to look Mum or Bran in the face.

"Since it's a holiday, and everyone is off work, they're having an all-day service at the church, Glwadus," Mum said enthusiastically. "A wonderful letter has arrived from our beloved Brother Paul the Apostle. Everyone is excited, for it is to be read today."

"I can't go to church today," I mumbled, avoiding her gaze, trying not to see her disappointment. "There's something I have to do."

An innumerable multitude, from all classes of people, thronged the arena, ascending in endless tiers of stone seats. Since Pudens belonged to a family of the senatorial class, we were given "good" seats in the front row, along with the lewd poet who accompanied us as a "chaperone."

Amid a clash of cymbals and a flourish of trumpets, a parade of knights and charioteers in vibrant costume entered the arena, mounted on magnificent, proud-stepping horses. Their harnesses were wrought from richly ornamented scarlet leather, with golden fittings. Leopard and zebra hides, held in place by gleaming buckles, adorned the backs of the horses. Next came the Indian elephants, whose outrageously garbed brown-skinned drivers perched atop them in throne chairs encrusted with emeralds and rubies.

These were followed by a parade of burly gladiators—the retiarii, or net fighters; the agile, light-armored Thracians; and everyone's favorites, the gigantic heavyweights. A great roar, accompanied

181

by thousands of clapping hands and stomping feet, went up from the crowd as the swaggering, lion-like brute Licentio appeared, whom they all apparently idolized. Foolish women tossed bouquets of flowers down to their favorite gladiator, and screamed when he flexed his burly muscles. His chest swelled with self-importance.

Next came a procession of cheetahs, lions, tigers, and long-necked giraffes. Then a troupe of men and boys wearing purple tunics, carrying swords and lances, danced the Phyrric sword dance. With another flourish of trumpets, a long train of dancing black-and-scarlet robed pagan priests and priestesses swayed and gyrated before the high priest and the Vestal virgins, who were borne in on gilded sedan chairs.

An offering of wine and incense was made before paraded effigies of the gods. I shuddered, for I knew that the gladiators who fought and died on Saturnalia did so for the purpose of appeasing the god Saturn, who was akin to the Celtic god Bel.

Finally, the Emperor Nero was carried in, whom the mob greeted with deafening applause. The gladiators stood beneath the Imperial box, arms uplifted, and spoke the terrible words:

"We who are about to die salute you!"

Nero raised his arms for the games to begin. I squeezed my eyes tightly shut, determined not to watch. But they fluttered open as a blood-curdling cheer thundered from the stands. A young net fighter about my age entered the arena, obviously an untrained newcomer, a prisoner of war, Batavian perhaps.

Led out from his dim prison, he stood for a moment squinting as the glare of the sun struck his pale face. Lost and bewildered, wearing virtually no armor, he had little chance of survival in the arena. As he marched past the grandstand, his frightened blue eyes held mine for an instant. How I yearned to tell him about Jesus!

The armor-clad, black-maned Licentio was brought out amid a passionate roar from the cruel audience who thirsted for the Batavian's blood. He flung his net with dexterous aim, attempting desperately to entangle Licentio, but the more experienced gladiator evaded his throw with remarkable agility. Twice more he escaped the net, and in return he plunged his sword into the smaller man, who was clearly no match for him.

The Batavian crumbled to the sand on his knees, raising his arms to the audience to implore the pity of the people. But there was no pity in Rome, no human compassion. Even the matrons flashed the death sign, their well-manicured thumbs pointed ominously downward. The air was rent with shouts of "*Habet*! He has it!" The brutal mob, drunk with bloodlust, clamored for his early death.

"Why does he rush so timidly upon the sword?"* They cried out, with not one ounce of regret for the slaughter of a human life.

---

* Seneca

Finally Licentio, his face contorted with rage, inflicted the terrible death stroke, and his opponent collapsed in a bloody heap. I screamed in horror, and bolted from the carnage, staggering into the marble stairwell, my stomach heaving violently, hands clenched in tight fists. Even while the arena slaves dragged the young man's body away with a hook, through the "gate of death" to the *spoliarium*, and swept the sand, the wretched audience clamored for fresh combatants to be brought forth.

Pudens followed me into the stairwell, his eyes like blazing coals. "What is wrong with you anyway?" he demanded, grabbing my arm roughly.

I jerked my arm away. "How can you sit there and enjoy watching a man being murdered?"

"You might know that you are embarrassing me, making a spectacle of yourself. This is just a part of our culture. Why can't you understand that?"

My face flushed red with anger. It was not my Pudens, but a cruel stranger who stood there. As I had already begun to suspect, the grace and genteel beauty of his countenance was not necessarily reflected in his soul. The man that I loved had never really existed. He had only been an illusion in my mind. I was left with but one desire—a desperate urge to flee the place.

"You people are all insane!" I screamed at him. Taking one long last look at my cherished engagement ring, I tore it from my finger and flung it in his haughty face.

Fire leaping from my eyes, I dashed through Rome's dangerous streets, pushing angrily past a group of drunken bullies. A fat man leered at me, a garland of flowers encircling his bald head. It seemed the whole city had become tipsy with the celebration of the holiday. I swerved to avoid a company of inebriated sots who linked arms and swept the street in a crazy rush, whooping uproariously. The "Lords of Misrule" presided during the feast of Saturnalia. Loose reins were given to revelry, and all that was flesh. The porticoes and shops, decorated for the festival, resonated with ribald laughter and shouting.

Exhausted and out-of-breath upon reaching Manlius' and Priscilla's house-church, I slid into a rear seat, just as Brother Rufus was reading these words from the new letter from Paul the Apostle:

> . . . Be not conformed to this world; but be ye transformed
> by the renewing of your mind, that ye may prove what is
> that good and acceptable and perfect will of God.

I closed my eyes, letting the words wash over me. There was some comfort in knowing I had finally done the right thing, but pain sliced through me as Pudens' face floated vividly before me, filling my soul with a dull gray ache. I had expected that God would open the way before me, but now I must journey on alone. Yet still He whispered peace. *My love for you is greater than any need in your heart,* He seemed to say.

I avoided Acilia and her family during the remaining days of Saturnalia. They'd been so kind, and our failed betrothal would be hard for them to bear. Surely they would be angry with me. The betrothal gifts would have to be returned, of course, and the contracts annulled.

The next school day I arrived early, anxious to give some explanation. Acilia met me at the door, her eyes red-rimmed and swollen. "There was a terrible scene here last night, Claudia," she said. "Pudens came home drunk. A lot of harsh words were flying back and forth. Mama is so upset, she hasn't even come out of her room yet. And Papa stormed out of here early to go to the office."

Priscilla finally came downstairs to help the freedwoman Mary prepare the midday meal for the students. Trembling, she folded me in her arms. "I fear that my foolish mind has been stuffed full of romantic notions," she said, her speech ragged. "But you must not make the tragic mistake of marrying an unbeliever, child, even if he is my . . . own . . . son."

Seeing her tears, the pain washed over me anew.

"How our hearts rejoiced when we first found Christ!" Priscilla went on. "My husband and I thought the whole world would want to know the Saviour. Pudens was one of the first children ever to be raised in a Christian home. How carefully we taught him the Scriptures . . . and all the right answers. It never occurred to us that our son could . . . turn his back on the Lord."

"I'm so sorry," I whispered, crushed by the sadness in her eyes.

"We have tried to minister to broken people. Now it is we who are . . . broken," Priscilla whispered, through a new outbreak of tears. "Last night we said a lot of things to him that we . . . regret. Our Pudens has left home; he says that he will stay with his friend in some squalid apartment until he's finished with school, then he plans to join the military."

"We must leave him in the hands of God, and trust Him to do what is best," I heard myself say.

"Manlius and I feel that we have failed utterly . . . all words too poor to comfort . . . or to soothe. Pudens once seemed so promising, we loved to speak about him. But now . . . oh, how I dread the endless questions . . . the well-meaning advice from friends."

In the afternoon I sat in the atrium with Acilia, Bran, Linus and some of the others in our youth group, transcribing the words from Brother Paul's letter to the Romans into codice books, so that everyone might have his own copy. The Jewish preacher Apelles Aristobulus was visiting, and his friendly dark eyes sparkled when he saw what we were doing.

"You remind me of the Jewish scribes who carefully copied each word of the Old Testament," he said, resting his large hand on Bran's shoulder. "You must take pains to print every word exactly as it is written, letter by letter, as they did, for it is a most sacred task."

Pudens swept past us when he came to retrieve some of his belongings, but he pretended not to see me. The black-bearded poet was with him, and he sneered at me with what appeared to be triumph . . . yes, triumph. With a small pocket-knife, I savagely attacked the tip of my goose-quill pen underneath the table, shaving it into a stiff point. A tear rolled down my cheek then and left a stain on my parchment sheet, when I gazed on these beautiful words for the first time:

> "We know that all things work together for good to them that love God."

How thrilling to worship a God who knows and understands our deepest grief! He alone can bring peace and blessing out of sorrow, and use our trials to bring us closer to Himself.

The dismal winter rains passed slowly, and spring blossoms burst across the land. At breakfast one morning, Bran gazed at Mum, his dark eyebrows drawn together.

"Now that my education is finished, it's time I returned to help my father in his duties as King of Siluria," he said. "As you know, his health is failing. He writes in his letters that the Romans are transforming the old Silure capital of Caerwent into a splendid town, not far from Caerleon, the fortress of the II Legion."

A stunned silence filled the room. The thought of losing Bran too was beyond bearing. Yet always we had known this day would come.

Bran brushed crumbs from his tunic, and reached for another cinnamon biscuit. "Some of the Silures are still fighting the Romans in the hills, but I will not be required to fight against our own people. I am to be 'Captain of the Fleet'—can you imagine? My duties will be to clear the pirates from the Irish Sea and from the Severn Estuary, and to repel foreign invaders from our shores."

"Going home," I murmured. "How I wish Mum and I could go with you."

"The other surprise is that Apelles Aristobulus and Ilid plan to accompany me as Britain's first missionaries!"*

"Praise God!" Mum exclaimed. "My most fervent prayers have been answered. The Gospel will be going out in Britain! I have so longed for this day."

"It has been my fondest dream to tell our people about the Lord Jesus," I said. "If only Mum and I hadn't been forced to make that dreadful oath to the Emperor Claudius, never to return to Britain."

---

* The "Welsh Triads;" "British Achau of St. Prydain;" Dorotheus, Bishop of Tyre (A.D. 303); and Nicephorus the Greek. [Not to be confused with St. Augustine's famous 597 A.D. mission to the Anglo-Saxons, who pushed the Roman Celts west into Wales, Cornwall, Cumberland, and the Strathclyde region of Scotland in the 6th century.]

"I don't think he gave you much choice at the time," Bran said wryly.

When the shipping lanes became safe for travel, it was time to bid farewell to Bran, Ilid and Aristobulus. The brethren from the various house-churches rose early, while it was still dark, to journey the ten miles with us to Rome's port of Ostia. When the sun was just peeping over the mountaintops, we spread picnic cloths in a meadow, where bright purple, gold and white crocuses, glowing violets and sweet-smelling hyacinths pushed up through the lush grass. Baskets of pastries, dried figs, dates and almonds were passed around to the multitude. Aquila offered up a prayer for their safe journey, and for the missionary work.

Brother Rufus stood up to speak. "My brothers, it is your great mission to reveal the sunshine of God's love to those who walk in darkness. The Lord will be the Light to guide your footsteps. Let Him form your plans in everything you do. 'For there is no good apart from God. 'Trust Him. Do not fear, nor grow weary, for the 'peace of God which passes all understanding, shall keep your hearts and minds in Christ Jesus.'"

As we stood on the granite quay, the ship's immense sails unfurled, and billowed impatiently in the stiff breeze. Stewards rushed up the gangplank with several crates filled with Bran's belongings.

"It seems only yesterday that you and I roamed the wild hills of Britain, scrambled up ropes, and skinned our knees on the jagged rocks," I said.

Bran laughed. "Not to mention a certain bloodied nose."

His freckles were faded, and he had finally grown into his long, spindly legs. He was a handsome prince, tall for a Silure, with glossy raven-black hair curling in thick waves. His bronzed hands were fine-boned like Mum's, but had a grip of crushing force. I embraced him for what might be the last time.

"I will miss you. Please write soon, dear cousin, and God go with you."

I hugged Ilid, whose sparse hair had by this time turned iron-gray. Tears of joy flooded his eyes. "Praise God, Glwadus, I can finally teach them of the true God, who loves His children, and about our beloved Messiah, the Lord Jesus Christ!"

Mum and I clung together, eyes misted with joy and sorrow, and watched until the ship disappeared beyond the western horizon.

Chapter 11

"The brethren . . . came to meet us
as far as the Appia Forum"
—Acts 28:15

February, A.D. 61

A commotion erupted at the back of the house-church after the evening prayer service. Everyone stood clustered around a young man who staggered across the threshold. He reached out and grabbed the edge of the arched brick doorframe to steady himself. His lips were outlined in blue. Rain spurted from his boots, and dripped from his waterlogged cloak, spreading in pools over the fine mosaic floor.

Manlius and Patrobas ran to him, supporting him on each side. They assisted him into the warm *balineum*, and into a dry change of clothing. Wrapping him in blankets, they laid him on a couch next to the large ornate brazier that heated the room. Linus led his overtaxed horse out to the stable to groom him. Messengers were quickly dispatched to all of the other house-churches in Rome.

"But who is he?" I asked curiously.

"He is a messenger who has traveled all the way from Puteoli, some 160 miles," Acilia explained. "Our beloved Apostle Paul has arrived in Italy, and is on his way to Rome! He came in on one of the enormous grain ships, *Castor and Pollux*, that shuttles between Alexandria in Egypt and Puteoli, Italy's deepwater harbor."

I followed Acilia as she dashed into the kitchen to prepare a plate of food for the young man.

"The fleet left Alexandria the minute the weather broke, its captain being anxious to bring the first grain of the season to Rome's hungry citizens, in order to receive the Emperor's prize. They stopped just long enough to pick up the survivors from Brother Paul's ship, which had been wrecked off the coast of Malta. Papa is praying about making the journey down to meet Brother Paul, and everyone insists on going with him!"

In the darkness of the early morning, the clatter of hoofbeats and iron-rimmed wheels announced the arrival of the farm wagons and the old salt wagons from the Via Salaria. They had been covered with leather hides, to protect from the cold February downpour, and were already half-filled with enthusiastic brethren from the Via Salaria house-church. Morag Julia motioned to us, and cleared a spot for Acilia and me to sit, while Mum rode in the plush *carruca dormitoria* with the older women.

I threw my arms around Morag Julia's neck. "It's so good to see you again. Isn't it too exciting! Imagine Brother Paul coming here."

Manlius stuffed as many as he could into the wagons. But he had to rent more from a grumpy liveryman, awakening him from a sound sleep. Finally our strange caravan consisting of various carts and wagons lumbered along Rome's slick cobbled streets, splashing in out of the black puddles. We huddled together, swathed in blankets and straw, listening to the rain drumming steadily against the roof. The wagon lanterns cast eerie shadows on the bleak, rundown tenements and dark alleyways.

When we reached the tall gate of the Porta Capena, that marked the entrance of the Appian Way, we found groups from Aquila and Priscilla's house-church, and from Sergius Paulus' church already gathered.

"Let's wait awhile longer for the brethren from the Trans-Tiber," Sergius Paulus said. "The stormy weather probably slowed them down. Some of the streets in low-lying areas are nearly impassable with the flooding."

"Amplias and Narcissus Maurus are organizing another huge group of slaves and laborers who needed to ask their masters for time off work," Aquila said. "They plan to follow in a day or two on foot, Lord willing."

When the pale winter sun struggled to break through the overcast sky, Morag, Acilia and I wrapped our blankets around our shoulders and jumped down from the wagon with the other young people. We trudged along the smooth paving stones of the Appian Way, to ease the burden on the team of mules, as the flat *campagnia* gradually slanted upward into the Alban Hills. The purple mountains ascended proudly in a gray-misted veil, their snow-covered peaks all but shrouded by the fog. Birds hung in the brisk wind that roared out of the highlands, and swept across the fields of winter-brown stubble.

At noon we stopped to eat a picnic lunch beside the gardens of the Quintilii brothers which sprawled in splendor for almost a mile along the side of the road. Avid horticulturists, their blankets of hardy, bright-faced pansies streaked with jet, crocuses, violets, narcissus and daffodils exploded with color, glistening with the recent rain. Statue-lined walkways connected to elegant marble balustrades, with steps descending among goldfish ponds and ornamental fountains.

Our young friend Sergia Paula caught up with us, holding tightly to the hand of a small, sturdy boy with a mop of black hair, and huge brown eyes with long curling lashes. He was Ionnes (John) Alexamenos, the child that I had rescued from the wild dogs.

"How you've grown," I exclaimed.

Ionnes held up four fingers. "I am already this many, four years old," he said. "I helped my mama and papa find a new brother and sister for me. We might get another sister someday. But I'm the biggest. And I can write my name and read some letters. And I love Jesus. Do you?"

I lifted the little chatterbox in my arms. "Yes, I love Jesus very much, too."

"I am having a birthday in August, and I will be five," he rattled on. "Mama and Papa will take me to the Saepta Julia and buy me lovely toys, and Grandpapa and Grandmama, too. And when I grow up, I want to be a missionary in Britain, for Mama said it was you, a British girl, saved my life."

I hugged him tightly, and a tear fell on his forehead, knowing how close this beautiful and well-loved child had come to being slaughtered before he'd even had a chance to live.

"Why are you crying, pretty Claudia?" he asked curiously. He reached up to pat my cheek, and wiped my tears away with his chubby fingers.

As we neared the village of Bovillae, the road ran downward suddenly into a low-lying area, past a trash heap, melancholy in its dirt and stench. Rain and melting snow had created a mud bog, and pools of brown, stagnant water stretched across the roadway. We'd have liked to climb into the wagon, but the mules were having difficulty pulling it.

Suddenly one of the rear wheels slipped off the roadbed, and stuck fast in the muck. The mules strained against the quagmire, but to no effect. For every inch they moved forward, they slipped and fell back two. The men cut evergreen branches to spread in the ruts underneath the wheel. Rocking the vehicle back and forth, they struggled to lift the wagon free from its miry prison, until it finally returned to the sodden roadway. We waded gingerly, ankle-deep, through the cold slough, the mud sucking at our boots as if to swallow us into the earth.

"I hope there's no snakes in here!" Sergia Paula exclaimed.

Our caravan soon came upon a crystal waterfall that tumbled with a mighty roar through a steep chasm, then over a rocky stream bed. We rinsed the mud off our boots in the icy torrent. Then I shivered, the biting wind tugging at the border of my wet tunic.

In late afternoon the wagons rumbled into the ancient village of Ariccia, whose white mound of buildings crowned the summit of a gentle hill, encircled by tangled woodlands. The jagged slopes of the Abruzzi towered in the clouds above it. A crumbling inn stood near the junction of its two main streets, facing the square.

Inside the inn's wide entranceway was a public room and banquet hall, which occupied a good deal of the first floor. Tendrils of smoke drifted upward and into the room, from a fire that roared in the cavernous hearth.

Romans rarely traveled during the winter, so we believers had the place to ourselves. The innkeeper and his family scurried about, doing their best to accommodate our enormous party.

"The only food we can rustle up is some coarse bread with pale cheese, and soup," the innkeeper said apologetically.

"That's fine," Brother Manlius assured him. "We had no way of notifying you ahead of time. It was a spur-of-the-moment situation. So we will be quite content with whatever you can find."

The bread was stale, and the soup studded with a few slimy beans. But I cupped my reddened hands around the Samian-ware bowls, grateful for the warmth. After the meal, Brother Aquila read to us from his tattered-edged copy of the book of Isaiah. We sang a psalm, and offered up prayers.

When night fell, the men and boys retired to the stable to feed and care for the mules. Then they would bed down in the piles of hay. The inn boasted three plain, dreary guest rooms downstairs, and four more upstairs, where the older women slept on straw mattresses, three or four to a bed, on rather dubious-looking linens.

Exhausted, Acilia, Morag, Sergia Paula and I rubbed salve on our blistered feet, then curled up beside the weary children huddled together on the rough flagstone floor of the public room, next to the dying fire.

"Ouch, a flea bit me!" Acilia howled in the darkness. She slapped at her leg.

I chuckled. "I don't mind the fleas as much as the mice and roaches. I hope they don't run over us while we sleep."

"You wouldn't know the difference, if you would go to sleep," Morag Julia pointed out.

Sergia Paula giggled. "*If* we sleep. No matter which way I turn, I can't get comfortable on this hard cold floor."

At daybreak we sputtered back to life.

"We must start out early," Manlius said, "for this will be a strenuous day."

Acilia moaned. "I thought yesterday was strenuous."

Just beyond Ariccia, the Appian Way separated, circling around the extraordinary tomb of the Curiatii brothers, formed from a square and five large conical towers.

The road proceeded steeply downhill, through the Villariccia Ravine, then upward, our feet crunching through patches of old snow. From the lofty heights of Lanuvium, the view was spectacular, with row after row of rugged, snow-covered peaks to the east, and the Mediterranean Sea and the town of Antium to the west.

"If you squint, you can see the white marble of Nero's seaside villa," Acilia said.

"I wonder if poor dear Octavia is down there," I mused.

The wagons clattered across a great arched stone viaduct, and into Tres Tabernae, a bustling town that lay at the junction of the road that led to Antium. The sun was melting into the west by the time we reached Appia Foro, traditionally the second night's stop on the Appian Way, some fifty-six miles from Rome.

"Appia Foro lies on the northern border of the Pontine Marsh, which is the haunt of desperate outlaws and military deserters," Acilia said. "Caesar Augustus tried to drain the malarial marsh, and dug a canal through it. The canal extends twenty miles south, creating a shortcut across the rugged Terracina peninsula."

Manlius sat on a stump, and with his forefinger, carefully traced the *itinerari* spread out on his knees, as we all crowded around to see. "We have a problem, brethren. We don't know if Brother Paul is traveling by canal, or by the coastal road. If we take the one way, we may miss him. I guess Appia Foro is about as far as we can go."

"Yes, I think it wise to remain here," Sergius Paulus said, "though it is well known as a town of ill repute, the home of insolent bargemen, surly innkeepers, horse thieves, and swindlers who prey on unwary travelers."*

"Yes. Keep any money well hidden," Aquila warned, "for it is rumored that many have been robbed here during the night while they slept."

In the morning a watch was set up over both the canal and the road, to search for Brother Paul. "Look for a thin, wiry, balding man with a pointed beard," Aquila said. "And he will probably be chained to a soldier."

Brother Paul's group took the faster canal route, arriving early, having traveled all night on the water, in order to push ahead toward Rome during the day. The bargemen tossed ropes onto the wharf, and

---

* Horace

secured them to iron rings. The gangplank snapped down into place. Teams of mules strained forward, hauling wagons heavily loaded with grain.

Brother Paul didn't see us at first, from where he stood on the deck of the barge, his eyes downcast. I knew well the shame and humiliation of that chain on his wrist. How he must have dreaded the taunts and jeers from cruel onlookers, an object of malice and ridicule. He was an aging man, broken in health. This was surely not the arrival in Rome that he had always dreamed of—a prisoner with ugly charges against him, cast out by his Jewish kinsmen, and uncertain as to his appeal before Nero.

"Brother Paul!" everyone called out.

His close, prominent eyebrows lifted, and his gray eyes fell with wonder upon the large group of Christians who waited to welcome him into their hearts. As he hurried down the gangplank to meet us, a bright smile spread across his face and his eyes flooded with joy. We smothered him with so many hugs and holy kisses that even his guard, Julius the Centurion, grinned. Luke, the Syrian physician, and young Timothy accompanied him, for when a Roman citizen was brought to Rome for trial, he was permitted to bring two attendants. Brother Paul prayed, and thanked God for us all.

"You have given me courage," he said. "I have never before received such a warm welcome, made even more precious by the fact that most of you are strangers to me. The weariness fell off my spirit, and my labor has become great joy."

As our party journeyed back toward Rome, we were greeted at Tres Tabernae by the second group of slaves and freedmen who had followed a day later on foot. There were more hugs and happy tears. We traveled together uphill through the evergreen forests until we reached Ariccia.

In the evening we all crowded into the public room at the inn, and sat spellbound, by the light of a greasy fire that spat and sizzled, amid the fleas and roaches, surrounded by garish, peeling walls scrawled with graffiti. Brother Paul told us the tale of his imprisonment at Jerusalem, of his shipwreck, and how our Lord Jesus had been his strength and comfort through it all.

"Thanks be to God, the anchor of our soul, both sure and steadfast. He causes us to triumph in Christ, and makes manifest His knowledge in every place!" he exclaimed.

Before we separated for the night, someone started singing, and we all joined in with those beautiful words from our well-loved Letter to the Romans:

> *O the depth, O the depth of the riches*
> Of the wisdom and the knowledge of God!
> How unsearchable are His judgments,
> And His ways past finding out.

Ears cocked, the innkeeper and his family listened intently. "I have never seen anything like it," the man said, scratching his head. "We must hear more about this God and His Son Jesus."

In the morning, the brethren clambered up an elevated ridge just beyond Ariccia, on the western edge of the Alban Hills. From its rocky heights we gazed across the wide, flat *campagnia* dotted with melancholy tombs and magnificent aqueducts, as the city of Rome burst into view. Its rooftops gleamed golden in the sunrise. And so, gray eyes unswerving, his heart prayerfully fixed on the goal, with the zeal of a mighty conquering Caesar at the head of a victorious, albeit ragtag procession, Brother Paul prepared to march on Rome.

Chapter 12

"Put on the whole armor of God"
—Ephesians 6:11

M um arrived at school just as classes had been dismissed for the afternoon. "Glwadus, can you go with me to take this basket of food to Brother Paul's house?" she asked.

We threaded our way through the narrow streets, past a maze of ancient crooked alleyways, where little sunlight reached through the rows of bleak, groaning tenements and rickety overhanging wooden balconies. Laundry flapped on clotheslines that criss-crossed high overhead. Sluggish guildsmen, wearing coarse brown tunics stained with sweat, shouted oaths and curses, amid the monotonous clanging of hammers, chisels, and the screech of double-handled saws. A money-changer rattled coins on a dirty table, while a maker of musical instruments in an adjacent stall loudly tested his flutes and auloes.

"Has anyone heard how long it will be before Brother Paul's trial?" I asked.

"The Emperor's court docket is always crowded, and a man might wait two or three years before his appeal can be heard," Mum said. "But being a Roman citizen, and having received a good report from Porcius Festus, the governor in Judea, and from Julius the Centurion, he has posted bail, and is at liberty to rent a house while awaiting trial."

The street was obstructed by pushcarts, and benches set in front of stalls smelling of hot olive oil, garlic, onions, and scorched, overcooked food, where the poor, whose apartments lacked proper cooking facilities, often ate their meals. Food vendors shouted out, each with his own particular cry, peddling bean and lentil stew, pastries filled with cheese and shredded pork, or *tomaculi,* greasy sausages carried about in hot portable ovens. Underneath one lone spreading shade tree full of languid cats, merchants hawked their gaudy wares, set out on boards perched precariously atop crates or battered amphorae, in a haze of dust and smoke.

"Paul's house, however, must be in the vicinity of the Praetorian camp, the Castra Praetoria," Mum went on, "for he is under house arrest, chained to a soldier. Every four hours a different guard comes on duty. Some of them are kind, and enjoy listening to Brother Paul speak about Jesus, but others mock him."

As we neared the Castra Praetoria, we sidestepped hordes of swaggering chickens scratching between the flagstones, and brown barefoot children that darted in and out of small, bright-painted stucco houses. A mangy, disagreeable hound lay motionless across the sidewalk. He opened one eye and growled as we slipped past him, sniffing at our loaded baskets of food. I sighed with relief when he turned away to snap noisily at the flies that buzzed about his head.

Brother Paul lived across from the parade ground, where thousands of soldiers practiced their military exercises daily, complete with trumpets, the constant rat-a-tat-tat of drums, and the shouted commands of officers.

"Isn't that the same field where our family met the Emperor Claudius for the first time?" I asked.

"Yes. And it is rather a raucous neighborhood. Circus animals and wild beasts bound for the amphitheaters are kept in the area as well. So the roar of lions or the trumpeting of elephants is not uncommon," Mum said. "The brethren have patched and painted Brother Paul's cottage a quiet shade of beige, but its previous bold orange color still seeps through in spots."

The front door to the small rented workmen's cottage was always kept propped open. The sun made bright patches on the stone floor spread with colorful rugs from the leper colony; matching woven pads cushioned the newly painted chairs. A yellow stray cat with chewed ears wandered in, and stretched itself out to doze on the windowsill. A rooster poked its nodding head inside the doorway, glanced at the cat; then with a squawk and a rustling of feathers, scampered quickly out again.

Mum and I bustled about in the kitchen. We set out plates of grilled mullet, snow peas and beetroots shining purple, a pottery bowl filled with tender leaves of crinkly lettuce with cucumbers, onions and slices of egg, and fresh baked bread and honey. For dessert there was blackberry dump cake with thick whipped cream.

Brother Paul smiled. "You ladies in Rome are spoiling me," he said, taking a second helping of cake. "Sister Eurgain, I also wanted to thank you for the eye salve you brought last time. It helped me much more than that Laodocean salve I had been using. I was even able to see well enough to write a letter with my own hand."

After dinner I poured out my heart to him about my disastrous broken engagement. "I am already twenty-two years old, far beyond the age of marrying, and without a proper dowry. I cannot marry a pagan, yet seem to have only brotherly feelings for the young men in the church. Pudens was the only man who could make my heart sing. Sometimes it seems that life is passing me by."

"Marriage is honorable, dear Claudia, but don't despise the single life," Brother Paul said. "We are espoused to a Bridegroom nobler, richer, more wondrous by far than any of this sad earth. Let Him fill the empty spaces in your heart. An unmarried woman is at liberty to go wherever she is needed, to undertake any mission that God may entrust to her."

With his free hand he passed his plate and beaker to Mum, who had begun clearing the table. "You have time to devote to prayer and the study of the Scriptures, and I've heard that you are able to reach your many students and the suffering folk of the tenements with the wonderful Gospel of Christ. But a married woman must first care for her husband and children. Learn to see things as God sees them, my daughter. 'Commit thy way unto the Lord.' "

"I never thought about it that way."

"God may someday provide you with a Christian husband," he went on. "God has his own 'set times and seasons.' It is not for us to know them. Jeremiah 23 says, 'it is not in man that walketh to direct his steps.' But God's way is always so much better than we could have chosen for ourselves."

The tall, curly-haired soldier chained to Brother Paul's wrist watched us closely. "I have heard you before talking about God and Jesus," he said to Paul. "But I always belittled you, thinking you were beside yourself. Yet I have no joy or peace in my heart, and am very anxious about what lies beyond the grave, for I know I deserve to be punished for my life of sin."

"The wages of sin is death, but it was God's plan to send His Son Jesus to die for you," Brother Paul explained. "Only the blood of Jesus Christ can take away sin. There is now no condemnation to those who are in Christ Jesus. If thou shalt confess with thy mouth the Lord Jesus, and shalt believe in thine heart that God hath raised Him from the dead, thou shalt be saved."

The proud soldier's hands trembled, and his fervent expression revealed that God's light had penetrated his dark soul. He and Brother Paul fell on their knees and prayed. Before he relinquished the chain to the next guard coming on duty, the young man beamed, assured that all his sins had been washed away by the blood of Christ.

"I will soon be traveling to my home in northern Italy," the young soldier said, as Brother Paul gave him several Scripture portions. "I cannot wait to tell my family and other relatives about our Lord Jesus!"

During the afternoon, Mum and I washed the dishes, and scrubbed the kitchen, swept the floor, emptied the rubbish pail, beat the rugs, and hung the coverlets out to air. Then we carried the basket of laundry out to the tiny courtyard to wash in a vat set on uneven planks stretched between two tree stumps, beside a dry, cracked fish pond. I watered the ragged geraniums that languished in terra-cotta pots.

Brother Timothy took out quill and ink and parchments, and above the noise and clatter of the neighborhood, Paul dictated a letter for the church in Philippi. Mum and I heard snatches of the wondrous words as we went quietly about our tasks:

"That at the name of Jesus every knee shall bow . . . every tongue should confess that Jesus Christ is Lord . . . Be blameless and harmless . . . the sons of God . . . in the midst of a crooked and perverse nation, among whom ye . . . shine as lights in the world; holding forth the word of life."

If Brother Paul's tiny rented cottage seemed like a glimpse of Heaven, returning to the Imperial palace quickly jolted Mum and I back to earth. Within the splendor of its jewel-encrusted marble corridors, an aura of evil lurked. Tryphena met us at the door of our apartment, sniffling and dabbing at her eyes with a handkerchief.

"The Empress Octavia is in residence," she said. "She is asking to see you. I'm afraid that her disastrous marriage to Nero has gone from bad to worse. He threatens and abuses her, and indulges in every kind of fleshly abomination."

I was shocked at Octavia's appearance. Thin and sallow-skinned, her eyes seemed hollow, sunk in sockets, and ringed with dark circles of fatigue. Her small white hand clasped mine.

"I've missed you so much, Claudia," she murmured. "You just can't know how wretched my life has become. Agrippina and Burrus, the Praetorian Prefect, tried to help, but it only put me in a worse position. Nero finally grew weary of his mother's constant interfering in his affairs, and insisted that she was plotting with Rubellius Plautius to seize his throne. Nero bribed that brute Anicetus to murder her. My own life is also in danger. Three times Nero has tried to strangle me, but the servants prevented him. I am hardly a living person anymore."

"Dear Octavia, if only you could know Jesus," I said. "Your poor heart, however crushed by fear and sorrow, can find in Him the peace and hope you long for. He is the Resurrection and the Life, and when we die, we will awake in His likeness, in His happy home in Heaven, where no tears can ever come!"

Octavia sighed, resting her sharp little chin in her hands. "No day is joy to me, no hour not filled with terror. Oh that Fate had given me her wings, that I might fly above this cruel world! I've tried all the gods, Claudia. But none of them will help me."

"Those gods are made of stone," I replied. "But we serve a living God. Jesus said, 'Come unto me, all ye that labor and are heavy laden, and I will give you rest.' He can make 'all things work together for good.' He will cradle you in His arms, and lead you in a way such as you never dreamed your eyes could look upon. Nero may never love you, but to the Lord Jesus you are the most priceless treasure."

"Tryphena and Tryphosa tell me the same sorts of things," she said, "but I just don't know what to believe."

"Glwadus! No! Don't stand by the window!" Mum shrieked.

But it was too late. The amber-glass window in the banquet hall shattered, and splinters of glass tumbled over the polished marble floor. I winced in pain as a palm-sized rock struck my shoulder, and sharp pieces of glass stung my face and hands. Mum, Tryphena and Tryphosa rushed to my side, pulling me back as another boulder thudded against the side of the building.

"Oh, pray that none of the glass got into her eyes!" Mum exclaimed as she made me lie down on a banquet couch and carefully removed the shards that had become imbedded in my skin.

Tryphena and Tryphosa screamed as a fiery projectile sailed through the broken window, scattering flames and pitch. Amplias and Stachys moved quickly to close the shutters. Narcissus Maurus hurried in with wet brooms. They beat out the fire, and swept up the glass on the floor.

"Will the mob break through the gate?" I asked.

Nero was determined to marry his new love, the wicked Poppaea. He divorced Octavia, and banished her to an estate in the *campagnia*. However, this situation was denounced among the common people of Rome, for Octavia was popular among them.

Menacing, angry mobs had rampaged through the streets for days, knocking over statues of Poppaea that Nero had erected, and hacking them into pieces. The dismembered limbs they dragged away with ropes, kicked, stamped them underfoot and befouled them with dirt. The crowds thronged the broad pavement that surrounded the palace, refusing to leave, trapping us inside the building.

"If only the people could understand that we are all on *their* side," I said. "But there is nothing any of us can do."

"They carry statues of Octavia on their shoulders, and have put them up in the Forum and in the temples, festooned with wreaths and flowers," Narcissus Maurus said.

Swords drawn, royal guards rushed in to quell the howling rioters, and trampled some of them underneath their horses' sharp hooves. The furious mob fought back, pelting the soldiers with rocks, bricks and clubs.

"Matricidal beast!" the people shouted.

"Give Octavia back her kingdom!"

"Disperse, you filthy peasants!" the Prefect bellowed. "You shall all pay dearly with your blood for this, of such revenge that Time shall never forget!"

Nero paced through the banquet hall, terrified of the mob. Poppaea, always full of hate, threw herself down, grovelling at Nero's feet.

"Can't you see that both our lives are in danger?" she screamed. "If these evil beasts can get away with rioting, they will stop at nothing! If you love me, and value your own life, you must do something! I can't understand why you don't stand up and act like a man. Are you the Emperor or not?"

"What am I supposed to do?" Nero shouted. "I have appointed Tigellinus as the new Praetorian Prefect. He has put the guilty ringleaders to the sword, and will soon have the situation under control."

"Where is Burrus?" I whispered to Tryphena. "I thought that he was Praetorian Prefect."

"He took Octavia's side, so Nero had him poisoned," she replied.

"I cannot rest until Octavia is executed!" Poppaea cried. "Then these loathsome people will realize that all their efforts are for nothing. How I hate them. It would be fine with me if all of them were dead! No, death is far too small a punishment!"

"We shall see if I have strength enough to crush this brutish rebellion!" Nero exclaimed. "As for Octavia, whom these crazed citizens would have to rule over me, she will be brought to stand trial for her crimes! Nothing but the sword can rid me of my enemies. Who stands highest must fall!"

Tigellinus arrested Octavia at the villa in the *campagnia*, and brought her back to Rome. No prisoner had ever evoked such sympathy and compassion within the minds of the people. There were few dry eyes when she was dragged into court, and accused of monstrous offenses.

Tigellinus tortured Tryphena, Tryphosa, Paezuza, and Octavia's other maids, tearing away pieces of their flesh, trying to force them to denounce her.

"Testify, and you shall be spared from these torments!" Tigellinus roared.

"Nay, I will not speak ill of her, for she is innocent!" Tryphena affirmed. "Do with us what you will."

"It's so unfair!" I cried out, and leapt to my feet in anger. But Mum and Narcissus Maurus pulled me down.

"Glwadus, your wrath will accomplish no purpose," Mum whispered. "We are powerless here."

When Nero and Tigellinus realized that their tortures were in vain, Nero's horrid friend Anicetus was summoned to the witness stand. He had been rewarded with a hefty bribe to trump up false charges against Octavia.*

"I order Octavia to be punished in the ancient style for her hideous crimes against me, banished to the island of Pandateria." Nero thundered.

Another riot broke out among the populace when Octavia was taken into military custody, surrounded by a crowd of soldiers. A pall settled over the palace.

Choked with tears, I threw myself into Mum's arms. "I didn't even have a chance to say good-bye to her," I said. She held me close, and stroked my hair. "And poor little Paezuza. She suffered so from her tortures that she was taken to the infirmary. They don't think she will live."

Within a week, news came that Nero had given the command to murder Octavia. My heart wilted like a crumpled Sabine rose, realizing that my dear friend would never be coming back. I never knew if she found Jesus in the end, but I pray that she did.

When Tryphena and Tryphosa's dreadful injuries finally healed, they accompanied Mum and I through the streets to Brother Paul's house, food baskets in hand.

Brother Paul studied the odd wounds on the diminutive sisters' faces and arms. "What are these scars, my daughters?"

Tryphena, between sobbing breaths, related the whole sordid story while we toyed with our dinner. "Their mother long ago entrusted Octavia and

---

*Suetonius

Britannicus into our care," Tryphena said. "Whatever her other faults, she did love her children dearly. Now both our little lambs are gone."

Tears of compassion flooded Brother Paul's eyes.

During the afternoon he continued on with the letter he was dictating for one of the churches. His voice choked a time or two:

> Finally, my brethren, be strong in the Lord, and
>   in the power of his might.
> Put on the whole armor of God, that ye may be
>   able to stand against
> the wiles of the devil. For we wrestle not against
>   flesh and blood, but
> against principalities, against powers, against the
>   rulers of the
> darkness of this world.

How the words calmed our wounded spirits, and armed us for the dark days that lay ahead!

Chapter 13

"... walking in the midst of the fire ..."
—Daniel 2:10

July 19, A.D. 64

It was the hottest summer anyone could remember. Clouds disappeared from the skies, and the sun scorched Rome with a drought that cracked the very earth. The hot scirocco winds that gusted across the seven hills offered little relief from the oppression, but did guarantee that the city was parched and dry as a tinderbox.

Unable to sleep in the suffocating heat of that July night, Mum and I dragged our mattresses onto the balcony, which was several degrees cooler than the apartment. We sipped chamomile tea, while gazing out onto the dark rooftops of the city, outlined in the moonlight.

"I surely do miss dear Brother Paul," I said.

"Yes," Mum sighed, "but it's a great relief that Nero finally set him free, for his Jewish accusers failed to come forward to denounce him.* Perhaps they feared to do so because of his friendship with Nero's tutor, Seneca and his brother, Annaeus Gallio. It seems that Seneca and Gallio respected Brother Paul as some sort of persecuted philosopher, perhaps like Socrates."

I read to her a chapter from Brother Luke's wonderful new book about the life of Christ, then blew out the lamp and drifted off to sleep. But a dull roar thundering from the west awakened me in the night. Stirring in a fogged half-sleep, I thought a storm was brewing, and we would have to move our mattresses inside the apartment. How we needed rain! But suddenly Mum and I were brought to our senses by frantic screams and curses.

"Fire! Jupiter's city is lost!"

"All is burning!"

"Call upon your gods!"

A tremendous explosion in the Circus Maximus had apparently ignited sparks among stores of combustible material. Already raging out of control, and driven by strong winds, a wall of fire quickly swept through the Forum Boarium, where the stinking slaughterhouses and the cattle market stood.

The flames fanned outward onto the Tiber plain, then leapt upward in a frenzied glow into the surrounding hills. One by one, the city's proud buildings fell. Wherever we looked, the landscape sprouted

---

* Many Bible scholars believe Paul was released; then was arrested a second time about 65 A.D., after Nero had begun to persecute Christians.

flames. Human shapes silhouetted against the hideous red sky danced and tumbled like ghoulish specters.

Mum and I began to feel the warmth of the growing light, as tongues of fire licked their way with scornful impudence up the magnificent Palatine itself.* Wispy tailings of smoke began to drift through the apartment. The flickering light rose and fell, shedding alternate glare and darkness about the ornate walls. Wordlessly we gathered a few belongings in a sack, including gold coins, Scripture portions, and a change or two of clothing. I reached up and removed my father's wooden sword from the wall, where it had proudly hung for thirteen years. At the last minute, my fingers curled around a tiny alabaster box with blue flowers painted on its lid.

Holding wet cloths to our faces, Mum and I stumbled and groped our way along the murky stairway, which was rapidly filling with smoke. Nero and his entourage were vacationing at Antium, but a handful of servants remained at the palace. Tryphena, Tryphosa, Stachys, Amplias, and Narcissus Maurus and his cousins huddled together by the atrium door.

"How can we go out there in all that confusion?" Tryphena cried.

"Remember the words of our Lord," Amplias reminded us, "'Lo, I am with you always.'" He prayed, entrusting our lives to the Lord. We joined hands and inched our way out into the tumult of the street.

---

* Tacitus

"Whatever you do, don't fall down!" Narcissus Maurus warned. "Should you fall, they will quickly trample you to death."

When I dared to look back, a fiery halo crowned the Palatine with a bloody glow. The terrified mob was a babble of tongues and shrill voices and whirling limbs. Some were unable to speak at all except for mindless utterings. Heartbroken mothers screamed for children lost in the confusion. Some people supported invalids, or carried prized household possessions on their backs. They pushed and pummeled one another, not knowing which way to turn. Many in the crowd stretched out their hands to implore the heathen gods, while others cursed them. As we fled from the fire at one end of the street, flames rose in front of us. There seemed to be no source or pattern to it.

"Fires are breaking out everywhere," a man next to us stated. "Gangs of torch-wielding brigands are intentionally setting them. They insist they are following orders of some kind, perhaps from the Emperor himself. If anyone tries to extinguish the flames, they are set upon by armed thugs."

"They used military siege engines to demolish the granary," another chimed in. "Nero has always coveted that particular piece of land."

"If we get out of this alive, we shall have nothing to eat."

I had passed this way every day on my way to work. But in the eerie light that spilled its radiance over the sea of desperate faces, the *via* appeared as a strange and haunted wasteland. A crescendo of impassioned shrieks arose as a blinding cloud of smoke rolled down the narrow lane, close to the ground. Nothing could be seen but the flashes of fire through the cloud. The very air seemed to be burning. Then just as quickly, the wind snatched the acrid haze away again.

We watched in alarm as a tenement, its windows ablaze with light, rattled and shuddered to its very foundations. People were trapped on the upper floors, many hanging out of windows. Some jumped, preferring a quick ghastly death to the terror of the flames. A pulsating backdraft sucked oxygen from the air and nourished the fire, until the whole building became engulfed. Having burned through its supports, the tenement gave one last quiver and melted into the earth with a deafening groan. Chunks of broken glass and burning plaster flew upward, and we had to shake off the shower of sparks that singed our hair and clothing.

"Surely no one could have survived it," I said.

But a dusky man staggered from what had once been a doorway, disoriented with shock and grief. "My whole family is dead," he wailed. "People panicked and hid in crevices and under stairwells."

Amplias reached out to steady him, beating with his hands the flames springing from the man's clothing; but before our horror-stricken eyes, the distraught man turned about and dashed back into the fire. The screams were terrible for a few minutes, the shape of his burning body clearly outlined in the inferno. Then there was an eerie silence, pierced only by the hiss and crackle of the embers.

The searing heat and smoke subsided as our weary band neared Patrician Row, on the Esquiline Hill. We passed a squad of *vigiles*, the proud, well-trained firefighters who had long ago been commissioned by the Emperor Augustus, standing idly by with their newfangled Heron-built fire-fighting pump mounted on the back of a massive horse-drawn fire wagon.* Their fire station was well appointed, with a pleasant courtyard and fountain visible through the black iron-work gate.

A man in the crowd put words to my growing suspicions. "The *vigiles* have been ordered by Nero to stand aside in certain neighborhoods!"

"Death to Nero and his incendiaries!" the cry went up.

"I hope it isn't true about Nero," Mum said. "So much suffering and loss of loved ones. Yet a man who is capable of murdering his own mother, his stepbrother and dear Octavia, would think it of little consequence if thousands of Romans died, in order to further his own maniacal schemes, whatever they may be."

"The absinthe that he and his new wife Poppaea indulge in heavily has done much to impair his already twisted mind," Narcissus Maurus said. "He fancies himself a fine actor and playwright, and he believes the absinthe helps him to create."

Despite our grave circumstances, we couldn't help but laugh.

---

* Peter James and Nick Thorpe, "Ancient Inventions."

After several hours we collapsed in the arched doorway of the familiar house-church on the Via Urbana. Priscilla gasped as she threw open the heavy door.

"The Lord be praised!" she cried, drawing us into the safe refuge of her home. "We have all been praying for you!"

Mum and I found a space to sit on the second-story loggia among scores of other dazed refugees. Acilia and Priscilla brought armloads of quilts and blankets, and cold milk to soothe our parched and burning throats. We watched the wall of smoke and flames below that streamed high above the treetops and thundered at the night sky, leaving ash and rubble where our homes had been. The moon and stars appeared blood-red through the thick haze. A rooster crowed somewhere, confused in the weird light as to the time of day, and dogs howled in the background.

"Can it be the end of the world?" Tryphena whispered.

I fell into a troubled sleep. A few hours later a hand clutched my shoulder and shook me awake. "Get up, Glwadus," Mum said. "Patrobas and his rescue party are bringing in many wounded people. We need your help desperately."

Obediently I scrubbed my hands and splashed cold water over my face, donned a fresh apron Mum gave me, and tied my hair back in a kerchief. But my stomach wrenched as I stepped into the *balineum*, revolted by the odor of burned flesh, the sight of grisly charred faces and limbs smeared with blood. All the victims writhed and screamed in agony.

With much fervent prayer, Mum, Olympas, Manlius and other volunteers lowered the burn victims into the water of the large bathing pool, to cool the excruciating pain and to stop the burning process. They removed charred bits of clothing, taking care not to break any blisters, and with fine scissors debrided the tattered sheets of dead skin. This was essential for healing, but was accompanied by agonized screams of pain both during and after the procedure.

I helped Priscilla create soft pallets on the elegant marble floor of the *balineum*. As the victims were carried out of the water, we moved quickly from one to another, applying aloe ointment to the burns, and covering them with loose bandages. Priscilla brought pillows and blankets to prop the burned limbs above the level of the heart, and we served cups of cool water, mixed with a little honey.

A din erupted from the entrance hall. "They're bringing more of them in," I said wearily, my head pounding.

Patrobas stumbled across the threshold, carrying a small, badly burned child. "Wherever we turned, there was a sea of fire! The poor people who live in those dilapidated wooden tenements suffered most. This child's parents tossed him to me from a window, just before they were engulfed in flames. Bodies of people who jumped to their deaths, or who were overcome by thick smoke are piling up in the streets. Many were crushed by the mob. Some just lay down and died, surrounded by fire, with no way out."

When night cast off its murky veil, the sun's dim rays filtered through an ashen fog, people and objects appearing like phantom shapes. The firestorm still crackled across the black windswept hills. I helped serve bowls of chicken soup and crusty bread to the homeless families who camped in the courtyard and crowded into every room of the house, and spoon-fed broth to the burn victims who could eat.

The third day the wind shifted, carrying showers of ash and cinders toward the Esquiline Hill. Manlius brought farm wagons to begin evacuating the refugees to the safety of the *campagnia*. The *vigiles* and the Praetorian Guard set up a command post at the base of the hill to assess what methods could best be used to combat the blaze, and protect the fine houses on Patrician Row.

The earth trembled when the soldiers used siege engines to knock down several blocks of rickety tenements, where many of the students from Priscilla's school had once lived. These were set alight by carefully controlled backfires to create a firebreak.

During the fourth night Mum and I were left alone for a time with a few of the severely burned patients, the last of the group to be moved to the *campagnia*. Exhausted, I nodded off to sleep sitting in a chair, but a loud pounding at the front door startled me. I almost didn't recognize him, dressed as he was in the uniform of a military Tribune, but it was Pudens who stood there. Soot darkened his face, and his eyes were red and swollen. He stared, obviously as surprised to see me as I was him.

"Rufina!" he exclaimed. "The fire is coming this way. You must leave at once. We have established a firebreak, but no one knows if it will hold, or if it will be over-jumped by the sparks."

"Your father and Patrobas will be back soon, and we will try to carry the rest of these people to safety. But how did you happen to be in Rome? I thought you were in Germany."

"I worked my way up through the ranks of infantry, and then commanded a cavalry division. Now I have received another promotion as Quaester, so was already on my way back to Rome when we heard about the fire. I'm just trying to help out where I can."

His eyes glittered, and he seized me suddenly in his arms, crushing me against his blackened leather breastplate, stifling my protests with fierce kisses. A flood of emotions whirled around me, sentimental feelings that had been locked away for years. I did not return his kisses, but stopped struggling for a moment and pretended that I belonged in his arms.

I reached up to caress his rough cheek, worried that he was thinner than he ought to be. Heavy cares and responsibilities had etched new lines on his face, and made me realize that we were no longer in our youth. My tormented heart still yearned for him with that same undying love, which for us could only be a cruel and tragic thing. For we were worlds apart, and I could never go back.

"I wondered how you were," I whispered, fighting to clear the cobwebs from my brain.

"How do you think I am? I've missed you so much, *carissima*. There is no one else like you in the whole world."

"I will always love you, and pray every day that you will find Jesus. For He has given me the peace and joy that I had searched for all my life."

He pushed me from him then, and his brown eyes raked my face with anger. "Why can't you love me the way I am? Why must this martyr God forever come between us? Christianity is only for slaves and women and weak men. My mother would spend our entire family fortune on widows and orphans, so there will be nothing left."

Finding his arrogance intensely irritating, I prayed silently for wisdom. *God, please give me the right words.* "Your mother 'lays up treasure in Heaven, where moth and rust do not corrupt, and thieves do not break through and steal.' And what would you spend the money on? Drinking binges for your wild friends, or for gambling at the chariot races? Besides, your parents have given you the very finest education. It isn't likely you should ever starve to death!"

"I live by the philosophy of the Stoics," Pudens retorted. "It is a great ethical system which believes in moderate living, and freedom for women and slaves. Seneca says that 'knowledge is the source of all virtue,' and that 'every right-thinking man is a pilgrim in search of the good; that life can be lived on the loftiest heights, with steadfast confidence in man's own divinity.' "

"So that's what Seneca has been teaching Nero all these years!" I hooted. "Little wonder then that he fancies himself a god. The Stoics are moralizing immoralists, full of empty boasting and curious paradoxes. They deny the power of the true God, whose Holy Spirit comes to live inside of us and helps us to do good. Seneca is an outrageous hypocrite. He speaks out against slavery, yet he owns hundreds of slaves. He denounces extravagance, yet he has acquired a fortune. His houses rival the Emperor's own. And you know as well as I do how he looked the other way when Nero and Agrippina plotted to wrest the throne from Claudius and his rightful heir, Britannicus."

"Claudius had plenty of innocent blood on his hands too, a fact which you have always stubbornly avoided," Pudens said.

"That may be," I said, "but Britannicus was an innocent child."

Pudens leaned his length against the arched frame of the doorway, the firm line of his jaw grimly set. "I might have known I'd be outdone by a crazy blue-face Briton. You've won this round, Rufina, so I will go away and leave you to your work, you being such a proper girl and all!"

His words twisted like a knife-edge in my heart. He shot a quick glance over his shoulder, before he turned and vaulted onto his horse and angrily tapped its flanks. It didn't seem possible that two people who loved each other could go on hurting ourselves this way. Tears sprang into my eyes, and my fevered brain begged me to call him back. Yet these words of our Lord kept coming to mind: "How can two walk together unless they be agreed?"

Chapter 14

"Jesus wept."
—John 11:35

The dawn of the fifth day revealed that the fire-break had been a success. When the fire reached the bare scorched earth at the base of the Esquiline, the flames slowly extinguished themselves. The wind subsided, so the sparks could be easily controlled. The blaze rekindled in another section of the city, but was not judged to be as serious.

I stood beside Manlius, Priscilla and Patrobas on the *loggia,* and as the golden sun climbed into a perfect azure sky, the magnitude of the disaster became apparent. Between the Esquiline and the Aventine Hills, nothing was left but burned-out, blackened rubble. Survivors grieving for lost loved ones, wandered blankly through the still-hot, smoking ruins of buildings, searching for their charred corpses.

"Blocks of tenements, mansions, temples and ancient monuments were leveled in three districts,"

Patrobas said. "Scarcely a family inhabiting those neighborhoods survived intact. Seven other districts were also severely damaged."

"Thousands of hungry and homeless people are still wandering about in a daze," Manlius said, "camping out wherever they can find space, in fields or alleyways, in mausoleums, or on the muddy flats along the Tiber. Families sleep on the bare ground, without so much as a blanket to warm them."

Patrobas sighed, and rubbed aloe ointment between his badly burned palms. "Typhoid and dysentery menace the camps, and hundreds are dying from a cholera epidemic that has broken out, due to poor sanitation."

"Decaying bodies are beginning to pollute the city," Manlius said. "The death wagons, laden with their foul-smelling cargo, lumber through the streets night and day. Law and order has broken down, and violent thugs rob and plunder at will."

Our apartment had burned, though sections of the palace walls still stood intact. The Imperial slaves returned and cleaned up the smoke damage, and tried to salvage as much as possible. But Mum and I remained among the homeless refugees that crowded into Manlius' and Priscilla's house-church.

"Nero has thrown open the Saepta Julia, the Pantheon, and other public buildings, and had tents erected in the Campus Martius and in his own gardens, allowing thousands of destitute people temporary shelter," Patrobas said. "Food supplies have been rushed in from Ostia."

"But despite Nero's benevolence, the outraged people suspect that he was responsible for the disaster. Rumors are flying about that while the fires still raged, he had donned a stage costume, and sang a song about the burning of Troy, while he watched from the Tower of Maecenes, exulting in the beauty of the flames. It is said that he wished to clear ground for construction of a grand new Rome, to be called Neronia, built to his own specifications!"

The people began to invoke curses upon Nero, as a tide of hatred welled up against him, especially among those suffering souls who had lost loved ones in the fire. They thirsted for vengeance, and grew ever more threatening.

"Death to Nero and his incendiaries!" the cry went up everywhere in the streets.

Not long after, during an evening prayer service, Narcissus Maurus rose to his feet, his expression grave, and broke the dreadful news to the congregation. "Nero, fearing a revolt, called a conference with Tigellinus and his advisors. 'We must find someone on whom to shift the blame for the fire,' Nero insisted," Narcissus' voice choked off.

Amplias went on with the horrid tale. "Then his wife Poppaea said, 'why not blame the Christians? Does not their religion teach that the end of the world should come by fire? You don't have far to look, for your own palace is infested with the wretched vermin. Like Tryphena and Tryphosa, who always sided with Octavia, and all those who refuse to serve at your orgies; nor will they worship you as a 'god,' as you have requested, even when punished with the whip! The Empire has no end of slaves. Surely you can find others more congenial."

"The Praetorians, while doling out free bread to the populace, have begun to whisper about the hideous lie that the Christians burned Rome," Narcissus Maurus continued. "They encourage people to inform on Christian friends and neighbors."

A shocked tension settled over the congregation, as the bitter reality sank in. Someone cried softly.

"We will pray for the Lord to deliver us from the trial," Manlius murmured.

"Nay!" Narcissus Maurus exclaimed. "Pray not that we should be delivered, but rather that we will be found faithful. We must ask God for strength to endure the trials, that we might not deny the precious Name of our Lord Jesus, who willingly gave His life for us."

The diabolic Nero and Tigellinus, the Praetorian Prefect, stretched out their claws in every direction. My pen falters to tell of our hearts' anguish as we watched our beloved brethren being dragged off to prison. The Carcer Mamertine and the larger Latumiae became glutted with captives.

A nip of autumn cooled the morning air. Morag Julia and I fastened the hoods of our Gallic cloaks tightly about our throats as we made our way toward the Mamertine, weighted down with enormous baskets of food, water and a few medical supplies.

"Most of the accused are foreigners or poor people. I don't understand why Nero does not seem to be arresting Roman patricians," I said.

"It may be because they have the right to appeal, which can take two or three years," Morag Julia replied. "He needs instant scapegoats to blame for the fire, and doesn't want Roman citizens clogging up his jails and court dockets, unless they are specifically denounced by an accuser. It is said that Nero plans to open the Imperial Gardens across the Tiber, and throw the Christians to the wild beasts."

I shuddered. "Such a monstrous way to die! I'm thankful that we are still able to help our dear brothers and sisters."

"Yes, that's why I chose to stay in Rome, after Manlius moved the orphan children and many of the other Christian families to his vast lands in the Sabine and Umbrian hills," Morag Julia said. "Some have moved to the leper colony, too. That is one place the Praetorians refuse to go!"

We pressed several denarii into the greedy outstretched hands of the prison guards. Turning our backs on the sun's golden rays, we made our way down those steep, narrow steps that led to that subterranean dungeon. The dampness and the petrifying stench suffocated us as we descended into the murky blackness. Terrifying ghosts from my childhood rose up and haunted me.

Morag Julia pulled out a tinderbox and, hands shaking, lit her red terra-cotta oil lamp. As she turned up the wick, its beam swept the dark abyss, illuminating the sea of faces crammed into the upper chamber of the prison. But instead of groans and wails of despair, we heard singing of psalms and the chanting of Scripture verses, memorized and carried in their hearts for such a time as this. Tears streamed down my cheeks when I recognized many of the dear Imperial servants.

Narcissus Maurus' eyes glowed in the flickering light. "Do not weep for us, dear Claudia," he said. "This will pass quickly, and we shall look upon the One who died for us, and set us free from sin. He has turned the shadow of death into the morning!"

Morag produced a loaf of bread and a flagon of wine, which Amplias laid out for a communion service. There were few dry eyes, when we realized that for some it would be the last time we would share the communion cup. Amplias rose to pray, giving thanks that they were counted worthy to suffer for His Name.

"We long for that country not made by human hands," Amplias said, as he broke the bread. "Now we see our precious Lord Jesus 'through a glass darkly, but soon . . . face to face.'"

Afterward, Morag Julia and I stumbled about in the shadows, distributing bread and cheese, apples, grapes and cool water. We wrote down all their names, and took any last messages to be delivered to relatives, or requests for epitaphs to be carved on their gravestones. Tryphena was silent, her face twisted with pain, and she slumped against her sister's shoulder. Dried blood stained her skin and was matted in her long dark hair.

"During her trial she spoke very boldly for our Lord Jesus," Tryphosa explained. "Nero's magistrate couldn't abide it, so he had her tortured."

Penelope of the tenements, who had won so many souls for Christ, sat in a corner with her daughter Marcia, one of my former students, now in her early teens.

"She's just a child!" I exclaimed.

I swayed, clutching the sides of my face, faint and overcome with horror. Had the entire world gone mad? Surely it was all some dreadful nightmare. Rome had always claimed to uphold law and order. Roman magistrates had often protected innocent Christians from cruel mobs that intended to harm them.

As Morag Julia's lantern lighted a dark corner of the room, she came upon a grieving family gathered about a tall blond young man lying prone in the rough straw. His wife knelt anxiously beside him, and also his parents, a stocky, olive-skinned couple, Syrian perhaps, or Jewish. I had seen them once or twice before at various gatherings, but had never learned their names.

The mother explained. "The magistrate ordered him to be scourged when he would not denounce Christ. The wounds are festering, and now he has grown septic with fever."

"Please, ma'am," the young man whispered. "I must die with my family, to help them endure the wild beasts. I don't want to rot here in the dirt."

Morag Julia dug her fingers into her leather bag full of medical supplies. She placed a flask over the oil lamp, and set willow bark tea to boil, to bring the young man's fever down. With lightly salted water, she gently cleaned his wounds, and slathered aloe ointment over them. Suddenly she gasped, and jerked the lamp up quickly, to make sure. There on the back of his right shoulder, just above the festering wounds, was a familiar heart-shaped birthmark. She examined his feet, where the third and fourth toes were curiously webbed. Overcome with emotion, her shoulders began to shake with sobs.

She turned to the mother. "I thought he had surely died. How . . . where did you find him?"

The small woman smiled. "One of the farmers who brought vegetables to our little market in Trastavere found him by the side of the road. He was such a beautiful baby, like an angel, and he has been the light of our lives these many years. He has grown up to be a fine Christian. We call him Lucius."

When Morag Julia finished wrapping the linen bandage rolls around his torso, she lifted Lucius' head and cradled him in her arms, helping him to drink the willow tea and a large dose of elderberry extract.

"I'm so sorry," she murmured. "You are my own son, dear Lucius, whom I wickedly abandoned many years ago, before I came to know the Lord Jesus. Please, please forgive me."

She kissed his cheek, and gently laid him back down to rest. Even in the poor light I could see that he looked just like her. The prison guards clanged on the iron bars then, signaling that it was time to leave.

"I'm staying here, Claudia," Morag Julia declared firmly. She lapsed into Gallic speech. "I will die here with my son, to help him face what has to be faced. He needs me. And I can care for Tryphena and the others who require medical help as well."

"Morag, my sister," I pleaded, "have you quite thought this through? Your forefathers in Gaul were given Roman citizenship by the great Julius Caesar himself. You are entitled to a fair trial and appeals, and even if convicted would be beheaded, not torn apart by wild beasts!"

"I abandoned my son once, Claudia. I won't leave him again. My husband is dead. There is no one left to mourn for me. Even a few hours spent with my son will be the joy of my life, and we shall meet our Lord together."

My heart shattered as I hugged my friend for the last time. "I will see you in Heaven then," I whispered.

She quickly removed her heavy blue cloak, and handed it to young Marcia. Then she claimed the child's ragged one. "Brother Manlius will see that she escapes safe to Umbria," Morag said.

If the guards noticed the difference as we slipped by them, empty baskets in hand, they didn't say anything. Before they could get a second glance, Marcia and I scurried around the corner and blended into the crowded Forum.

Pudens was in fine spirits that warm, golden afternoon. He had a few days leave coming to him, just in time for the opening of the grand new arena in the Imperial Gardens. He had laid aside his military garb in favor of a snow-white toga, with the wide purple *laticlava* of the senatorial class proudly displayed.

On the way to the arena, he and his black-bearded poet friend passed by hundreds of workmen clearing land, hauling rubble in wheelbarrows to be loaded into rude wagons. Every block seemed to sprout new buildings. Winches and modern cranes, powered by giant treadwheels, lifted here a beam, there a massive block of marble. An enormous network of scaffolding teemed with construction crews. Masons stood armed with set-squares and compasses, while daubers mixed mortar in huge vats. Workmen from the plumbers' guild were laying water pipes.

"Streets in the new Rome will be wide and spacious," Pudens said. "Although Nero has practically beggared Rome's citizens and the colonies with his Fire Relief Program."

The lewd poet laughed. "I suppose that's why you were appointed financial officer. It is said that the Acilian Glabriones possess more riches than the Emperor himself. Nero knows that you will see that the soldiers get paid, even if you have to dip into your father's estates."

Pudens shrugged. "Well, no matter. No more wilderness camps for me, and fighting pesky Germans!"

The public spectacles Nero had arranged for that week were designed to take the minds of the beleaguered populace off the wretched living conditions they were forced to endure. Despite the rebuilding program, thousands still remained homeless. Nero has promised the grandest sort of multiple extravaganza the Romans craved, a holocaust to satisfy their gluttony for blood.

"The handbill says that all fights today will be without quarter," the poet said enthusiastically. "We will see 'Bacchus devoured by ferocious beasts! Spartacus crucified on a cross! Osiris cut to pieces!'"

Nero had long prided himself in his theatrical "achievements." Here was an opportunity to turn the debacle into a most elaborate production that would last all afternoon and into the night, all that his most infernal imagination could contrive. A multitude streamed into the arena. Pudens and his friend found seats next to Vespasian's brother, the wealthy Flavius Sabinus; his son, the quiet and studious Flavius Clemens; and young nephew, Domitian.

Gold and purple banners fluttered on the autumn air. The sun glinted on the highly polished brass trumpets that heralded the entrance of the pagan priests and priestesses, splendidly attired in scarlet and gold, and carried on gilded chairs. The Emperor Nero and the Empress Poppaea were brought in, and took their places in the Imperial box.

The high priest stood at the altar and uttered these terrible words: "To Jupiter, the 'greatest and the best.' Accept these thine offerings, and heal our city and our Empire!"

"And to the great Sun-God Apollo, who first revealed to the Emperor Nero the Christians' plot to burn Rome," the high priestess of Apollo echoed. "Accept their blood as a token of thanksgiving—these loathsome wretches, haters of mankind, who refuse to sacrifice and do obeisance to all the gods of Rome!"

A large group of Christians were driven into the arena, amid the deafening tumult of the crowd. The enraged lions and other wild beasts roared, pacing back and forth in their cages, insane with hunger, for they had not eaten in three days. Pudens' face blanched, realizing in horror that he recognized many of the captives. There was the kindly Amplias, and Stachys; the diminutive sisters, Tryphena and Tryphosa; and the black-skinned Narcissus Maurus, who had several times bested him at handball.

A few of the Christians cowered at the thought of so painful a death, but their comrades encouraged them. A hush fell over the thousands of spectators when the martyrs joined hands and knelt in a circle, while Amplias led them in prayer.

Possessed of a confident faith in their Lord Jesus Christ, and an unshakeable hope of eternal life with Him, the martyrs then lifted their voices in song, eyes raised toward Heaven, even as the beasts were released from confinement:

Who shall separate us from the love of Christ?
Shall tribulation, or persecution
Or famine or nakedness, or peril, or sword?
    As it is written, for Thy sake we are killed all the day long;
    We are accounted as sheep for the slaughter.
    Nay, for in all things we are more than conquerors
    through Him that loved us.
        For we are persuaded that neither death, nor life,
        nor angels, nor principalities, nor powers,
        nor principalities, nor powers, nor things present,
        nor things to come, nor height, nor depth,
        nor any other creature
            Shall be able to separate us from the love of God,
            which is in Christ Jesus our Lord.

"Be strong, brethren, in the power of His might!"
Stachys proclaimed. "Let us be faithful unto death,
and we shall receive a crown of life!"

Pudens felt an overwhelming desire to bolt from
the arena, but he found himself frozen to his seat,
drenched in perspiration, his eyes fixed on the frenzied scene before him.

"Aren't you one of the Christians?" his seat-
mate Flavius Sabinus asked him curiously. "Your
mother and father surely are, and they make no
secret about it."

Pudens winced. There was nothing he could say.
Hot molten iron simmered and churned within his
soul like a thousand demons. His mind had lost all
fascination for the hideous "games."

"I worry that the Christians' God will take vengeance upon us," Flavius Sabinus went on. "I have

heard about strange and startling events concerning this Jesus Christ, the Messiah of the Jews, from some of my brother Vespasian's soldiers in the east."

A sob escaped from Pudens' throat when Tryphena went down, only a few cubits in front of his eyes, blood spurting from her torn throat. A massive Bengal tiger uttered a savage growl, and lunged at Tryphosa beside her, knocking her to the ground. It was quickly over.

"I came to see a fair fight between trained gladiators!" the usually reticent Flavius Clemens declared. He slung his arm protectively around the shoulder of his young cousin, Domitian. "How can it be 'sport,' watching innocent, defenseless women being mutilated. This is only depravity! The glory of our beloved Empire is fallen this day! Let's go home, Father. I can't bear to see it anymore."

The songs of the Christians blended with those of the angels in Heaven, as one by one the martyrs collapsed in the blood-soaked sands of the arena. But their spirits soared with triumph into Glory, victorious over death itself, the brightest jewels in His crown. They were beholding the face of Jesus, even while the arena slaves dressed as Charun, the Etruscan demon of death, hurried out to drag the mangled corpses into the *spoliarium*.

Linus sat clouded in agony, his chin in his hands, watching his beloved brethren suffer in a savage orgy of blood. He would rather have been anywhere but here. But he had volunteered for this job, and he was determined to see it through, blinking back the tears. He wrote down the names of each of the martyrs who had died that day, with descriptions, so that their remains could be identified later.

When night came, he and others would return and carry the bodies away. They had vowed to give each martyr a decent Christian burial, where their precious bones would await the promised Resurrection at the Lord's return. He wondered if this was to be the end of the fledgling church. Yet had not the Lord said, "the gates of hell shall not prevail against it"?

"They die well." A boy sitting next to him woke Linus from his reverie. It was young Tacitus. "Father says we shouldn't like the Christians; but it's not right what Nero does to them. Everyone knows these people didn't set the fires."

Linus glanced around him then. Amid the fiendish shrieks of derision and applause from the spectators, callous to their terrible guilt, there were some who wept, shielding their faces from the slaughter.

"They're singing!" a woman behind him said, with a muffled sob. "What peace these Christians have."

"See how they love one another," her companion sighed, dabbing at her eyes. "What do you suppose they're looking at up in the sky?"

"We shall have to find out more about a God Who can give such peace, even in the face of so horrible a death!"

On one side of the battle were arrayed all the forces of Hell, and the Emperor Nero, Satan's proud servant, whose evil will dictated to most of the known world. On the other, a few poor innocents armed not with weapons, but with psalms and prayers.

Linus winced in pain as each of his dear brothers and sisters went down under the gaping jaws of the wild beasts. But he began to understand that their deaths would not be in vain; that the blood of the martyrs would somehow become the foundation of the church. Suddenly it seemed not the end, but the beginning.

Roman law allowed for the bodies of the dead to be given up to friends or relatives, often for an exorbitant fee. But most of the relatives were in hiding, afraid to come forward. If a body went unclaimed, it would be thrown into the enormous *carneria* pit with the dead animals. This would have been unthinkable!

Late that night Linus, his young friend Eubulus, Acilia, Sergia Paula and I came with horse-drawn wagons and stole quietly into the arena. Linus paid the fee to the guards, and we were waved ahead, entering the *spoliarium*, a murky, torch-lighted chamber. The precious tattered remains of the martyrs had been carelessly strewn about its macabre interior. Overwhelmed by the stench of blood, my eyes watched, but refused to see the torn and ravaged limbs, the bits of flesh already decaying. Beads of sweat ran down my face, despite the cold and clammy air.

"I can't!"

Shrinking back, I crumbled against the doorway of the *spoliarium*, and buried my face in my trembling hands. My stomach turned and turned, and bile climbed into my throat. I tried to force it down, but had to duck away abruptly and vomit outside the door.

Linus' hand tightened on my shoulder, as he gave me his linen handkerchief. "Claudia, please. There is no one else. Only Roman citizens are able to come and go. The older women will be of some help, but they don't have the stamina to run about all night."

His voice sounded hollow. "The other girls look to you, for you are the daughter of a brave king. You have seen battlefields. This is one of those times when we must put on the 'shield of faith and the helmet of salvation, for we wrestle against the rulers of the darkness of this world.'"

"I loved them so much, and cannot bear to think of them this way. No one could have imagined it would be this bad!"

"If we love them, then let us put our love into practice," Linus replied. "We promised to give them a Christian burial. See them as they are now, beholding the face of Jesus, wearing their glittering crowns of glory. Their suffering is over. He has gathered His lambs in His arms."

I had reached the end of human resources. Only God could have given me strength to guide me through that night! Acilia, Sergia Paula and I accomplished the grisly task with little conversation, our eyes half-blinded with tears, tending to the mutilated women, matching up the shredded pieces as best we could. We wrapped the beloved martyrs in shrouds, labeled each one with her name, and laid them in the wagon beds. Linus and Eubulus tended to the men.

Some of our beloved brethren had been dressed in tunics made stiff with pitch, fixed to axletrees suspended around the perimeter of Nero's Imperial Gardens, and had been set afire as human candles, to illuminate the evening games.* My heart strangled with nightmarish sorrow, I helped Linus and Eubulus sift through the charred remains, carefully gathering up the pitiful ashes with the blackened scraps of teeth and bones, and arranged them in burial urns.

---

* Tacitus

Chapter 15

"The way of the transgressor is hard."
—Proverbs 13:15

Pudens followed his poet friend to the Baths of Claudius Etruscus, on the Quirinal Hill, hoping to find relief from the despair that overwhelmed him. He paid his *quadrans* to the attendant, and entered the atrium, where mighty pillars chiseled from green Laconian marble rose to support its high vaulted dome.

Issuing from the open door of the gymnasium could be heard the grunts and groans of men exercising, their hands heavy with lead weights.* Porticoes along the sides of the bath complex were filled with shops and eating and drinking establishments. The bath complex enclosed lush gardens, with a fountain that splashed over rocks and plants and ferns in a nature-like setting. But the cloying scent

---

*Seneca

of the gaudy, exotic flowers that bloomed in the thick green foliage mingled with the odor of sweat and mold, giving off a sickening aura.

The late afternoon sun pierced the long rows of skylights along the ceiling with all its flaming rays, flooding the baths with ruby light. The over-decorated walls and gables glittered with mosaics in vibrant colors, and niches embraced obscene statues of the gods. Pudens wandered down a dimly lit promenade to the changing room hung with towels and clothing, then past small private cubicles, to the steam room, where fat men and simpering boys reclined on green marble benches. Some of them called out his name. Vapor hissed in rasping echoes off the gray walls that dripped with ugly beads of moisture. The heavy damp air suffocated him.

Pudens laid on a table while a masseur slathered sweet fragrant oil over his back, and slapped and pummeled the tense muscles, his hands cupped or flat, a different thump for each, fiercely kneading away the physical aches and pains. But Pudens suffered from an anguish deep inside his heart that could not be so easily soothed.

He plunged first into the steaming *calidarium*, the hot pool nearest the boiler, or *hypocausis*, that lay underneath the baths, and channeled the heat upward. A haze ascended, and there was a vague odor of smoke. Distantly he heard the off-key strains of some oaf who enjoyed the sound of his own voice, singing in the bath.

Pudens wished that the steaming water could wash all the sin and ugliness out of his body. How could one be so clean on the outside, yet so unspeakably dirty on the inside? He dipped his face in the water to hide the tears that streamed from his eyes, for a Stoic scorns the shedding of tears.

"I know the martyrs went to Heaven," he whispered. "But if I died tonight, where would I be?" And well he knew the answer—he would go to that place of darkness and everlasting fire, from which there could be no escape.

Pudens jumped next into the warm *tepidarium*, a wide blue river that ran perfectly clear between snow-white marble "banks." A rowdy group of his friends splashed noisily about, and beckoned for him to join them in a vigorous game of water ball. They cursed and laughed uproariously with every stroke.

When the baths closed for the evening, Pudens wandered across the dark alleyway with his friends to an open-fronted *caupona*, which kept its doors open and its lamps aglow late into the night, serving strong drink and cheap food to their usual unsavory clientele. Pudens had a terrible thirst, and he gratefully accepted a goblet of the bitter absinthe.

He knew better than anyone, except for God Himself, that the sickly green-colored liquid had somehow become his master, gnawing at his insides, killing him bit by bit. He, a proud Roman officer, was little more than a slave to that demonic wormwood nectar, wallowing in shame and degradation.

He raised glass after glass to his lips and drank deeply, hoping to quiet the horror that raged within his breast, waiting in pain for that oblivion which would allow him to forget this life with all its misery. How he welcomed the warmth that quickly permeated his body!

He closed his eyes and sat in stuperous silence, while his friends' coarse, filthy jesting and shrieks of hideous laughter droned on unendingly. The absinthe gave him a slight euphoria, causing his arms and legs to tremble. And there was a loud ringing in his ears. But the faces of the martyrs still haunted his dark soul.

"You all missed Nero's greatest 'games' ever!" the lewd poet exclaimed. He passed around the souvenir handbill from the arena to his crude friends, and enthusiastically described every atrocity they had witnessed, right down to the last theatrical detail.

One of them sniffed, his lip curled back in a look of utter loathing. "It's time Nero finally did something about those Christians!"

"I can't abide the way they complain about the words we write in our poems. As if they knew anything about art and culture. They always want to spoil everyone's fun."

The lewd poet chuckled, a cruel gleam in his eyes. "The Christians always think they're so much better than everyone else, like that stern-minded, self-righteous Linus, and Pudens' girlfriend, the high and mighty 'ice princess,' Claudia Rufina."

"Nero ought to write a piece for the next spectacle about her. With all that long red hair, she could play the part of Boudicca when Suetonius Paulus thrust her through with a sword in the British revolt!"

A sharp pain stabbed Pudens' heart. What of his own loved ones? Anyone who was a Christian was automatically suspected of lighting the torches that had burned Rome. And what defense could they offer? They were all guilty of being Christians. He knew they would never deny it.

It was rumored that Nero wasn't arresting Roman patricians, but the madman was subject to change his mind at any moment. He had many times padded his beleaguered Treasury by murder, and confiscating estates. The wealthy Pomponia Graecina and Claudia Procula were both of noble birth, related to the Emperor Augustus or Tiberius—though in his muddled state, Pudens couldn't remember just what the connection was—and his own family and Sergius Paulus possessed great riches.

He had to know if they were safe. Staggering to his feet, he wandered out into the dark, cobbled street, reaching out a hand to steady himself, as his body smashed against a brick wall. Pudens had never before swilled such a large quantity of absinthe. His head was spinning in a fog, and cold beads of sweat gathered on his forehead as he stumbled along the dark street near his parents' home. Eyes glazed, he stared up at the shuttered windows which hours ago had been bolted against the dangers that lurked in the night.

Weird images and shadowy objects whirled about, like dark death angels carrying flaming swords. Then the shaking began. Suddenly paralyzed by the numbness in his legs, he pitched forward onto the filthy pavement, and began to convulse with the peculiar "absinthe epilepsy." The blood tasted salty as it spurted from his nose, and ran down into his mouth. Through half-opened eyes he saw the bobbing headlamps and the dim outline of a heavy freight wagon hurtling toward him, drawn by a team of massive German horses. His fingers clawed helplessly at the cobblestones.

"I'm going to die and go to Hell!" It was his last thought as he plunged into oblivion.

Timothy and Luke had arrived from Asia just that day, in the company of Brother Paul, who had been arrested again in Ephesus, and cast into the Mamertine Prison. They had been invited to stay in the comfortable home of the Acilian Glabriones, on the Via Urbana. With envy, Timothy could hear Luke's deep, even breathing as he slept soundly in the adjoining bedroom. Timothy had not yet become accustomed to the hubbub of Rome's streets at night: the constant thunder of wagon wheels, the squeak of axles, the loud braying of mules, and the angry voices of the teamsters who were obliged to deliver their supplies after dark. It seemed Latins thrived on noise.

His head bursting, he wandered out onto the second-story *loggia*. Timothy saw the young man fall; and he saw the heavy freight wagon turn into the dark street. Even with his lantern glowing, there was no way the teamster was going to see that limp form lying there in time to stop his spirited horses. Without hesitation, Timothy scaled the iron-work railing that bordered the *loggia*, and let himself down with his hands, dropping onto the sidewalk. A sharp pain shot through his ankle, but he couldn't let it hinder him.

He dashed into the middle of the street, just in time to pull the man to the side of the pavement, as the wagon wheels thundered by. He cradled the man's injured head, to keep him from banging it repeatedly on the cobblestones while he convulsed. The eyes seemed to roll back. Timothy mopped perspiration from the pale forehead, and felt for the weak, uncertain pulse. Then he beat on the door just loud enough to wake the freedman Patrobas. They hoisted the young man inside, very drunk and reeking of liquor, muttering in delirium about the "absinthe."

Patrobas groaned. "It's young Master Pudens."

"We need some strong dandelion tea," Timothy said, "and a bit of charcoal to absorb the poison in his stomach."

They tickled his throat with a feather to make him vomit the alcohol. Then Pudens felt the bitter dandelion tea being forced between his lips. After that, the preacher Timothy and Patrobas were standing on either side of him, making him walk, walk, walk on his numb legs, when he desperately wanted to sleep. He tried to shrug off the two men, and started to get loud and mean, knocking away the helping hands.

"Please try to restrain yourself," Patrobas chided him gently, with tears in his eyes. "You don't want to waken your dear mother. She has been through enough today already."

Something penetrated Pudens' muddled brain, and he began to cooperate, drinking quantities of the tea and pacing. The lamp flames flickered strangely in their iron receptacles; he sobbed at the monstrous faces of the gargoyles that danced and grinned at him from the shadowy corners of his mother's kitchen. Patrobas helped him into the bath, scrubbing away the dried blood, and the stinking vomit and grime from the street, and brought him a clean tunic. When he and Timothy were satisfied that he hadn't poisoned himself, they allowed Pudens to fall asleep on one of the banquet couches.

Daybreak found him sober and shamefaced. Through slanted eyes, he watched Timothy tying a strip of linen tightly around his painfully swollen ankle. "My mother told me about Jesus when I was a boy," Pudens said, "but I thought Christianity would hold me back in the world. I became a Stoic. But last night I thought I was going to die. It was so terrifying! I cannot endure the agony a moment longer. My sins keep coming up before me. I have broken my mother's heart, and am not worthy to carry my father's good name."

"The first step to becoming a Christian is to realize that we are miserable sinners, and can do nothing to save ourselves," Timothy said. "That is the reason Jesus came to die for us. The Scriptures say 'there is none righteous, no not one.' But God's gift of salvation is free. We only have to receive it. Isaiah 44 says, 'I have blotted out, as a thick cloud, thy transgressions, and as a cloud, thy sins.'"

"I don't think you understand." Pudens buried his head in his hands, and his shoulders shook violently. "You just don't know . . . the Greek Stoics claim to believe in good works, yet they embrace certain vices . . . things I can't even talk about."

Timothy hobbled to a nearby shelf, and reaching inside his leather *capsa*, drew out a letter. "I am half Greek myself," he replied gently. "There's not a whole lot you could tell me about our culture that would shock me. But you don't have to confess your sins to me; you only have to confess them to God."

"But I am such a wicked sinner, God would never want me."

Timothy opened the letter. "Brother Paul sent this to me some time ago," he went on. "Here it says that 'Jesus Christ came into the world to save sinners, of whom *I* am *chief*.' If Brother Paul was the chief of sinners, then you could only be the second, at the very worst—and God forgave him! When we trust Christ, repent and ask Him to forgive us, He makes us new creatures, and helps us to live a clean new life that we would not be ashamed of."

"I should like to do that right now," Pudens whispered. He fell heavily upon his knees, begging for mercy and forgiveness, trembling before the great Lamb of God. As he prayed, the love of Jesus filled his heart and washed away the sin and depravity. A sweet peace flooded over him, such as he had never known, swallowing up the last shred of darkness.

Priscilla's shoulders drooped as she plodded down the narrow back stairway to the kitchen. She didn't see him at first where he stood in the far corner of the room. Her eyes, red and swollen from weeping, were fixed on the cold stone floor. She lit a fire in the hearth, and set over it a large pot of water to boil for polenta. Pudens thought how she seemed to have aged a great deal; perhaps it was just the pain in her eyes, or the sluggish, plodding way she went about her tasks.

"Mama," Pudens said. Standing behind her, he wrapped his arms around her waist. "The Lord has saved me!"

She turned to look at him, clasping his face between her hands. "God has finally answered my most fervent prayer." Overwhelmed, tears spilled from her eyes.

He chuckled. "I thought you would be happy, and not cry."

"I have called out to God for your soul with anguished heart these many years," she said. "Oh, to have an unwavering faith that waits patiently for the Lord, to know that His delays are not denials . . . to be assured that the refining fires were part of His promised blessings . . . that He might make us come forth shining as pure gold!"

The brightness in her face erased the weary, tormented look. The refugee women, many of them scarred from the Great Fire, began to shuffle in one by one, to set out spoons and bowls for breakfast.

"My son has found the Lord!" Priscilla exclaimed.

There was a great deal of rejoicing, and hands reaching out to clasp his, as Pudens was welcomed as a brother in Christ.

Sister Eurgain smiled. "Claudia will be so happy for you."

Pudens felt a sudden cold fear. He'd seen Claudia and Acilia coming home very late last night with Linus, when they thought he was passed out on the couch. He wandered to the hallway and gazed at his reflection in the silver mirror. He needed a shave, and his nose was scraped, from where he'd struck it on the cobblestones. It was difficult to look into his swollen, pink-veined eyes without flinching. And he could still taste the vile liquor on his tongue.

Claudia had been the sweetest love that he had ever known. But he had cast her cruelly aside, while chasing dreams of sin and pleasure that had always disappointed. He hated himself for the pain he had caused her. Pudens yearned to tell her how desperately he loved her. There had been others, of course, but no one could ever thrill his heart as she had. His lonely arms ached for her, and he craved the touch of her soft bright hair, which was the color of the setting sun. She had no need of face paint, nor kohl for her eyes that sparkled blue as the Mediterranean. They had captivated him since she was a child.

But it was not her outer beauty that set her apart from the others. He'd learned long ago that many who were known for their lovely features often harbored ill qualities just underneath the surface. But Claudia was a virtuous woman, whose "price was far above rubies." She did not think it beneath her noble birth to apply her hands to the most difficult task, often stretching them out to relieve the poor and suffering, asking for nothing in return.

But he was being presumptious. He knew that he had hurt her deeply. She was probably in love with someone else by now, someone worthy of her, who treated her kindly, Linus perhaps. Good old Linus, who had never strayed from the right path, from the faith he had learned in childhood. If Claudia loved another man, he couldn't bear to know. Pudens' mouth felt dry, his head dizzy, bursting with sick dread. If only he could turn back time.

He was due back at the Castra Praetoria in a few hours. Wandering out into the sunshine, he closed the heavy front door, and leaned wearily against it. "I will always love you, Claudia," he murmured, "more than you could ever know."

But his words were swallowed up in the clamor of the street, and by the raucous cries of the fruit vendor.

Chapter 16

A.D. 66

"I met a new friend this week, name of Cornelius Severus," Pudens said, while he sipped a beaker of chilled cider in his mother's kitchen. "He has lately returned from Nero's expedition to Ethiopia, where he ran into all sorts of adventures, including being captured as a slave. We have joined a class devoted to the study of the Scriptures among the Praetorian soldiers. Brother Paul had led many of them to the Lord during the time he was held under house arrest."

"That's splendid, dear," Priscilla said. Her brows furrowed. "But I'm worried about you all. The persecution of the Christians rages on. Everyone has been devastated to hear that the beloved Apostle Peter was crucified on a cross, head down, for he considered himself unworthy to die in the same manner as did our Lord Jesus. And the Christian Praetorians . . . how long will Nero and Tigellinus continue to look the other way?"

Pudens leaned back against the wall. "We are not overly concerned about ourselves. We have counted the cost, and will pay the price willingly. Our lives are not our own, for we were bought with a price, the precious blood of our Lord Jesus. We only wish to do God's will, to open blinded eyes, and bring rest to weary, sin-laden souls."

"Praise be to God!" Priscilla said.

"Have you heard that Nero has appropriated some 125 acres of Rome's burned-out property to construct his elaborate new palace, the 'Golden House,' which will eventually join the Palatine and the Esquiline in a labyrinth of ornate porticoes and buildings," Pudens said.

Priscilla clucked. "Such folly!"

"Some sections have already been completed, actually overlaid with gold. The dome of its circular main banquet hall is studded with 'moon and stars,' and revolves in imitation of the cosmos. The Emperor who sits in its center sees himself as ruler of the universe!"

Priscilla frowned. "Multitudes of Romans murmur against Nero, for his crazed spending habits and lavish lifestyle have bankrupted the Treasury, while thousands still remain homeless."

The kitchen door creaked open, and Pudens raised his eyes as Claudia entered the room. No words passed between them, only a shy smile. How he loved her smile! The soft blue radiance of her eyes made him forget what he was thinking. He felt his face blush red as a schoolboy, as he listened to the wild, painful beating of his heart.

But though he loved her completely, was obsessed by her, he knew now that he must never rekindle the love that had once bound them together. She must be free to find a husband who was worthy of her. The thought was almost beyond bearing, but he could only be her friend, nothing more. The smothering heartache would be his own private torment, penance for the years spent in sin. There was no one to blame but himself. He would learn to build high walls around his heart against the pain, so that he might never feel anything again. Perhaps God wished him to travel on alone, devoting his life entirely to the service of the Lord.

Surely Claudia sensed the tortured agony of his soul by the way he looked at her, the way his hands trembled. He set his beaker down on the marble countertop, for it had suddenly become very heavy. He felt an overpowering urge to crush her in a fierce anguished hug, to tell her he loved her over and over. But once she was in his arms, he knew that all his resolve would vanish. He kissed his mother's cheek instead.

"It's time I was gone, Mama," he said. "I'll try to get back tonight to help with the . . . burials."

By night the Christians transferred the remains of the martyrs to the cemeteries. Many were interred in the cemetery on the property of the Acilian Glabriones, near the Via Salaria. Rome's poor pagans were usually cremated, but that was contrary to the Christians' beliefs. Yet only wealthy Romans could afford tombs. Therefore the Acilian cemetery filled up quickly.

Manlius and Pudens hired laborers from the fosser's guild to excavate deep into the soft limestone to hollow out a catacomb, as the Jews had done for years, which was called the "Catacomb of Priscilla." The fossers worked night and day by the faint light of olive oil lamps and hauled the dirt and rubble away in baskets and buckets.

In these tombs were laid to rest the precious bones of those who slumbered in the Lord, to await the Call of Morning. Wrapped in their burial shrouds, they were laid in niches, or *loculi,* and closed with a slab of marble or tiles sealed with mortar. Their names were carved in the stone or mortar, often with a short verse they had requested, such as "In Peace," or "Asleep in Jesus." Slashes of vermilion paint were emblazoned across the martyr's tombs, an old Roman custom signifying that they had given all.

Pudens' stomach clenched sharply as he made his way into the *spoliarium.* Never would he become accustomed to that cold chamber choked with grisly images, crushed and dismembered bones, the tattered flesh. He was staggered by the fact that civilized men could inflict such atrocities on fellow human beings, on innocent men and women who had committed no crime. It nauseated him to think that he had once counted the vile murderers among his friends. He had, indeed been one of them. His wasted years lived in sin could never be recalled without a shudder of revulsion. Yet the Saviour gently whispered, *I will restore to you the years that the locust hath eaten.*

Forcing one foot in front of another, he crossed the bloodstained floor to where Linus, Eubulus, Brother Luke and Cornelius Severus were piecing together the bodies of the men. Priscilla, Claudia, Acilia and Sergia Paula had just begun to tend to the female victims. Pudens would never forget the expression of horror that clouded Claudia's eyes as she gazed upon the shredded remains of Morag Julia, attached to a long mane of blond hair soaked with dried blood. Nearby lay the body of what appeared to have been a tall blond young man.

As the whole long nightmarish scene rushed over her, Claudia winced, as though she was enduring the most incredible torture. Closing her eyes, she sagged against the wall, her spongy legs giving way beneath her, and collapsed on the cold stone floor.

"Son! Carry her outside, please, into the fresh air!" Priscilla cried out, alarmed at how Claudia's face had lost all its color. "I'm afraid it has all been too much for the poor lamb. She hasn't been sleeping or eating well lately, and has been driving herself, working too hard."

Pudens bent down and lifted Claudia gently in his arms. Her head sagged, rolling back against his chest. Outside the grating the guards were casting dice. They smirked and voiced ribald remarks when he laid her down on a stone bench. He had no choice but to stay until she revived. All thumbs, he sat down and wrapped his cloak about her shivering form, supporting her head in the crook of his bent arm. *Just to warm her,* he whispered to himself.

Pressing her cheek close against his aching heart, Pudens rocked her gently back and forth like a small, injured child. He could not take his eyes from her face, which was deathly pale and drawn, her eyes ringed with purple shadows, the long curling lashes resting on wax-like cheeks. The light from the torch on the wall rose and fell, glimmering on her burnished hair, the silky strands soft against his arm.

Pudens lost track of time. His mind twisted and twisted. *I am going mad,* he thought. His hand lingered on the side of Claudia's face, then entwined itself deep in her hair. He rubbed his jaw against its gossamer warmth, while several brass hairpins clattered to the stone floor. He blinked back tears, tormented by his love for her. A groan of despair erupted from his throat. His lips brushed her forehead, just as her eyelids fluttered open. The feathery lashes tickled his stubbled cheek.

"Forgive me, Rufina," he said in a deep strangled voice. "I had no right to kiss you. It was a foolish thing to do. I must have swallowed too much of the night air, which got into my brain apparently."

But his arms wouldn't let her go. Her gaze fastened on him curiously for a moment in silence, trying to focus, not quite comprehending, but seeming to draw strength from the dark glow of his eyes.

"I thought we could be mere friends, a brother and sister in Christ," he said, "but that can never be. I cannot go on in this agony. I have received orders to leave for Pannonia in a few weeks, to function as Senior Tribune of the 13th Legion. I will go far away where I can't see you anymore."

Her eyes were filled with love for him. She reached up timidly and touched his chin, and her fingers traced the outline of his cheek.

"I couldn't have expected you to wait all these years for me," he blundered on. "Perhaps there is someone else. You could have married a thousand men better than me . . ." His voice choked off. He couldn't face life without her. Not now. Not ever again.

"It has always been you, *caro mio*," she whispered. "There could never be anyone else."

His arms tightened around her.

God's "set time" had come at last. Out of that long night of sorrow, when hope seemed at an end, the rugged cross too difficult to bear, the Lord reached down and made a new beginning.

After his second arrest, Brother Paul was imprisoned in the lower chamber of the Mamertine, chained to the wall like a savage beast, while he awaited his appeal. To reach him, the brethren had to shinny down a rope from the cell above, through the round aperture in the floor. The tomb-like dungeon had been carved from solid rock some six hundred years before. It was nineteen feet long, ten feet wide, and only six-and-one-half feet high.

It would be difficult to imagine any more appalling conditions: the filth of centuries, the bitter cold, the overcrowding, the pitch darkness, the fetid atmosphere, the company of dangerous criminals. The only oxygen entered through the small hole that led to the upper cell. Yet I heard them singing psalms as I scrambled down the long rope the next Lord's Day afternoon, their voices ringing out in the close, damp air, for Brother Paul had led many of the prisoners to Christ.

I lit a torch, while Pudens held the rope for Linus, and Eubulus, who slid down behind us, carrying packs of food, ink and writing materials, a small oil lamp, and a *barguenio*, a sturdy wooden book box with a lap desk. The dungeon's one luxury was a crystal-clear underground spring that bubbled miraculously through it.

"We bribed the guards so that you can be released for a time each day to bathe in the spring," Linus said to Brother Paul, "and to exercise your aching limbs."

"Thank you very much. That will be so refreshing," he replied. "I thank God every day for you young folks who have been such a great encouragement during these trying times. I had to send dear Timothy back to Asia to help combat false teachings. Grievous wolves have crept in among them, not sparing the flock. Many of the Christians in Asia have had difficulty making a clean break with the intellectual philosophies of men, and old pagan and Jewish dogmas."

"I'm afraid we have also brought bad news, for we learned that all court cases have been suspended until next year," Linus said apologetically. "It appears that you will have to spend another bone-chilling winter down here."

I shivered, thinking of Brother Paul's creaky old joints. But he accepted the news calmly and patiently. "You know how I long to go Home to be with Christ, which is far better," he said. "But I have a few more important letters to write, to the young preacher Titus in Crete; and also to dear Timothy, which is what Luke and I have been working on this week."

"Be sure to send our greetings to my Brother Timothy, and from all the brethren in Rome," Pudens said.

Brother Paul beamed. "Yes, I surely will do that."

The Apostle Paul was probably beheaded by Nero in 67 A.D. Within a year, as General Galba's troops were advancing on Rome, Nero learned he himself was to be executed in the "ancient style" for his crimes against humanity. Seeing escape was impossible, he stabbed himself in the throat. As he lay dying, his eyes glazed over and protruded from their sockets, in a ghastly expression that terrified all witnesses.

Then followed a struggle for power among four emperors; Flavius Vespasian emerged the victor, and ruled for nine years. Though he persecuted Jews and taxed them heavily, he seems not to have oppressed Christians. He dismissed corrupt officials, and appointed honest and sober trustees to bring the Empire back from the brink of financial ruin. His son Titus reigned from 79 A.D. to 81 A.D., and after his early death, his younger brother Domitian assumed the throne. Vespasian's nephew Flavius Clemens and his young wife Domitilla became Christians, and apparently used their fine home near the Coliseum as a house-church, school, and boys' college.

Part III

The Second Day

". . . and ye shall have tribluation ten days"
Revelation 2:10

Chapter 17

A.D. 93

Pomponia Graecina Lucina reached for another spinach-and-cheese pastry. "These are delicious, Claudia," she said. "I must have your recipe."

My dear husband Pudens helped himself to a generous portion of pepper-roasted duck with peach sauce. "We've struggled to keep the government operating efficiently," he said. "Everyone hoped for peace after we pushed back the barbaric Chatti and Dacians who threatened Rome's peaceful subjects in Pannonia."

"In the early years of his reign, Domitian ruled wisely, and established humane reforms," Manlius said. "But ever since the rebellion of Saturninus three years ago, some savage paranoia has possessed his mind. He has formed the irrational belief that there are everywhere conspiracies against his life and throne."

"He recently had the walls and colonnades in his new palace faced with glittering plates of phengite stone," Pudens added, "and keeps them polished until they shine like mirrors, to allow him to watch for an assassin who may be creeping up behind him."

"And he favors informers," Manlius went on, "those boot-licking flatterers whom his father always despised. They listen in on private conversations, which are often misconstrued. Nor are they above trumping up false charges. Innocent men have been executed, often due to nothing more than jealousy and malice."

Pudens speared the last stalk of broccoli from a serving platter as it went by. "It's Domitian's pattern to lavish favors on those whom he is about to murder. Afterward, the victim's estate is confiscated, and the informer receives a substantial portion of the property as a reward."*

"When Domitian was younger, he used to spend hours every day in his chambers, tormenting houseflies to death by stabbing pins into them," Manlius said. "Once when I asked if someone was in there with Caesar, Vibius replied, 'No, not even a fly.' It was a joke then, but now he tortures his human victims with physical and mental cruelty."†

I grimaced, irritated that the menfolk would discuss such dreary topics during our *agape* feast. I waved my hand back and forth to shoo away several houseflies that hovered above the colorful fruits, vegetables and meat dishes that overspread the table.

---

* Suetonius
† Cassius Dio

Buzzing fiendishly about, they now and then zoomed down to dine with us, nervously wringing their little hair-feet. At that moment, the thought of murdering houseflies seemed like a splendid idea.

Like many of his ancestors, Pudens had become a Consul two years before, along with Trajan, who had also distinguished himself in the Dacian wars. The Consulship was always held for one year. The Consuls presided in the Senate, became commander-in-chief in case of war, represented the Senate in treaties, and received foreign dignitaries. Pudens was allowed to appoint an alternate that year to perform pagan religious functions when necessary. This year Pudens and Manlius were serving as members of Domitian's cabinet.*

I smiled at our two sons, Acilius Glabrio Novatus and Timotheus, who sauntered into the room, and I fixed plates for them. Glancing from underneath fringes of long eyelashes, a group of adolescent girls sighed and giggled as the two walked by, the one golden-haired, the other darkly handsome. But seemingly oblivious to the many pairs of staring eyes, they perched on the edge of their father's banquet couch, stretching their long legs out in front of them, and joined in the grisly conversation.

"If you look in Domitian's eyes, there is something that is not in the eyes of normal people," Pudens said.

Novatus spoke up. "It is said that the world is filled with Domitian's images, plated with silver and

---

* Juvenal

275

gold. And he rewards those fawning, sniveling toads who fall down and worship him, calling him 'My lord, the god'."

Timotheus shuddered. "He has put up so many statues of himself, some prankster wrote on the newest one *Arci* (it is enough)."

Novatus smirked. "I hope it wasn't you who did it!"

"The Praetorian Guards claim they will always be loyal to Domitian because of the huge pay raise he gave them. He knows that with the military behind him, he can do whatever he likes."

"Wicked men will always place financial gain ahead of Truth," Patrobas said. "Seeking their own ease and prosperity, they would sell their very souls for filthy lucre. 'The love of money is the root of all evil.'"

Manlius nodded. "Where your treasures are, there will your heart be also. 'But what shall it profit a man, if he shall gain the whole world and lose his own soul?'"

"We must pray, brethren, that we might continue to live quiet and peaceable lives," Patrobas said.

I gazed fondly at our teenaged daughters, Potentiana and Prassede, surrounded as usual by hordes of neighborhood youngsters, as they paused to wipe the small hands and sticky faces. Having devoured their food, the children gathered in a corner of the atrium, while Potentiana read them a story about Jonah and the whale. Prassede and her friends in the youth group pulled out parchments, quills and ink, and sat at a table to copy Scripture portions.

A rainbow glistened outside the window, and shining rivulets that followed the recent rain chased each other down the panes. Every leaf and blade of grass sparkled, awash with yellow sunlight, and a chameleon scuttled along the windowsill, proudly exhibiting its puffed-up crimson throat. At that moment it was difficult to comprehend that a strange horror had settled over our city.

I stood in the dark recesses of the arched entranceway and peered anxiously through the intricate ironwork grille. Thunder clapped behind me, as masses of threatening clouds raced across the sky, blotting out the stars. The blustering November winds pulled down frigid air, and rattled the branches of the trees. Loose shutters clattered on rusty hinges, and trash and debris swirled along the vacant street. I twisted my golden wedding band until it pained my knuckle, and pressed my forehead against the cold iron bars.

Wandering back into the warmth of the inner chambers, the heavy door slammed behind me, caught by the wind. "The men should have been home by now," I said, while closing shutters and drapes against the cold.

Priscilla, Mum, and the four children dawdled over a late supper of gruel-thin polenta, the only sustenance our nervous stomachs would bear. We sat huddled together until long into the night, crying to God in prayer, haunted by anxiety, and questions that had no answers.

After many fearful hours, Mum's age-mottled hands, now cramped with arthritis, smoothed my icy brow. "You must try to sleep, dear. Tomorrow is a school day."

I rested on my bed as the deeper night drew on. But sleep wouldn't come, only images of an evil Emperor who, due to his own cruelty, had become suspicious of all mankind. I pressed my face into my husband's pillow, where the faint scent of the sandalwood liniment that the barber always splashed on his cheeks still lingered. Despair crept into my soul. But in my weakened state, when it was impossible to think clearly, the Saviour drew near, and comforted me with one odd Scripture verse from the book of Exodus, that went round and round inside my head:

"The Lord caused the sea to go back . . . all that night."

Pudens and Manlius were among a group of senators who had been "invited" to a banquet hosted by Domitian. In frightened silence they were herded by heavily armed Praetorian Guards, along an airless subterranean passageway into a cave-like vault draped entirely in black.

The low-roofed chamber was dark, except for the eerie blood-red glow from the two small iron lamps hanging on wall hooks, the kind of oil-filled lamps normally found in mausoleums. Bare stone banquet couches, painted black, rested on a lava-rock floor. At the head of every banquet couch stood a slab shaped like a tombstone, with each guest's name inscribed.

A group of servant boys, dressed all in black, brought food of the type that was generally offered to the ghosts of the pagan dead: dark boiled cabbage, eel, leeks, and brown speckled pike, served on plates of costly jet-stone. While the guests trifled with their meal, the servant boys entertained them with a ghoulish "dance of the dead." Then they came and sat at each guest's feet, to represent familiar spirits. Their eyes peered starkly white from behind black-painted faces.

After an agonizingly long pause, Domitian entered the room, draped in a black toga. He closed the door behind him, and the flickering light glinted on the weapon in his hand. His face, no longer handsome, wore a haunted, feverish expression, as if he was a bull about to charge. Pudens sensed Domitian's rage and fury as he paced about the table.

"You won't kill me!" Domitian ranted. His bloodshot eyes glowed like lanterns, and darted nervously about. "I'll kill you all first."

The senators sat stunned, mesmerized by his maniacal gaze. Pudens caught a shallow breath, anticipating the sharp point of a sword thrusting through his body at any moment. He prayed silently, committing his soul into the hands of the Lord.

Domitian perched on an ebony throne, the lantern light casting eerie shadows over his face as he read aloud for hours, poems and stories related to death and slaughter.*

The night lifted, and the pale morning dawned, a few uncertain rays of sunlight poking through the mantle of gray clouds. A rooster crowed somewhere, and the fruit vendor underneath my window shouted loudly, advertising his wares.

The neighborhood children would be arriving for classes soon. I dragged my face to the wash basin, and flung open the shutters for a bit of fresh air. Mournful breezes sighed among the dripping trees that stood like phantom shapes, while sparrows kept up a timid chirping. The blue-tiled fountain overflowed in streams, and the dirty brown puddles threw back a grim reflection. Broken branches and palm fronds littered the ground.

Running down the stairway, I heard the front door open and close, and there was a rush of footsteps. Manlius and Pudens had been carried home in a litter. They limped into the house, faces white and drawn. Priscilla and I rushed into their arms, and we collapsed on our knees in a prayer of thanksgiving. But scarcely had they arrived home and be-

---

*Cassius Dio

gun to catch their breath, when messengers from the palace clamored at the door. The elderly Patrobas' hand trembled as he unbolted the latch.

Imperial slaves filed in, carrying two tombstones from the banquet, crafted of solid silver, with the name Acilius Glabrio inscribed upon them. Other slaves brought various dishes made of the black jet-stone that had been used to serve the food. A note from the Emperor was attached, which read:

> I dreamed that my beloved patron goddess Minerva came forth
> from her hallowed shrine, and informed me that she could no
> longer protect my life. The lot of emperors is most unhappy, for
> when they discovered a conspiracy against their life, no one believed
> them unless they were already dead! Now you know how it feels to, like
> myself, expect to die at any moment, the blade twisting in your throats.

Daffodils bloomed, and the cold, rainy winter weather broke. The bizarre incident was nearly forgotten as Priscilla, my daughters and I rushed to complete our school activities before the spring holiday, and anticipated a week relaxing in the *campagnia*.

But a thunderous pounding of the brass knocker on the front door shattered our sleep in the murky hours of the morning, bringing Pudens quickly to his feet. A detachment of Praetorian Guards filled the entranceway.

"Our Lord the god Domitian has summoned you and your father to his palace at Lake Albano," the sergeant-at-arms declared. "You must rise and leave at once!"

Priscilla and I hastily packed a few belongings, while the men helped our newly-hired wagon-driver harness a team of horses to the *raeda*, the swift four-wheeled carriage of Gallic design. We joined the crush of vehicles that rumbled through Rome's streets. The dark hulking mass of the new Coliseum, that evil scourge of mankind, loomed sinister in the waning moonlight. I clutched Pudens' arm. Behind us, Priscilla huddled next to Manlius, still handsome in his official robes, though now past eighty years of age.

"For Domitian's cabinet to be summoned thus hastily usually means that a crisis has broken out somewhere in the Empire, perhaps among the Chatti or Dacians," Manlius said grimly.

Pudens sighed. "There will never be peace in this poor world until our Lord Jesus returns to reign. What a glorious day that will be!"

The newly-hired wagon-driver stirred in his seat, and glanced quickly over his shoulder, a curious expression on his face. But I put it out of my mind as drops of water spattered down my neck when the *raeda* passed underneath the Porta Capena, the so-called "dripping arch," for the water that sprinkled like rain from an overhanging aqueduct. It stretched its massive spines some forty miles across the flower-strewn plain, toward the mountain springs.

Domitian's magnificent three-storied palace, surrounded by a thousand evergreens, and a private game park full of exotic wild animals, was even larger than Nero's Golden House had been. It floated in a maze of terraced gardens and porticoes, connected by winding promenades. The *raeda* swept along an avenue of oaks and chestnut, whose luxurious foliage shaded us from the noonday sun. Marble fauns and wood nymphs danced in the green shadows, emerging from wisps of delicate ferns.

Haughty black swans glided on the surface of a long, narrow reflecting pool, between pink lotus and blue water hyacinths. Fat tropical fish, striped with red and black, flitted among exotic plants and coral shells. A marble octopus, its creeping tentacles spattered with gold flecks, thrashed about on the pool's mosaic floor. Beyond the reflecting pool were elaborate quarters for the Praetorian Guards.

We arrived early, at the same time as the elderly Vibius and the portly old gentleman, Montanus. Priscilla and I relaxed in a nearby gazebo, and watched while the other senators disembarked. The dreadful Crispinus alighted from his gilded sedan chair, borne by slaves. His black hair was artfully styled in oiled curls that rimmed his forehead, and he was draped as usual, in soft Tyrian purple-dyed robes, fringed with gold. He sported a bright earring and layers of gold chains and jewels hung about his neck, that glittered and trembled at every step. Even from where we sat, I could smell the clouds of exotic perfume that surrounded him.

"He will attract every bee and wasp within miles," Priscilla murmured.

I giggled, wrinkling my nose. "And flies, too. Pudens said that, as Domitian's favorite, Crispinus has been appointed Praetorian Prefect."

Senator Viento, a well-known informer, followed in the company of the blind Catullus, who, with his malicious tale-bearing, had won many favors from Domitian. Pegasus Proculus, the Praefect of Rome, and Rubrius Gallus, who had been one of Vespasian's generals, arrived with the other senators, their faces grave. All were noblemen of lofty rank, government officials who had served under all the Flavian emperors.

Domitian had not specified the reason for calling his Council together so hastily. It was the most trivial of crises that disturbed the mad Emperor that day. For Crispinus had purchased a rare six-pound red mullet, but no vessel could be found in all the palace large enough to cook it in! The senators looked from one to another, not quite comprehending.

The gourmand Montanus, his wide face blank, scratched his bald head. "It must not be stuffed into a dish too small," he said lamely.

"Nor should it be cut up into stew!" Pegasus Proculus insisted.

"Perhaps a copper laundry vat could be used," Rubrius Gallus said.

"No, a dish must be created especially for it," Montanus affirmed.

Pudens glanced at Domitian, curious to know if he had indulged in cannabis, or absinthe perhaps, but he seemed to be quite sober, his eyes clear. The lesson the Emperor hoped to instill in these respected statesmen was that he could exert supreme power over his subjects, even on the most trivial of whims. Rome was his estate, he was its master, and even high-born noblemen were nothing more than humble slaves in his all-powerful hands.*

When the "conference" was dismissed, we followed the servants who carried our few belongings up the semi-circular stairs, between gleaming white pillars, and the pair of enormous marble lions whose stony eyes guarded the entrance porch.

The balcony in our suite of private rooms overlooked the shimmering Lake Albano, and Domitian's gardens, where swollen green buds were bursting forth into colors of springtime. Beyond, frozen snow-patches lay at the summit of Monte Cava, which towered above a belt of trees into the clear azure sky.

Red silk draperies, fringed with gold, curtained the elaborate teakwood bed that stood upon a platform at one end of the large room. Twin brass side tables with delicately curved legs and eagle-claw feet

---

* Juvenal

supported tops of high-polished pink-veined marble. A garish fresco on the wall depicting Hercules clad in a lion skin, battling the many-headed Hydra, was painted in red ochre, blue, purple, greens and yellows, heavily accented with gold leaf.

I glanced at the wall, then jumped up, terrified. "A human eyeball is staring at us through a hole in the eye of Hercules!"

Muffled footsteps echoed through the hallway as I threw open the door. No one was in sight, but the unmistakeable odor of cloying perfume lingered in the air.

That evening we reclined at the Emperor's table for a magnificent sixteen-course banquet, on couches inlaid with ivory and precious gems, upholstered with soft cushions thickly stuffed with goose down. Domitian's haughty servants were attired in splendid livery of white Chinese silk brocade, ornamented with gold trim and sparkling glass beads. *A bit overdone*, I thought.

I stood with Pudens and Priscilla on the balcony in our suites for a few minutes before retiring. Pale moonbeams shimmered across the lake, drifting like silver rain over the statues of Venus and Neptune and Minerva that rested on a soft black mat of rotted leaves. The forests and gardens teemed with flitting shadows, and the occasional glitter of steel.

"There seems to be an unusual number of Praetorian Guards about today," Priscilla mused.

"I fear we have unwittingly allowed ourselves to become the prisoners of a madman," Pudens muttered, drumming his fingers nervously on the marble balustrade.

Masses of wisteria vines, those gorgeous purple-flowered parasites, trailed down the latticework into the terraced gardens below; and gleamed pale among the boughs of the trees, while they slowly strangled the dark green foliage.

A platoon of hard-faced Praetorian Guards burst into our chambers just as we were finishing a sumptious breakfast. "Our lord the god Domitian has decreed that the senators must perform some entertainment for the children at Juvenalia!" The Centurion declared.

The guards herded us into the amphitheater which was of fabulous size, partially carved out of the mountainside, and had been lavishly decorated to resemble a fantasy world. Many wealthy Romans were visiting their lakeside villas during the spring holiday. A multitude of people, including many children, had turned out for the "games," arrayed in festive costume, in anticipation of a grand spectacle. Manlius, Priscilla and I were forced into the "best" seats in the closely packed arena, near the Imperial box. But my beloved husband was taken away.

"Every year during the Ides of March, at his villa in Albano, Domitian celebrates the festival of Minerva, whom he worships with superstitious veneration," Manlius said.

"These festivities include Juvenalia, that crass holiday inaugurated by Nero, in which adults attempt undignified feats designed to provide amusement for the children," Priscilla said.

Trumpets blasted, and an orchestra began to play. Offerings were made to Minerva, goddess of wisdom, that demonic creature who symbolized human intellectualism—that a man's own thoughts and opinions were his gods. Domitian, clad in a purple toga and a gold mural crown, was carried in on an ivory sedan chair along with his haughty-eyed wife, the Empress Domitia, who was adorned like a painted doll, her hair arranged in elaborate tiers of curls. Her slender white fingers caressed the string of heavy pearls that encircled her pale neck. A thunderous cry went up from the throng:

"Long live our lord the god and his lady!"

A twisted smile spread across Domitian's face, and he raised his hand for the entertainment to begin. The circus paraded in, with elephants wearing outlandish costumes, performing monkeys, prancing horses and dancing dogs.

The blind Catullus, attired as a clown, was forced to perform a juggling act with clubs and balls. A roar of laughter rang from the foolish crowd, as the blind man was hit more than once in the head by the descending clubs. The aged Montanus had been stuffed into a jester's costume, which was much too small for his heavy frame, leaving little room for his large round belly. He was forced to sing and dance and attempt to do cartwheels, all of which was met with much hilarity.

"Isn't it obnoxious, teaching children to disrespect their elders in this way," I said.

The crowd went wild when Pegasus Proculus performed splendid riding tricks on horseback. Then servants who had been posted in the upper tiers showered the audience with gold coins and sweets wrapped in red paper and ribbons, to be scrambled for while the scenery was being changed. Mock glittering trees and rocks and green shrubbery in large pots were brought in and arranged to create a "jungle," with bright-plumed birds with clipped wings perched in the trees. A buzz of excitement echoed through the audience as a tropical paradise burst forth.

Then, amid a blast of military music, my fifty-five-year-old husband was led into the arena, wearing a scarlet cape. I gasped when the slaves swept the cape from his shoulders, for he was dressed as a gladiator, wearing little armor except for a few leather strips and some light mail. His only weapon was a short sword. Priscilla and I clung together, as an unearthly roar erupted from the den where the hungry wild beasts were confined. Now it became clear why we had been given the best seats, where Domitian could watch our stricken faces, for he loved to toy with his victims.

"I feel like one of the houseflies he tormented to death," I whispered. "He knows that as Christians, we're not afraid to die. But it is to be our peculiar torture to sit as front-row spectators while our beloved one is mauled to his death."

Manlius, his voice husky, led us quietly in prayer as the iron grating creaked open, and an enormous lion emerged, his coat of shining yellow gold.* He sniffed the air, and a deep ferocious growl escaped from his gaping jaws. The awful noise tore at my heart. Lashing his great long tail, and tossing his bristled mane, he fixed his tawny eyes on Pudens. The evil beast crouched low, and I covered my mouth to stifle a scream as it sprang toward him.

Pudens had received years of military training, but that was long in the past. He was, however, possessed with the agility of a much younger man. He darted quickly to the side in the sort of active military motion that had been drilled into him. The lion turned about in surprise, then stood and uttered a roar that echoed about the farthest reaches of the amphitheater. Women and children trembled at the sound. The lion charged with astonishing speed, and swiped his claws across Pudens' arm.

The spectators were looking for an effective hit. They howled with appreciation when Pudens dealt the creature a sharp blow. But the short sword struck a bone and glanced off. The weapon fell to the sand, out of his reach. The wound only made the lion more agitated.

Pudens jumped behind the artificial trees, and the beast followed close upon him. In a series of nimble maneuvers, Pudens was able to leap out

---

*Suetonius

and retrieve his sword. Both of them now dripping blood, the lion jumped atop a rock, and gazed down through narrow, slitted eyes. Again it sprang toward Pudens, but this time his aim was true; the sword pierced the brute's heart. Dark blood gurgled from the jagged wound and from the yawning mouth. The spectators leapt to their feet, throwing their hands into the air, as a deafening cheer thundered about the arena.

"Bravo, Acilius!"

"Long live Acilius!"

But the Emperor Domitian rose, his round face a purple cloud. This was not the ending he had planned. He signaled to the arena slaves to open another grate. Out bounded two fierce Numidian bears, one of those rare species rendered almost extinct by the bloody Roman games.

The hungry bears were driven mad by the scent of freshly spilled blood. Pudens, his foot braced against the lion's carcass, jerked his sword free, then retreated into the "jungle" to plot his strategy, and waited for them to find him. The bears' noses searched the air, and catching his scent, they padded after him, stalking him through the foliage.

Pudens thought to apprehend the larger and more aggressive of the two bears first. The monster reared up on its great hind legs, hair bristling, and uttered a low, menacing growl; then hurtled toward him. Pudens drove his sword into the chest of the headlong-rushing bear, but the brute refused to die. The smaller one then made his attack, but Pudens sidestepped him. The larger one, maddened by the pain of his wound, his snarling mouth open, caught Pudens from behind, and scraped his claws down his back, exposing strips of raw, tattered flesh.

Cringing from the torment, Pudens shook off the injured brute, and with thrusting sword, fell upon the smaller one in a riot of dust and fur and blood. Both bears finally toppled to the earth, stretched out in death.* The audience screamed and clapped, but Domitian exploded with fury, his prominent eyes bursting from his head. Pudens limped off through a gate. The crowd begged him to return, but he ignored them.

He stood without wincing, as the medics threw salted water on his wounds. I waited by the doorway until they finally set him free. Groaning, he collapsed into my arms, his face gray and twisted. The crimson stripes on his back spurted blood at every step. I led him back to our gilded prison suite, while Priscilla begged the medics for some bandage rolls and aloe ointment to bind up his wounds, for the filthy bites and scratches of wild beasts would quickly fester.

I held him close all afternoon, as he lay awkwardly on his side, each movement agony. I gave him sips of willow tea for the pain, until he calmed himself.

"I was so afraid . . . I thought you would die," I whispered, kissing his cheek and his soft hair.

---

* Juvenal

"Domitian meant to kill me, Rufina," he said in anguish. "Yet I don't even know why. If Domitian had sent me out to fight with a man, I should have been already dead. For I could not murder in such a cold-hearted way. It pained me enough killing those poor beasts for no good reason."

Manlius and Priscilla entered the room, their faces grave. "We have just received word from Rome. The Praetorian Guards have orders to round up Christians all over the city," Manlius said quietly. "Domitian's cousin Flavius Clemens has been arrested, and also his wife Domitilla. This has caused a tremendous political scandal, since after Domitian's young son died, he named their children, Vespasian and Domitian, as crown princes, heirs to his throne."

"Domitian has become convinced that the Christians are conspiring to bring one of Jesus' relatives from Judea, to murder him and steal his kingdom.* There was an old prophecy made by a sybil about eighty years ago," Priscilla explained, "that 'One should arise from the East, who would someday take over the Empire.'"

"And who among us has not spoken longingly of the Lord's return," Manlius said. "One of Domitian's informers, it seems, has a vivid imagination."

"We have worked so hard all these years, and dreamed of improving the laws and the government," Pudens said. "Is all our work to be for nothing?"

---

* Eusebius

"Their pagan hearts may not yet be ready to accept such changes, *mi amor*," I said. "Brother Timothy once said that changed lives would flow from changed hearts."

Manlius turned toward the window, his hands clasped behind him. "I fear that politics has failed to deliver what we had hoped it would," he said.

"Our kingdom is not of this world," Priscilla said. "We must remember we are only pilgrims and strangers passing through. 'We look for a city which has no foundations, whose builder and maker is God.'"

We were allowed to go free that day, since Pudens had become a folk hero among many of Rome's citizens. But it soon became apparent, from the stealthy footsteps, and furtive figures lurking in the shadows of the street, that we were being kept under constant surveillance.

Chapter 18

"The Days of Thy Mourning . . ."
—Isaiah 60:20

A.D. 94

An evening breeze rustled through the courtyard as we stood talking with some of the brethren after a midweek Bible study. Acilia and her husband Linus had recently returned on furlough from Britain and were visiting in our house-church, bursting with news of the missionary work. Acilia held a small portrait an artist had painted of Bran's family, his beautiful Jewish Christian wife Anna, and a roomful of dark-haired children.

"Bran's oldest girl is named Eurgain, and this one is Claudia Glwadus. The younger boys are Apelles, Daffyd (David), and Cynan. This is Caradoc, Bran's oldest son, the crown prince, who is named for your father, of course. And Bran's first grandchildren, little

Cyllin and the darlingest baby boy, Llin,* named after my Linus!"

At that moment we jumped back, startled as a detachment of Praetorian soldiers burst through the front door and swarmed through the house brandishing swords, a demonic gleam in their eyes. One of them, an enormous bull of a man, sent the elderly freedman Patrobas sprawling to the ground, and held the point of a spear against his neck.

"What can your God, Christus, do for you now, old man?" the brute asked, laughing.

"He can allow me to pray for you," Patrobas replied with quiet dignity.

I shrieked when the soldier thrust his spear through the kindly old saint's neck, leaving a frightful gash. I knelt by his side and clasped his head in my arms. When I looked down, a river of dark-red, sticky blood was dripping between my fingers.

"My Lord Jesus . . ." Patrobas murmured. His countenance shone with an amazing luster, as though in response to some celestial being that I could not see, and sweet, harmonious melodies I could not hear.

Others were falling now, amid the clink of steel weapons slashing and mutilating, women's screams and the cries of children piercing the night air. Rough hands clenched my throat, and a soldier struck my head again and again and spat at me. I shrank back as the side of my face went numb, and rivulets of gore and slime trickled down my swollen cheek.

---

*Llyfr Baglan

Then they were grasping my hair, dragging me half-dazed across the floor. They chained me with Pudens to a pillar, and forced us to watch in agony, powerless to intervene, while our beloved brethren were massacred in a horrifying bloodbath.

While most of the twenty-three victims were men whom the soldiers believed to be leaders of the "conspiracy" against the Emperor, the eighty-three-year-old Pomponia Graecina was butchered when she dared to rail on the centurion.

"You will never get away with this! Many here are Roman citizens, entitled to a fair trial!" she exclaimed, wagging her finger back and forth. Her quavering voice was horribly cut short.

A soldier lunged toward Linus.

"No!" Acilia screamed.

She reached out her arm in a vain attempt to shield her husband. The sword pierced Linus' body, and he doubled over, clutching at his midsection. He took a step or two, then pitched forward, sprawling face-down in the rose garden. His life gushed out in a crimson pool. Linus and Acilia locked in a final embrace, her hand a bloody stump. An anguished cry tore from my throat.

It all happened so quickly, and with so much violence. Surely it was all some ghastly nightmare. But dark stains dripped down the walls, spattered the broken furniture, and crawled across the marble floor. Bloody footprints tracked everywhere, and splintered wood and crockery were strewn about the place. The tears that flooded my eyes made everything a blur. For the dear martyrs, sudden death meant sudden Glory, but my heart cried out in sorrow for the bereaved families whose loved ones would not be returning home with them that night.

The centurion grabbed my daughter Prassede by her long golden hair, and twisting it around his wrist, he forced her to her knees like a dog, to clean up the hideous bloodstains with a sponge.* With shouts and curses and peals of fiendish laughter, the soldiers lunged at Pudens, pinning his arms behind him, and slammed him repeatedly against the cold floor of the atrium with their heavy hobnailed boots. They kicked him in the stomach, and stomped on his face and head until his lip was split, and his cheeks were bruised and lacerated. He lay limply on the floor, blood oozing from his mouth and nose.

"See how handsome you are now, war hero!" the centurion smirked.

Pudens and I were shoved into the street and thrown in the back of a rough wagon. At the point of a sword, the soldiers forced everyone else out of the house and sealed the entranceway. They nailed an edict across the front door that read: "Property of the Emperor Flavius Domitian."

The last thing I heard was our daughters crying out, "Mama, Papa!" Their anguished voices rang in my ears.

The soldiers kicked us down the stone steps of the Mamertine prison. Our ankles were clamped in

---

*St. Ado

shackles, with heavy chains that bound us to the rings imbedded in the wall. I felt sick in body and spirit as the iron grate jolted into place behind us. It had been years since I'd been inside the place, but the terrible stench and the thick darkness were not easily forgotten. Groping blindly, I could just reach Pudens, and felt the warm sticky blood that still poured from his nose. I held his battered head and tilted it backward, in an attempt to stop the flow.

"Does it hurt much, *mi amor*?" I asked.

"Our Lord was beaten, too," he murmured. "It is an honor to suffer for His Name." Our voices echoed off the dank stone walls of the dungeon. "We must find it in our hearts to forgive Domitian, for every soul must be subject to the higher powers."

Tears scalded my eyes. "Would that God had taken us Home with the others. I was sure we would awaken in His presence."

Pudens reached up to touch my face, and his injured fingers brushed my tears away in the darkness. "Our work on earth is perhaps not yet finished, *carissima*," he said. "The Lord will lead us safely Home in His own time. Now He asks us to be strong, and to trust Him for whatever is to come. In the Apostle John's book, Jesus said. 'Peace I leave with you, *my* peace I give unto you; not as the world giveth, give I unto you. Let not your heart be troubled, neither let it be afraid.'"

Finally brought to trial, Pudens and I entered Domitian's grand vaulted audience chamber. The Emperor sat on a prominent semi-circular throne high above the throng of spectators, to be perceived as some god-like personage.

"Attending trials is a favorite occupation of the Roman people, who have a voracious appetite for scandal," Pudens muttered.

Among the curious onlookers were a number of pagan priests, Chaldean astrologers, shorn followers of Isis, and representatives from the shrine and image-makers guild, whose craft had suffered greatly due to the growth of the Christian faith. Before the throne stood a white marble image of Jupiter, that demon who was called the "greatest and the best," at whose altar the witnesses must be sworn in. Pudens and I refused to take the oath to Jupiter, which in these troubled times was in itself enough to convict us.

One woman in the audience sniffed. "It is said that Acilius Glabrio Pudens fought with wild beasts in the arena."

"Hardly a fitting pursuit for a senator, if I may say so!" her companion said. "In my opinion, a gladiator is the lowest form of man."

Surely this can't be real. I stared down at the chains that bound my wrists together. My fingers had grown purple and swollen from lack of circulation.

Right and left, on a lower level, sat the jury boxes, and in front of Domitian's seat was the bench for the prisoner and plaintiff. The jury filed in, and each laid his hand on the altar of Jupiter, and swore to render a "fair and just verdict."

Domitian had assembled a motley band of witnesses, including our newly hired wagon driver. Each in turn was called to the stand, examined by Domitian, and cross-examined by Pudens, who had chosen to represent himself as his own advocate.

"Manlius Acilius Glabrio Pudens, you are charged with conspiracy and high treason, which is a capital offense!" Domitian thundered. A heavy frown distorted his features. "How do you plead?"

"Not guilty, my lord."

"You must address me as your Lord *and God*!"

"I can address you as my lord the Emperor, but not as my God," Pudens answered him boldly. "The God whom I worship is He who created the heavens and laid the foundations of the earth. 'He that formed the mountains, and declareth unto man what is his thought . . . and treadeth upon the high places of the earth, the Lord, the God of hosts, is His Name.'"

"Don't you know that I have power to avenge these insults by having you put to the sword!" Domitian ranted, a rising fury in his voice. "You openly practice that subversive doctrine of Christianity, which sect has been forbidden by the government."

"I had no intention of insulting you," Pudens replied. "I merely declared what is written in God's Word. On the day that I met the Lord Jesus Christ, my eyes were opened, and I turned from darkness into His marvelous Light. We do not fear death, sir, for He has given us victory over death. We long to be with Him, to look upon the face of the One who loves us, and to live in His bright Home forever!"

Domitian's face turned livid with rage. In that Roman courtroom there was no patience with a religion that promised Love and Light. For "men loved darkness rather than light, because their deeds were evil."

"It pains me that I once considered you to be a friend," Domitian said. His voice broke. "I will have you stretched upon the rack, until you agree to sacrifice to the god Jupiter and to the goddess Minerva, and to divulge the names of all those who share in your conspiracy against my life."

"There was never a conspiracy against you, for our Scriptures tell us that we must submit to the powers that be, and to pray for our Emperor, for he is ordained by God," Pudens said. "And I will never sacrifice to gods of wood and stone, such as you worship. Your 'Jupiter' exceeds all men in murders and incestuous crimes, which you readily acknowledge. Yet you worship him as god, conferring upon him honor above all others."

Pudens lips set in a firm line. He went on. "But one day you will know that 'As I live,' saith the Lord God Jehovah, 'every knee shall bow to me, and every tongue shall confess. Neither is there salvation in any other: for there is none other Name under heaven, given among men, whereby we must be saved.' There is a true and living God, who will punish all those who sacrifice to devils. Do with me as you will."

"Blasphemer! I have heard enough. Enough! I will have you stretched upon the rack. Surely then you will offer incense!"

The crier called out, "Both spoken!"

The soldiers seized Pudens and suspended him between the wooden posts. His body wrenched upward as the leather strips tore into his wrists and ankles, and every muscle and tendon was pulled taut. He winced, and I saw the agony that crossed his eyes. But far from yielding to the Emperor, he sang a psalm:

> Though I walk through the valley of the shadow of death, I will fear
> no evil: for Thou art with me; Thy rod and Thy staff they comfort me . . .
> surely goodness and mercy shall follow me all the days of my life: and
> I will dwell in the House of the Lord forever.

"Sacrifice, and rescue yourself from these torments!" Domitian shouted. "Obey my orders, or you shall repent it."

"I will neither sacrifice, nor will I repent it!"

"Have compassion on yourself, and sacrifice."

"Nay, for I cannot do what my Lord Jesus Christ forbids me," Pudens replied.

I quivered, nearly losing by balance, as his head jerked backwards, making further speech impossible. Only his lips moved.

The jury was sequestered in a small adjoining room, and after a very short time, they returned to the courtroom.

"Gentlemen of the jury, have you reached a verdict?" Domitian asked.

They lifted their slates. Each had written a verdict of "C" for *Condemno*.

"Then I shall have to pronounce sentence," Domitian said.

When the soldiers cut his leather bindings, Pudens collapsed in front of me with a thud, all his limbs twisted at an odd angle. A bucket of cold water was thrown over him to hasten his revival. But he made no move at all, nor any sound.

Domitian fastened his dark brooding eyes on me. "You may choose execution or exile."

"We choose exile, my lord," I replied absently.

"You realize that, given a choice, most people prefer death. You will be stripped of Roman citizenship, and your estates will be given to the Treasury. Where shall we send you then? The rock quarries, the death pits of Crimea? The lead mines of Sardinia are also a popular destination this time of year. Or perhaps Britain, where the cold is eternal, and the snow never melts."

"Please, sir," I said dully. "My family was forced to swear an oath to the Emperor Claudius many years ago that we would never return to Britain."

Domitian's eyes narrowed, and his brow furrowed underneath his balding head. He showed his teeth in a crafty smile. "Surely then, you have no co-conspirators in faraway Britain plotting my early death. Then that is exactly where you *must* go! And I know the very place. I shall send you to my father's old friend King Cogidumnus, who helped him during the invasion of Britain. Cogidumnus and your blue-painted father Caractacus were always sworn enemies—what a nice ironic touch—Caractacus' daughter shall be his slave! And I think I shall throw in your dear old mother as well."

I looked up and met the hard, cruel glint of his eyes. "Please, my lord, my mother is not well . . . the arthritis . . ."

"You should have thought of that before you plotted against my life!" He snapped. "King Cogidumnus will be so pleased with me. He helped my father rise to fame in his early years, you know. In gratitude, my father built him a magnificent palace during the time when he was Emperor, the very finest palace north of Italy. You shall become tenant farmers on his vast estates, and quarry rocks from his great slag-heaps, which are being used to build Britain's new roads."

I turned my attention to my battered husband, who was beginning to stir, and feared he would never recover from his dreadful wounds. He moaned softly, and struggled to raise himself. Priscilla pushed forward to aid him, but the guards cast her roughly aside.

Domitian chortled on. "Only a great divinity such as myself could have devised such a scheme. I am becoming as wise as my beloved goddess Minerva. Everyone says the Flavians spring from humble origins. So you high and mighty Acilians will know how it feels to be cold and hungry, to live out your miserable days scratching in the earth with naked hands, and like me, to feel the constant threat of an assassin's blade in your back. If you attempt to escape from captivity, I shall leave orders for Cogidumnus to release his great black demon hounds to hunt you down and tear you into small pieces."

Chapter 19

"A light that shines in a dark place . . ."
—Peter 1:19

April, A.D. 95

A tear catches in the throat of every Briton returning home after a long absence, when the chalk cliffs of Duvrae loom into sight. They gleamed silver-white, stretching out in the afternoon sun, their steep-sided images reflected in the crystal waters of the Channel. The high-flying gulls that nested in the cracks and crevices ventured forth and screamed out a raucous welcome. Now a fifty-four-year-old matron surrounded by heavily armed guards, I met myself as the frightened child who had sailed these waters so many years before. Calamities roared about us, despised exiles from Rome, bound in service to a man who had been my father's bitterest enemy.

"We never thought to see our native land again," I said, clinging white-knuckled to the wooden rail as the waves swelled, and the *corbita* took a sudden dip. "We always dreamed of spreading the Gospel in Britain, but who would've thought we'd come home this way?"

Mum's gnarled fingers closed around mine. "'We are strangers, sojourners; our days on earth are as a shadow.' But the Lord is always with us, carrying us in His mighty arms. Even in the darkest trials He gives us His own peace, a peace which the world can neither give nor take away."

A cold Channel breeze drifted from the west, and I was grateful for the warm woolen cloaks our daughters Potentiana and Prassede had fashioned for us. They had sewn hundreds of small gold *aurii* between the thick linings, as travelers often did. And they had persuaded the soldiers to let them salvage a few of our belongings from our former house on the Via Urbana.

"I miss the children terribly, but thank God that dear Sergia Paula and her husband Cornelius Severus offered to watch out for them, and for Manlius and Priscilla, too, since they no longer have a home," I said, my teeth chattering. "The boys will be able to finish their education."

Acilia and Pudens came to stand beside us at the rail as the *corbita* glided into port. Pudens walked stiffly, leaning heavily on a cane, his weakened limbs still suffering from the cruel tortures on the rack. By now his fingers moved easily, and he could flex many of the joints. A long scar covered Acilia's cheek, and a horrid red slash ran down the length of her arm. Several of her fingers were missing.

She smiled. "Linus would be so happy to know that I was able to return to Britain, to carry on the work among the Silure children." At Duvrae, she would be boarding another ship bound for Caerwent.

"Yes. Bran wrote in his last letter that Ilid is headmaster of a fine grammar school and *collegio* with almost a thousand students."* I said. "Sure they are constantly in need of teachers."

Mum sighed. "How I long to see Bran!"

Tears filled my eyes as I clasped Acilia's one good hand. "If only we could go with you. Give our best to dear Bran and Anna, and all the children. They must never be allowed to visit us though, lest the massacre at our house-church in Rome should be repeated. As much as our hearts ache to see him, I could never live with the thought that he and his beautiful family had been slaughtered on our account."

Duvrae's busy harbor teemed with galleys, huge-bellied corbitas, dinghies and schooners moored beside weather-beaten quays that jutted far out to sea. Crooked stone cottages and brightly painted Roman townhouses sprawled along the narrow streets of the village, which was nestled in a green valley sheltered between two bluffs. The formidable gray battlements of the Roman fortress crowned the upper cliff, and a newly constructed polygonal lighthouse, a smoky beacon of fire and stone and reflecting plates, welcomed ships into the harbor.

---

*Achau St. Prydain

When morning dawned, we dragged our few pitiful belongings, well packed in sturdy crates, up the gangplank into a Channel packet for the journey along the coast to Chichester. The vessel plowed through the leaden waters like some enormous sea-monster, gliding past brown-and-white-speckled rocks and cliffs. Endless white-crested breakers crashed against the pebbled beaches, leaving snowy foam and dull patches of seaweed.

Clouds gathered darkly, racing across the wide gray sky, and I shivered in the thickening vapor. The schooner sailed into port just as a thin, persistent rain was beginning to fall. There was a scramble to claim letters, months-old news and gossip from Rome and Gaul, amphorae of oil and wine, and other supplies.

The village of Chichester, girdled with high stone walls, stood on the low-lying plains between the wooded South Downs and the sea. Like hundreds of other towns in the Empire, its streets were laid out in the typical foursquare Roman grid plan, sliced into neat quarters by north, south, east and west streets. The streets intersected at the public forum, where the main marketplace stood. There were gleaming white pagan temples dedicated to Apollo, Jupiter, Claudius and Vespasian, and a fine public bath. Just outside the gates stood a small amphitheater.

The soldiers in the garrison were civil enough, aware that Pudens was an ex-Consul. But it was clear that all the troops were fiercely loyal to Domitian, and to the memory of Vespasian and Titus, both of whom had once served in Britain.

The following day a rough military wagon carried us the short jaunt west to the palace of "King" Cogidumnus. The salt-laden air was in places overpowered by the scent of apple and cherry orchards thickly hung with snowy blossoms, and tangled bands of sweet-smelling pines. Glimpses of Cogidumnus' green-tinged limestone palace could be seen for some distance through the fringe of trees. It resembled a Greek temple, surrounded on all sides by broad colonnades supported with massive columns. A well-manicured lawn sloped gently down toward a tidal channel.

The guards led us through the palatial entrance hall, where a great central nave supported by six columns soared upward more than twenty feet to support the roof. Statues perched on pedestals within the alcoves along its sides, and bright frescoes decorated the walls. Beyond the entrance hall, we stepped into an elegant formal garden that bloomed pink and white with ornamental trees.

"This is quite amazing. I have never seen anything so magnificent in Britain," Mum said. She stopped to admire the bright beds of crocuses and narcissus. Rose bushes bursting with tightly closed green buds lined both sides of the stone walkway, the rows of trellises, and the latticed walls of the summerhouse.

"Yes. Vespasian made certain King Cogidumnus was well rewarded for his treachery," I replied with a twisted smile.

Across a long reflecting pool stood an enormous statue of Domitian. Behind it, a flight of steps led up to a porch supported by four massive columns. We entered an audience chamber, or throne room, not unlike the one Domitian had built for himself in Rome. The floors were formed from black and white marble, arranged in a geometric design; the vaulted ceiling painted in colors of blue, purple and red.*

Though he fancied himself the King of Britain, Tiberius Claudius Nero Cogidumnus actually ruled only the tribe of the Atrebates. He was a pudgy, unsmiling man with ample layers of chin, protruding ears, and thick, petulant lips. Over his toga he wore a long coat, richly embroidered. He sat high above his subjects behind a polished semi-circular bench, on a throne overlaid with beaten gold, studded with emeralds and bands of ivory. The cold gray eyes peering down showed little mercy.

"How nice to see you again," King Cogidumnus said to Mum in a mocking voice. "It's been a long time."

The King's pudgy, well-manicured hands, bejeweled with fancy rings, shuffled the pile of parchments our guards handed to him. Then he clapped his palms smartly to summon the slaves that were to show us to our assigned quarters.

A sign at the back of the palace read "*cave canum*" (beware of the dog). It was an understatement. I shuddered as we passed by a horde of frenzied black

---

*Barry Cunliffe, archeologist, "Fishbourne Palace"

hounds that bared their teeth and snarled, lunging forward from their chains, saliva stringing from their gaping mouths.

Across the fields, a long row of hardwood trees darkened the ridge of the Downs. Turning out from the main road, the wagon floundered on a deeply rutted mud track, badly churned up by horses and the recent spring rains. We forded a shallow stream that meandered between soft grassy banks in its lazy descent to the sea.

A great despondency settled over me as our party approached a drunken-looking mud hut, not quite vertical, that seemed uninhabitable for human beings. Its rotting wooden door hung limply from the rusted iron hinges that had once held it. Climbing down from the wagon, we fought our way through the yard strewn with rubbish and an overgrowth of straggling winter-brown weeds, brambles, and dead clumps of thistles that tore at our skin and clothing.

The powerful reek of damp earth and mildew assaulted me as I pushed open the front door of the squalid cottage. Its rough walls were stained darkly gray from smoke and water damage. Shreds of tattered sacking stirred in the breeze, the only covering for the two vacant, shutterless holes that served as windows. Millions of dust-specks rose in the air, making me sneeze.

"A whole family died here few years back," one of Cogidumnus' slaves informed us. "Place is haunted. We'll be leavin' now."

"It looks like something dead, all right," I muttered, swiping at the cobwebs that tickled my face.

The "kitchen" was nothing more than a blackened pot hanging on a wall peg over an old cast-off cupboard, and a bucket for drawing water from the stream. Shards of broken amphorae and other useless trash were piled in heaps on the bare earth floor. Ragged blankets lay in a corner, atop two sparsely-stuffed mattresses.

Tired, cold and hungry, I could no longer swallow the tears welling up inside. "We can't live like this. Look at these filthy mattresses. There is scarcely a sprig of straw left in them."

Pudens folded me in his arms, and buried his cheek in my hair. "Please don't cry, *carissima*," he said. "I can't bear to see you cry."

"Our Lord had no place to lay his head," Mum said. "We must look beyond this sad world, to our beautiful Home above."

She pulled out a tinderbox, and with twisted hands, lit a bit of charcoal in her small, battered brazier. It soon glowed red. She brewed a pot of chamomile tea, and served it in her good Arezzo-ware cups that had somehow survived the journey from Rome.

"Have some tea, dear," she said. "Things will look ever so much better in the morning."

Pudens wandered about the place, making lists. "There is little here that can't be repaired," he said. "We have some money hidden, and tomorrow we will go into town for lumber and tools, hinges and paint, while we buy seed for the spring planting.

Thatched roofs can be patched, and I can build sturdy bed-boxes, and buy wool and ticking for mattresses."

Night fell, bringing with it a cold bleak wind that swept upward from the sea, blasting through the hundreds of cracks in the walls. I looked out through the doorway, across the stubbled field, and behind the branches of the oak tree at the edge of the property, and saw strange and silent shapes creeping about in the moonlight.

"We are being constantly watched by Cogidumnus' guards," I said with a shudder, listening to the baying of hounds.

Lying that night in the dark, my nerves quivering, I tried to ignore the musty smell of the mattress, and the way the straw poked through its thin covering. The others slept peacefully, but I couldn't make myself comfortable, listening to the rustling of mice and bats, and an owl that hooted on the roof. Whenever my eyes closed, it seemed I stood face to face with Cogidumnus' black demon hounds and their fiery red eyes.

Pudens stirred in his sleep, and his arm fell across my huddled form. Another problem disturbed my thoughts, for during the voyage, I had noticed several small hard nodules growing underneath my arm. They seemed to be getting larger. Perhaps they could be tumors. I determined not to tell Pudens until it was absolutely necessary, for there was no need to worry him. But perhaps the tumors weren't serious— one could only wait and see.

Morning dawned with a cold, damp fog that chilled a body through to the bone. Groaning, I reached around to rub the stiffness out of my back. Mum had risen early to prepare bowls of steaming polenta, a fresh pot of blackberry tea, and applesauce made from dried apples.

"You must be suffering so with the arthritis," I said.

She only smiled, stubbornly refusing to admit to pain.

Pudens rummaged about in the yard till he found a few sticks of firewood to take the morning chill out of the hut while we ate our breakfast. Tendrils of smoke from the central fire-pit fouled the whole room before drifting through the smoke hole cut in the roof, and through dozens of other holes in the ragged thatch, which had been eaten away by the salt winds. Several disgruntled bats escaped from the rafters, flying off in search of more congenial quarters.

With strong determination we set to work scrubbing and cleaning. We uprooted thorn-bushes, weeds and rubbish, and stacked them in a pile for burning. Dead leaves, bracken, straw, ashes and other suitable materials were gathered in a trench to start a compost heap, as recommended in Pudens' old farming guide-book written by the author Columella.

After the midday meal, Pudens and I set out on the long walk into town. Banks of flowering rhododendron, ablaze with color, stood among the darker trees that shaded the roadway. Fat, crinkled sheep with their bleating spring lambs seemed to grow out of every grassy meadow, between rows of ancient drystone fences.

Chichester's main street was flanked on both sides with timber and masonry buildings and small shops with tiled roofs. A crowd of shoppers strolled leisurely, market baskets in hand, underneath a long colonnade that overhung the three-foot-wide flagstone sidewalks. A colorful mosaic pavement covered the floor of the main bazaar, where stalls and pushcarts bloomed with life, beneath a massive portico. A town crier circulated through the marketplace shouting out the news of the day.

But suspicious, hostile eyes peered at us from every doorway. Women turned away from us as if in fright, pulling their cloaks tightly about them, and snatched their children out of our path. Someone spat on the sidewalk at our feet, and handfuls of pebbles and rotting fruit were thrown in our direction.

"Oh!" I cried out, and buried my face against Pudens' arm as we pushed past groups of surly spectators who laughed harshly, or shook their fists in a threatening manner.

"Remember, they spat at Jesus, too, and mocked Him," Pudens murmured as we ducked around a corner.

"Knowing Rome's passion for scandal and sensationalism, I should have realized that our 'reputation' would have preceded us," I said. My downcast eyes studied every cobblestone forming the pavement. "The news of the arrival of an ex-Consul accused of plotting against the Emperor, and his wife, the daughter of Caractacus, and even Caractacus' elderly wife, would cause no small stir and public outrage in this quiet village."

Pudens' arm came around my shoulder protectively. "And when Domitian gave a substantial pay raise to military personnel a few years ago, it not only increased the standard of living for the soldiers, but for the merchants in the towns that surround each fortress as well."

"So. Even the barbarians have become obsessed with financial gain," I said, "caught up in the never-ending quest for the almighty *denarius*!"

An unflattering quill and ink poster was displayed prominently beside the entrance to the bookshop, portraying a senator who carried some paltry household items, followed by his red-haired wife, her tall frame grossly exaggerated. Then there was the white-haired crippled mother hobbling along behind, with predictably, a blue-painted face. The picture was part of an elaborate advertisement for a poem about a beggar and his redheaded wife evicted from their home, from a recently published book written by the lewd poet in Rome.

"Do you think he wrote that cruel poem about us?" I asked. "It wouldn't be the first time he slandered you and our family."

Pudens' squeezed my hand. "I don't think he meant to write it about us," he said. "Though the shop has apparently interpreted it that way. Anyway, we agreed to forgive him years ago. We must pray for him."

"I can't abide the way he loved to recount every detail of the old sins of your youth, bandying them about in his poems, as if you were a hypocrite, still living in sin. He also tried to tarnish Linus' reputation, and even Cornelius Severus, and anyone else who asked him to clean up his filthy words that corrupt the minds of Roman youth."

Pudens sighed. "He never did understand that when I became a Christian, I no longer cared to 'run with him to the same excess of riot.' I suppose it cut him deeply that I was no longer his friend. But he did have some nice things to say about you."

I grimaced at the very thought. "And he still claims we owe him money for those unsolicited pagan poems. I just worry that posterity will remember you as he portrayed you, not as the dear man of God that you are."

"It matters little, *carissima*. The Lord is coming soon to take His people Home. How many more years of posterity could there be?"

At exorbitant cost, Pudens rented mules and wagon from the livery, and we loaded lumber and supplies in the back. The old mules plodded slowly along, heads bent down with melancholy, as we drove out of town. A heavy thunk startled me, as a rotten apple exploded against our wheel, hurled from an open doorway.

"My fancy notions about evangelizing in Britain are going to be more difficult than anyone could imagine," I said.

"Our responsibility is to shine for our Lord Jesus," Pudens replied, "and to show our neighbors Christian love, even when they've made it clear that they hate us. Brother Paul and others were often persecuted, but they kept on even when things seemed hopeless."

I was actually happy to see the derelict hut when we arrived home. Mum was kneeling by the doorway, transplanting wild violets, cheerful buttercups, forget-me-nots and bluebells from other parts of the property. On her head she wore a funny wide-brimmed hat she had woven from reeds.

"The garden is beautiful!" I exclaimed. "Even the Quintilii brothers couldn't have done as well. But you shouldn't have worked so hard."

Mum smiled as, with knotted hands, she patted the earth down firmly to protect the tender roots. "I find it helps my fingers to keep them limber."

Mum and I set out a hearty meal of flat barley bread, "baked" on a cast-iron plate over the little brazier, bowls of lentil soup, and thick slices of cheese bought at the market. After supper, by the light of a quivering candle stub, Pudens read verses from the Scriptures and prayed, thanking God for our little cottage, while a frigid wind whipped about the eaves with an eerie moaning.

At the end of the week we surveyed our handiwork. "Perhaps we can survive here," I said, brandishing a stiff boar-bristle brush in my work-reddened hands. I had furiously slapped whitewash on the walls inside and out, and painted the trim and the furniture and the new shutters a brilliant cobalt blue.

Mum chuckled. "That is truly a loud color!"

I shrugged. "Well, they were selling it cheap."

"It will cheer us up, anyway, on gray days."

As she unpacked one of the crates, I began to laugh hysterically, as she held up a beautiful, thickly woven rug in shades of red, white, blue, tan and brown, that the lepers' wives had presented to us as we were leaving Rome.

"Wouldn't the lepers be shocked to know that we don't even have a floor!" I exclaimed.

Mum wandered down to the stream, where she gathered up long green rushes to spread over the dirt floor of the cottage, and laid the bright rug on top. When the packing crates were emptied, Pudens nailed boards across them, to fashion rustic benches. Other leftover boards were made into a trestle table. I sanded them smooth, and painted them all blue.

"In the words of Nero, when he completed his 'Golden House,'" I said, "'now we can begin to live like human beings!'"

Brush still in hand, I glanced toward the open doorway. The dreadful "King of Britain" himself rode down for a visit in his fine gilded carriage pulled by prancing white horses.

"Our lord and god Domitian didn't tell me you had brought money with you!" He said, a smile finally breaking through his coarse-pored skin. "Since you have made so many wonderful improvements about the place, I shall have to raise the rent a good deal. Or if you want to buy it outright, I will throw in that mule and plow your neighbor rented from me, and used in his field yesterday. I happen to have a deed for the property right here."

Pudens studied the contracts carefully, and counted out the necessary gold *aurii*.

"Mind you, this is just for the house," Cogidumnus said. "I will still expect the rent from the lands, come harvest time. I'm sure Caractacus would be pleased to know that his wife and daughter had at last established a foothold in Britain, though he himself was roundly defeated."

The next morning at breakfast Pudens said, "We must begin the spring planting, since we have already fallen behind schedule."

I smeared zinc oxide on my cheeks and borrowed Mum's wide-brimmed reed hat. Pudens was no stranger to farm work, having helped on his father's estates since childhood, but it would place a tremendous strain on his broken body. The iron-shod plow was an ancient contraption from the last century, not designed to plow even furrows, but to tear the ground open. The tight-yoked mule groaned beneath the plowshare, and often foundered in the dirt. Pudens, growing more frustrated by the minute, yelled loudly at the dull-witted creature.

"What is wrong with him? This has got to be the stupidest mule I have ever seen," he exclaimed. "I don't understand it, since he seemed to be doing fine when the neighbor was using him."

"Perhaps he is one of Domitian's friends, too," I said glumly. Taking the reins from him, I called out to the beast, then began to giggle. "This is a British mule! He doesn't understand Latin commands. The only solution is to teach him Latin, or to teach you Brithonic. And I should think it would be easier for you to learn."

It was slow and tedious work. The field had not been worked in years. The iron blade of the plow had to be cleaned from time to time with a scraper. I followed with a hoe, staggering over the uneven, rock-littered ground, breaking up the heavy clods, and pulling out the old dead weeds. We picked up piles of stones, hauling them off in twig baskets, and brought soil to fill the bare spots. Birds swooped down around us, pecking at the worms and grubs.

Twilight crept slowly across the Downs as we trudged homeward, our hands raw and bleeding, our hair and clothes bespattered with mud. Knife-like pains shot through every bone and muscle. A wonderful aroma of beef stew and dumplings wafted through the air as we neared the cabin. And I knew Mum would have water heating for a bath.

Pudens pulled me close, and scattered kisses across my forehead. *"Bellissima.* You are still as pretty as you were the first day I asked you to marry me." He grinned. "As I recall, you were up to your ears in dirt then, too."

After the spring planting, the "King's" wagon stopped up on the highway. The sound of a ram's horn and the jangle of harness echoed across the fields. Guards beat on the door of our cottage.

"The King commands you to join in the labor detail," one of the brutes said, while he fastened iron chains around Pudens' ankles. "You will be working in the great slag-heaps a few miles to the north, cutting stone for the new highway that will link Chichester with Londonium to the northeast."*

They whisked him away before I could even kiss him good-bye. *Dear Lord, give him strength, and keep him in safety!* I watched from the doorway, choking back the tears, as the wagon slowly made its way into the hills, not knowing if he would ever return. Quarry slaves were given very poor food, if anything at all, and were beaten by the cruel guards if they fell behind in their daily quota of rock-cutting. Rock falls and accidents were commonplace. At night they slept on the bare ground, without shelter or even a blanket to warm them. It was a slow, painful death.

The work in the fields became my responsibility, but Mum and I had some extra hours in the afternoons. We visited the various tenants' cottages, inviting the children to attend the free school we planned to start. But everywhere we were met with sullen stares and words of antagonism.

"I wonder if we will ever win the confidence of these people," I said to Mum, discouraged. "You would think they would want their children to go to school. For despite the many reforms carried out

---

*Stane Street

by the former Roman governor Agricola, existing schools in this part of Britain are few, and only for those who can afford to pay."

The next afternoon, as scheduled, I placed a few benches underneath an old spreading shade tree, out in the open so that Cogidumnus' guards could see that we were only teaching the children letters. Mum set up a wooden tripod hung with colorful charts and maps, and sheets of papyrus printed with large red letters of the Latin alphabet. It was a staggering disappointment when no children showed up for class.

As the afternoon wore on, I idly traced patterns in the dirt with a stick. "It's a rather sorry beginning to our missionary venture."

"We must continue to pray fervently," Mum said, as we gathered up our supplies, "that in some way we may reach them with the glorious Gospel of Christ."

The following afternoon, two pairs of curious blue eyes peered at us from behind a hedge while we assembled our charts. When we set out the stack of new wax slates that Sergia Paula had donated, the towheaded boy and girl crept even closer.

"Probably a brother and sister, by the looks of them," I whispered.

Mum smiled. "Do you children want to learn how to read?"

"More than anything!" the boy exclaimed. He stood in front of the chart and ran his fingers over the red letters. "How I wish I could make the words talk!"

"What are your names? We will write them down in our attendance book," Mum said. She handed each of them a wax slate and stylus.

"I am Hywel," the boy replied. "And this be my sister Lyneta. We live o'er yonder." He pointed with his chin across the field, toward one of the mud cottages. "We know how to speak some Latin."

By the end of the lesson, they were able to spell out their first letters, and were printing their own names in the wax. But on Friday, Hywel and Lyneta met us underneath the shade tree when we arrived for class, their eyes red with tears. Hywel held out his precious slate and stylus.

"My Granddad told us we must give these back," he said.

"He said your father was a very bad man," Lyneta said with a trembling voice. "He killed our best cow."

Hywel's ragged tunic had slipped from his shoulder, and I stared in horror at the angry red welts that covered his back. "Granddad will whip us again if we try to come to school," he mumbled.

After supper I pulled a bench out into the garden in the fading light, and sipped a cup of blackberry tea while reading from the new book of Revelation that Bran had sent. It had recently been written by the elderly Apostle John, whom Domitian had driven into exile on the island of Patmos.

I tried not to think about Hywel, the poor lamb beaten for wanting to attend school. My gaze ranged over the river and the plain, and along the gentle ridges of the South Downs, crowned with the flaming rays of the setting sun that swirled like the rosy glow of a fire, above the fringe of trees. In a flash, an odd image boiled up in my mind, and my pulse quickened. Many years ago I had stood in a spot very similar to this one!

"Mum, what did Lyneta mean when she said Daddy killed their cow?" I asked.

Mum's face blanched. She stood in the doorway of the cottage, wiping her hands on a towel. "It was so very long ago," she said lamely. "I hoped they had forgotten. You couldn't have been more than four years old. Your father felt King Cogidumnus and the Atrebates were traitors, and ought to be punished for betraying our country into the hands of the Romans. The battle didn't amount to much, since Vespasian's army was following close behind us. But there was a fire . . . some property damage, and a few . . . casualties."*

The pains came sharply, like iron bands tightening about my chest. "Why didn't you tell me?"

She gave a helpless Gallic shrug. "I meant to, but . . . it wouldn't have changed anything. We both loved your father so much. I didn't want you to have bad thoughts of him . . . in our eyes he could do no wrong."

I slumped forward, as desolate as if the world had come suddenly to an end. "These people have good reason to hate us then. They will always hate us. Would to God we were back in Rome, where we were able to lead many souls to Christ!"

---

* Charles Kightly, "Folk Heroes of Britain." (from archeological evidence)

Mum placed a hand on my shoulder to comfort me, but her words were firm. "God's ways are not our ways. In the book of Ecclesiastes it says, 'do not inquire why the former days were better than these.' He has placed us here to serve Him in this generation, in the very spot where we live."

My eyes strayed back to the book of Revelation that lay open across my knees. A sudden shaft of brilliant sun slid from behind the trees, and slanted down the hillside, gilding these words with light:

> "Thou hast a little strength, and hast kept my word, and hast not denied my Name."

Chapter 20

"They loved not their lives unto the death . . ."
—Revelation 12:11

Monday morning I inspected the seedlings in our small kitchen plot of turnips, beans and other vegetables, while hoeing between the rows with a blast of nervous energy. I slapped at the black cloud of gnats flitting about my head. We would probably never try to have school again. Heartbroken, I prayed about the hopeless situation, giving it over to God, listening for His voice: *Show me your ways, o Lord; teach me your paths.*

I lifted my gaze across the plain, shading my eyes with one hand to sharpen visibility. There seemed to be a great deal of activity on the road that day. A parade of refugees streamed northward from Chichester like an army of ants, their household belongings strapped to their backs. They fanned out across the meadow and into the wooded Downs, setting up makeshift camps. The smoke from many cook-fires began to spiral toward the sky in lazy blue tendrils.

Hywel and Lyneta came dashing through the field. "*Athra* Claudia, *Athra* Claudia!" Hywel shouted. "'Tis the dreaded pox!"

Dropping my hoe, I followed the children up to the road. "Sailors brought the pox from Duvrae and Boulogne!" one man said. "There's sick people everywhere, alone in houses or just lying in the streets. Some have been left on the steps of the Temple of Claudius. Everyone is afraid to touch them. We must run for our lives, must flee from the poison airs."

A woman sobbed. "My child took sick, very sick, and died. The soldiers have closed the gates to the fortress, and refuse to come out. Nor will King Cogidumnus help."

"We've heard grim tales about whole villages peopled with now't but corpses," another wailed.

"We will care for the sick," I said calmly. "Tell all your friends that we will try to contain the plague within the Temple of Claudius. You must comb the forests for elderberries and honey that we will need to make medicine. Lay them beside our cottage, along with anyone who has developed a high fever or chills, or a severe headache, before they erupt in pustules. The sick must be isolated from the others at once. We will make one trip back here every day and take them to the temple."

The "King's" wagon stopped on the road, and Pudens crawled out, lowering himself painfully to the ground. My heart pounded as I ran to him, and he fell against me, leaning on my shoulder, groaning with every step. He had lost much weight, and circles of blood seeped through his filthy, ragged tunic.

"*Caro,* what have they done to you?" I whispered through my tears.

"The mine has been shut down because of the pox," he said. "One very sadistic Roman guard, Picen Rodrigo, brought the pox to us after a wild night in town. He and several slaves collapsed at the site. The guards just left them there. I promised to go back for them as soon as I can, or they will die. There is no time to lose!"

After Pudens relaxed in a warm bath and found clean clothing, we loaded Mum onto the back of the mule, and trudged into town. Long before reaching Chichester, we began finding desperate plague victims lying abandoned in the long grass by the side of the road, where they had fallen prostrate with fever, shivering, teeth chattering, some already covered with angry, itching red spots or ugly blisters filling with pus. Dimly I saw the great black buzzards circling, circling overhead.

The stone cottages in the silent village stared forlornly, as if they sensed that a terrible calamity had fallen upon their inhabitants. Pudens purchased a rickety old wagon and a load of leather tents from the army quartermaster, and distributed them to the refugees in the camps. Then he brought straw and blankets and linens, and we laid the sick side by side in rows inside the Temple of Claudius.

All afternoon and long into the evening Pudens and I searched for victims. Some stretched out feeble hands, pointing out homes where more stricken people might be found inside. Mum borrowed large cauldrons and braziers, and set to work crushing and straining elderberries, and boiling the juice down to make her special medicinal extract. Chicken broth simmered in another cauldron.

In the black hours before dawn Pudens returned from the mine with the four victims who had been left behind. "I think this is the last of them," he said.

Many thrashed about on their mats in delirium, crying and moaning, without seeming to recognize anyone. Mum was everywhere, bringing hope with her calm smile, while her gnarled hands soothed and comforted. We moved quickly through the ward, sponging the patients with cool compresses, and coaxing white willow tea between flushed lips, to relieve the pain and to bring their burning fevers down. Mum administered elderberry extract, and spoon-fed chicken soup to any of those able to eat.

"Apply honey to any of the blisters that have erupted into sores," she said. "Perhaps we can prevent them from festering, and forming dreadful scars. With good care, hopefully we can also combat the secondary illnesses such as the brain fever and pneumonia that claim the lives of many pox victims. I've made up some vinegar eye drops too, to ward off blindness."

By the time we finished with the last patient, we had to begin again at the head of the row.

Mountains of dirty linens had to be washed and boiled in a huge copper cauldron, and hung out to dry. When finally overcome with exhaustion, we catnapped in shifts.

Within the next few days several new cases trickled in from the camps, and my heart broke to see that one of them was little Lyneta and her mother, Fiona.

"Why do y' help us? Ayen't ye afraid to catch the pox?"

I stared into the frightened gray eyes of a frail, elderly woman with skin like thin sheets of parchment. Just clinging to life, she breathed with a deep heavy rasp. Mum and Pudens had nodded off to sleep in the corner, and I was left alone to care for the sick, in the dark of night.

"We do not fear death, for our Lord Jesus will carry us in His arms straight to His beautiful home in Heaven."

"I feel I am dying," she said. "It is always more difficult for the old ones. Tell me how I might find peace, as you have."

Tears welled up as I read to her the wonderful story of our Lord Jesus, God's Son, who had been crucified on a Roman cross, and rose again the third day. "We need only to believe on Him, and ask Him to forgive our sins."

"I should like to do that," she said. "Your Jesus is surely a good and kind God. I can see Him reflected in your face."

I led her as she whispered a simple prayer. Other ailing patients clamored for attention, so I was obliged to wander down the row. By the time I returned to the elderly woman, she had slipped into eternity. A smile played upon her lips, and an expression of peace reigned in the faded, sunken eyes that had turned Heavenward, forever free from suffering and pain.

"The Lord has healed marvelously. After two weeks, no new cases of pox have been reported," Mum said, going over the records. "Out of sixty-three patients we treated, only twelve have died. None have been blinded, and the grossly disfiguring scars associated with pox have been kept to a minimum."

Lyneta followed behind me, while I ladled lamb stew into red-ware bowls. She insisted on helping to carry them to those still bedridden. "How is your fever today?" I asked her, while feeling of her brow, happy to see that her pustules had cleared, except for a few small ones on her cheek.

"I am feeling much better today, *Athra* Claudia," she said. "But it is you who must rest."

There was a strange lightness in my head, and my heart was beating too fast. I became suddenly very drowsy, while watching the bubbles dance in the cauldron of stew. The ladle clattered to the floor, and Lyneta, screaming, reached out to break my fall, as my legs gave way beneath me.

For four days I was delirious with fever, aware of little, save for the cooling cloths laid upon my skin, and the lukewarm fluids forced between my lips. The red, purple, gold and blue patterns on the frescoed ceiling of the temple shimmered and danced . . . an assortment of faces floated about, talking and nodding to each other . . . voices calling out my name . . . too disoriented to understand or reply. During the fourth night, I awoke drenched with perspiration. The fever seemed to be coming down. By the light of a little oil lamp, Pudens' tall figure knelt beside me, sponging my forehead.

He lighted with joy when he saw me awake and alert. "Oh, *carissima*, I thought we had lost you," he whispered. "You have spoken to us a bit now and then, but not very coherently, I'm afraid."

"Oh no, what did I say?"

He laughed, and gave a shrug. "Does it hurt much?"

"No," I lied. "I am getting well, *caro*."

But it was only the beginning; Pudens' beautiful face faded, and lost itself in the frescoed colors of the ceiling. Later that day an itching rash developed on my arms and trunk, at first red and elevated. Soon they turned into pus-filled vesicles. For another two weeks I tossed and tumbled with a sharp pain that coursed through my body, and finally lodged itself in my chest. Then only darkness . . .

I hovered near death, coughing and choking for every breath, lungs saturated with thick bloody fluid. Mum and Pudens constructed a tent of blankets over my head, and splashed water onto heated stones, creating steam to break up the secretions in the lungs.

"You are the last patient," Mum said, delighted when I finally recovered my senses. She bowed her head. "But the bad news is that we ran out of medicine more than a week ago. That has delayed your recuperation. And there is no more honey to control your festering sores."

"How bad are the scars, Mum?"

"You must rest, and not worry," she replied.

There was a strange expression in her eyes, and she would not look directly at me. Alarmed, I reached up to touch the scaly lesions on my face. They were already beginning to fall off, and underneath were deep, pitting scars. My features were grotesquely swollen and distorted, ravaged by the disease.

I gasped. "My husband will think me so hideous."

"Nonsense!" Pudens said as he knelt and cradled my head in the crook of one arm, holding a beaker of cool water to my lips. "I see you through the eyes of love. You are more beautiful to me now than you have ever been."

Two more weeks passed, and the refugees began trickling back into the village. It was necessary to burn the Temple of Claudius to the ground, to destroy the poison airs, along with the wagon, the bed linens, and everything else that had come into contact with the pox victims. Our faithful mule was roundly scrubbed with washing soda and ash, much to his distaste. His whole face wrinkled with disapproval, and he kicked up his heels. He brayed his loudest protestations, all the way back to our little mud cottage.

Hywel and Lyneta appeared the next morning, clean and neatly dressed, while I sat in our doorway beside Mum's tall pink, orange and red hollyhocks, resting from my chores, feeling rather sorry for myself. My arms ached, for after our long absence, there was much work to be done in the neglected fields. And the rabbits had damaged our little vegetable garden while we were away. Lyneta thrust a huge bouquet of soft yellow dandelions in my hand.

"Granddad said we might come for school whenever ye're feeling well enough," Hywel said.

Lyneta reached out and touched the dreadful scars on my face. "When I grow up, I want to be just like you, *Athra* Claudia," she said. "Mummy says that when ever'body sees your scars, it reminds them that you were the onliest ones who loved us enough to take care of us, even when we had treated you so badly."

"Granddad told us that hundreds died of pox in the other villages around us," Hywel said.

"Because no one would help, and ever'body panicked," Lyneta went on.

I hugged her close. "You go and round up any of your friends who may want to learn to read, and we shall have school this very afternoon. And I should like to tell you about One named Jesus, who also has scars because of His great love for us."

Chapter 21

"Until the Day dawns . . ."
—II Peter 1:19

The rains and the sun came at the proper times to produce a fine crop, a vast wind-rippled sea of grain stretching out tall and golden. The shadows lengthened as the days grew shorter. I dreaded the harvest, and wondered how we could ever gather everything in and pay rent to the "King" who demanded three-fifths of the yield. Mum was growing frail, and although Pudens would be granted time off work in the mines at harvest time, his broken body was wracked with constant pain. I'd been feeling fatigued lately, and feared that my tumors might be spreading.

Leaning heavily on the hoe, I stared off to the west, where a great whirlwind of dust moved ever closer. A small detachment of horsemen, followed by a luxurious *carruca dormitoria* and a supply cart, bounced along the rutted track, splashed through the creek, and pulled up near the door of our cottage. A wagonload of dark-haired children scrambled out. Crying and shrieking and waving both hands wildly in the air, I sprinted toward them, stumbling over the furrows and loose clods that blocked my way, and fell into the arms of my beloved cousin Bran.

His hair still gleamed black as a raven's wing, with only a sprinkling of gray. "I know you feared for us coming, but we just couldn't stay away a day longer," he said.

"I missed you so much!"

"I have for years offered sanctuary to refugees from Judea, including those of the House of David, whom Domitian particularly suspects. My enemies have surely reported my activities to Domitian by now anyway. So what more harm could be done by coming to see you and to help with the harvest? We seek to do God's will, and do not fear the consequences, even if I should lose my head to Domitian's executioners. But come and meet my wife Anna, and the rest of the family."

He scooped up a small serious boy in his arms. "This is my oldest grandson, Cyllin," he said, "one of Caradoc's children."

The Jewish preacher Apelles Aristobulus accompanied them, still robust despite his advanced years. Mum, wreathed in smiles, quickly acquainted herself with Caradoc's baby Eurgain and her brother Llin (Linus), who held tightly to Acilia's hand. My eyes widened as the young people began unloading salted and smoked hams, slabs of bacon, joints of beef, and crates of herring and mackerel from the back of the wagon. There were bushels of fresh apples, cherries, carrots, cabbages, beans and turnips, stacks of thick blankets, and bolts of warm woolen cloth.

"The brethren from the house-churches in the west wanted to send gifts," Bran said, "including your old friend Rhiannon, her younger brother Morgan and sister Rhondda, whom you saved from the fire many years ago. Everyone has been praying much for you all."

In the morning, Caradoc and his younger brothers brought comfortable chairs, set them in the garden, and padded them with thick cushions from the *carruca dormitoria*. Bran's teenaged daughter Eurgain and her sister Claudia Glwadus placed beakers of blackberry tea in our hands.

"You all relax and visit, while we young folks look after the fields," Caradoc said. "We'll allow you to watch the babies, though."

Reaping handfuls of stalks at a time with bright sickles, they began moving quickly down the rows, bundling the golden grain into sheaves, and singing psalms to help keep the rhythm. Pudens leaned back heavily and rested his weary head against the chair, while we sipped our tea and watched the pink morning sun rising over the Downs.

"You can't know how much this means to us," he said. "And I was released from the slag quarry during the harvest season, so I shall have a fine holiday."

"How is the Gospel work progressing in the west?" I asked Bran.

"There are now several fair-sized house-churches. The neighbors call our palace Abergwaredigion, 'The House of the Saved Ones.'" He smiled. "The fact that Christians have been persecuted in Rome may have actually helped the spread of the Gospel, especially among the mountain people who are still unhappy with Roman rule, though they stopped the fighting some years ago."

"Aristobulus, whom the British call 'Arwystli Hen' (the elder) and his son have worked tirelessly among them, even as far north as the land of the Ordivices," * Anna added, "though the remnants of the Druids have often withstood him."

"The main obstacle among our people is that the old superstitions die hard. Many cannot comprehend the difference between true and false, between real history and nonsensical myths. Some even think our communion chalice has certain magical powers! God did perform a few miracles, as He sometimes does among idolatrous people, and mightily demonstrated His power over the evil spirits. But instead of giving glory to God, some believe I am the ancient god Bran, come back to life!"

"Like in the Acts of the Apostles, when Brother Paul, at Lystra, was mistaken for the god Mercury, and Barnabas for Jupiter," I mused.

---

* Haleca, bishop of Augusta; and Dorotheus, bishop of Tyre 303 A.D.

"Yes. But we're thankful that there are many sober-minded brethren who treasure the Scriptures, God's voice to us, and have 'had the eyes of their understanding opened,' and who worship our Lord in spirit and in truth."

"Praise God! And whatever happened to your sister, Branwyn?"

Bran sighed heavily, and dropped his head. "My father gave her in marriage to a pagan king. It ended badly. She is no longer with us."

At midmorning another wagon pulled up in the yard, and Novatus and Timotheus jumped down. Overwhelmed, I could hardly take it all in, as I held my beloved children in my arms. But after exchanging hugs and pleasantries and news from Rome, they went out to take their places beside their cousins in the field.

In the evening, the boys began kicking a ball around in a rowdy game of T'su Chu, and even the girls joined in, their shouts of merriment ringing out in the cool air. I cuddled baby Eurgain on my knee. Mum watched them all with dancing eyes, and giggled like a schoolgirl when Novatus got off a particularly spectacular head shot past his cousin Cynan, which went straight into the goal.

"This has been one of the happiest days of my life," Mum said, "seeing the children enjoying each others' company."

Pudens kindled a roaring campfire as darkness fell, and moonlight flooded that vast, tranquil land. Underneath a clear indigo sky, our voices rang out in psalms of praise to the Lord, echoing across the South Downs: How Bran's family could sing!

"I know Whom I have believed, and am persuaded that He is able
To keep that which I have committed unto Him against that day."

But Mum felt poorly that evening before she retired to her bed. I rose during the night, lit the little terra-cotta lamp, and went to check on her. Her blue eyes were open, but they no longer held me in her gaze. For they stared past me, through the mud walls of that humble cottage into the face of Jesus Christ. She heard Him say, "Well done, thou good and faithful servant. Enter thou into the joy of the Lord." I sat beside her bed for a long while, holding the gnarled, age-mottled hand until it grew icy and stiff. Jesus held the other hand, but it was no longer old.

In the morning Anna helped me prepare Mum's body for burial, and we wrapped her in a shroud. "We will carry her home to be buried among her own people in the west," Anna said.

How I will miss her. Tears blurred my vision. But God whispered His love in the singing of the birds, and shouted it in the cool brisk autumn winds that swirled the red and golden leaves around my feet. Bran and Pudens constructed a simple wooden coffin. A memorial service was held in the yard, and the tenant farmers and many of the townspeople from Chichester came to pay their final respects.

"She tended to the sick, without fear of death, with nary a thought to her own danger," Fiona said, weeping. "Never will I forget her calm, sweet smile that gave me hope when the pox brung me close to death. She touched the hearts of many."

"Because she loved us, who were her enemies," Picen Rodrigo, the cruel guard from the slag mine murmured. "'Twas evident at every point."

"Aye. And she taught our children to read and write and cipher," Fiona said. "King Cogidumnus likes us to be ignorant, so we will stay and scratch in his fields forever. P'raps our children can have a better life."

Apelles Aristobulus preached a thrilling sermon. "I know where my sister Eurgain is at this moment!" he said, opening the new book of the Revelation. "In that great city, the holy Jerusalem, descending out of Heaven from God . . . and God shall wipe away all tears from their eyes; and there shall be no more death, neither sorrow, nor crying or any more pain . . ."

Even Cogidumnus' guards crept close to listen to the words as he went on.

"And the light was like unto a stone most precious, even like a jasper stone, clear as crystal . . . and the street of the city was pure gold, as it were transparent glass . . . and the city had no need of the sun, neither of the moon to shine in it: for the glory of God did lighten it; and the Lamb is the light thereof . . . But you, my sinner friend, where would you be if you died today?"

That afternoon Fiona, Hywel, Lyneta and Picen Rodrigo all gave their hearts to Jesus. But as eventide descended, I glanced toward the highway, where a large gilded carriage slowed down and stopped, clearly outlined against the blood-red streaks of the sunset. A stout man alighted, accompanied by pagan priests of Apollo and Jupiter, recognizable by the tall two-horned mitre worn on their heads, and stood silently watching, watching from the highway.

I shivered that winter morning, when forced to relinquish the cozy warmth of the bed. Outside, a thick mist drifted like smoke across the low-lying plains, and the Downs were lost in a pale gray cloud. Pudens had risen early and gone out. The slave wagon no longer stopped up on the road, for the slag-heaps were iced in for the winter. The last of Mum's bright flowers, even the sturdy heartsease, were all dead, wilted with a heavy frost. How I missed Mum's cheery smile.

The leaden skies did nothing to improve my spirits. Twisting my hair into a roll, I glanced into the tiny silver mirror that hung on the wall, and pulled down on my lower eyelid. Even in the poor light, there could be no doubt. The whites of my eyes had a decidedly yellow cast. The tumors must have invaded my liver. So far I had managed to keep it from my husband, though the pain was at times unbearable. Now there could be no denying it, for Pudens would see it in my jaundiced eyes.

I took my last sip of blackberry tea, and gazed tenderly at the warmly dressed students who crowded into the doorway and took their seats for class. It had been a great joy watching their progress.

"I'm proud of all of you," I said, while passing out parchment maps of the world. "You have worked so very hard. Today we will study our maps, and write in the names of the countries and the rivers."

In the afternoon I opened the book of Luke, and passed it to Hywel. He stood up to read a story about how our Lord Jesus had healed a blind man. His voice rose and fell, and his eyes sparkled as he made each letter come alive on the page. Though he stumbled over some of the bigger words, the children listened intently.

The sparrows first warned me with their startled chirping, rising up in alarm. The clatter of horses' hooves thundering across the frozen earth drew my eyes toward the window. Pulling aside the sacking, I cracked open the shutter. Fear stabbed at my heart, for a squadron of Praetorian soldiers rode into sight. The heavy swords dangling from their scabbards gleamed brightly, making my limbs tremble with fear. *There could only be one reason why Praetorians would venture this far from Rome, especially during the winter months.*

The soldiers stopped and took one long look at a British farmer who was splitting wood at the back of the property, and stacking it in a lean-to shed. The man, his features blurred in the mist, was dressed in a heavy red woolen shirt, a knitted cap, and plaid breeches tucked inside tall boots. I had wondered about that strange Briton all morning. Pudens hadn't told me he had hired one of the farmers to split wood.

A sudden gust of wind howled, whipping the bare-limbed trees about. Ominous black clouds boiled up, rolling across the sky, and large, smothering flakes of snow began drifting down. The Praetorians, unused to heavy snowstorms in Rome, wheeled quickly around and cantered back in the direction of the King's palace. *But I know they will return.*

Hastily gathering up all our Scripture portions, the gold coins that Bran had given us, the school supplies, and some personal items, I placed them in a large sack and thrust it into Hywel's hands.

"Tell your mum to keep these safe," I said.

The strange farmer trudged through the whirling snow toward the cottage, staggering under the weight of an armload of firewood. I opened the door, letting in a rush of cold air. Suddenly the children began to twitter, for it was Pudens, the grand Roman ex-Consul, dressed in British clothing. He piled sticks of wood in the firepit, and stirred up the dull gray ashes.

"Well," he grinned, while removing his warm cap, and stamping his feet to shake off the snow. "It was getting too cold for a tunic, and did you ever try splitting wood in a toga?"

Pudens and I strolled hand-in-hand, after seeing the children home, as a night soft as velvet settled over the South Downs, the snow spreading a fine layer of white over the frozen mud and brown stubble. The skies cleared, and the full moon ascending above the horizon illuminated the empty fields with a silver sheen. The ethereal radiance was shattered only by the crunch of snow beneath our feet. The black tips of the pine thickets on the windswept hills, silhouetted against the purple sky, hung low with a feathery blanket.

"Did you see the Praetorian soldiers this afternoon?" I asked.

"I suppose we always knew they would come," Pudens sighed. His red-sleeved arm came around my shoulders, and his other hand swept the mass of stars that glittered above our heads, almost close enough to touch. "Soon perhaps, we will fly above the stars, *carissima*."

"Did you ever wonder what it would be like?" I said. "To behold the face of our Lord Jesus, and to see the look of love in His eyes?"

"We go to plead our cause before the Lord, the righteous judge, who shall preserve us unto His heavenly kingdom, to Whom be all the glory forever! I have already enjoyed more blessings in life than any man should be allowed to have. The only thing I yet lack is a martyr's crown."

"'Eye hath not seen, nor ear heard, neither have entered into the heart of man, the things which God hath prepared for them that love Him,' " I murmured.

I watched my husband sleeping peacefully that night, the rosy glow from the dying fire flickering across his face. He knew the danger of his situation, but he harbored neither a worry nor a care. His faith had grown amidst the storms, and taught him to look beyond this sad world to that rest above, armed with an unshakeable faith in the promises of God, and in the nail-scarred hands that would soon carry him safe home. I reached out to stroke his bronzed cheek, and bent to kiss the long silky eyelashes.

The last stick of wood in the fire-pit burned through, sending up a loud crackle and a shower of tiny sparks.

Epilogue

Timotheus' Story

April, A.D. 96

I'm sorry. I did everything I could for your parents," Cogidumnus, the old "King of Britain" anguished, rubbing his pudgy white hands together nervously. "But they had started their subversive activities anew, using trickery and deceit to win over the townspeople and even some of my own guards to their cause. And right here on my lands! I had no choice but to report it to our lord the god Domitian, for the safety of the Imperial family."

His pale fish-eyes darted here and there, and a network of blue veins stood out prominently on the end of his bulbous nose. He spoke Latin with a thick guttural accent, as though he had a speech impediment.

"I'm sure you know that Domitian has now repealed the orders to persecute Christians," I said.

The old man pursed his fleshy lips and pulled in his chins. "Your mother and grandmother died of natural causes. We had nothing to do with that, even though they were teaching poor children to read, which can come to nothing but ill, puffing up their heads with pompous airs, and false hopes and aspirations above their station in life."

The commandment of our Lord to "Love your enemies" had often seemed to me the most difficult rule of all to obey. I gazed upon the old King Cogidumnus' bitter, unhappy face with utmost contempt, wondering how any one man could be so ignorant. But there was no use trying to argue or protest. I signed the release papers, and Cogidumnus' servants helped me and Picen Rodrigo, who accompanied me, load the two heavy lead coffins into the back of the wagon. It was a Roman custom to bring home for burial the bodies of loved ones who died abroad.

"Domitian's men confiscated the property as well," Cogidumnus went on. "I must ask you to sign these forms too. I have, upon the advice of the priests and priestesses, commissioned our stone-cutters to erect a temple to Neptune and Minerva on the site."

I shuddered with strong revulsion. My dear mother did not live long enough to realize her dream of spreading the Gospel in Britain. That task would have to be left to others. For He who "doeth all things well" had ordered it so. His message to her was "Come up hither, thy Father hath need of thee."

"Minerva is our lord the god Domitian's favorite goddess, his beloved patroness," Cogidumnus said, "and it was Neptune by whose favor Vespasian crossed the seas to reach our shores. With the new temple built, perhaps the gods will forgive me, and forget that I allowed a Christian church to exist right here on my lands!"

Afraid of breaking down in tears, or embarking on a most un-Christianlike tirade against the old man and all his ilk, I swung the team of horses around and started down the narrow road in the direction of the tidy stone-built village of Chichester.

"The Emperor Domitian unjustly murdered several thousand innocent Romans," I said to Picen Rodrigo. "His own cousin, the mild-mannered Flavius Clemens was, like my father, killed while in exile,* though his wife Domitilla survived. Domitian seized their property and constructed government buildings and a temple of Mithras over their house-church and school near the Coliseum. Domitian converted our townhome on the Via Urbana, with its fine *balineum* and underground springs, into a public bath."

My gaze swept the green fertile landscape, shaded by an archway of cherry and apple trees in pink blossom, and the freshly plowed fields, dotted with cottages, stretching out toward the rolling Downs. I thought how my Grandfather Caractacus had fought so bravely to defend this many-colored land.

---

* Suetonius

"Cornelius Severus and Sergia Paula watched over us and also our elderly grandparents, Manlius and Priscilla," I went on. "My golden brother repaid their kindness by stealing the heart of their raven-haired daughter Cornelia, after he got lost in her beautiful violet eyes. I teased him about what a poor catch he was, since we are now penniless."

Picen grinned. "Sounds like Cornelia loves the old chap anyway."

"They married in the winter, and already have a baby on the way, whom they hope to name Manlius Acilius Glabrio Severus, if it's a boy. My brother, like many of our ancestors, has an eye to the Senate someday. I have been studying the usual courses of mathematics and science, and Cornelius Severus says I will be able to start medical school in Alexandria in the fall, Lord willing, as Grandmother Eurgain always encouraged me to do. Though some say it's not a fitting occupation for the son of a senator."

"And is it true that Domitian has stopped persecuting Christians?"

"Yes. Domitian brought two of our Lord Jesus' surviving relatives to Rome from Judea. He asked them if they were of the House of David, and how much money and property they controlled. They told him that they possessed only the small plot of ground on which they paid taxes, and lived on by their own labor. They showed him their rough work-worn hands, and their hard-muscled arms accustomed to heavy fieldwork."

"Simple farmers. Sure no threat to his throne or his empire!"

"Domitian asked them questions concerning Christ and His kingdom. But they told him that it was neither of this world or earthly, but heavenly, and it would be at the end of the world, when He would come in glory to judge the living and the dead."*

A boy and girl were sitting by the side of the road, whom I recognized as some of my mother's students. The boy held out his hand for us to stop.

"My name is Hywel," he said. "Ayen't ye *Athra* Claudia's son?"

"Yes."

"We hear'd ye were in town. Me mum said for y'all to come to lunch," Hywel went on. "We have some things *Athra* Claudia gave us jest before the so'diers came. Mum said ye might be wantin' 'em back."

Hywel and Lyneta jumped into the wagon, and directed my cousins and I to their mud tenants' cottage, with its peculiar tall thatched roof. Pink puffs of rhododendrons burned brightly around the doorway. The place was clean and tidy, despite its poor situation. Scripture verses painted on sheets of parchment hung on the walls, sharing space with the rush baskets, pots, and bunches of herbs and dried flowers.

A smiling woman made her appearance, wiping rough red hands on her apron. She set out flat

---

*Eusebius

loaves of bread, thick bean soup and slices of roast beef, with beakers of blackberry leaf tea. While we ate, the family talked about the epidemic of pox. They seemed surprised that I spoke Brithonic fluently.

"We treated yer folks a might bit poorly when they first come here," the old granddad said. His white hair and craggy face bespoke a long life of hard labor. "But they saved me daughter's and me granddaughter's lives. I didn't understand nary about their new God, Jesus, for He seemed strange to me. But we all reckoned He must be a loving God. Jest want ye to know ye're welcome here anytime, young feller, and I think I speak for the whole village of Chichester as well."

"Thank you, sir," I replied. "And we very much appreciate your family taking care of my mother when she was dying. I only wish I could have got here in time . . . to say . . . good-bye."

"After the so'diers come, she took real sick," Hywel said. "But the so'diers put her out of her own house anyway. When she was a dyin', I promised her I would teach the younger children their letters and tell them about Jesus."

They showed me the maps, the gold coins, several personal items, school supplies, and some codice books she had left, including Strabo's "Geographies." There were Old Testament Scripture portions, and copies of the Gospels, letters of Paul, Peter and John, carefully translated into Latin from the Greek. My eyes blurred with tears when I recognized my mother's familiar handwriting.

"*Athra* Claudia told us about Jesus," the little girl, Lyneta said. Her small hand crept into mine. "We asked Him to come into our hearts."

"Ev'ry night me grandson reads stories to us from the Scriptures," the old man said. "Hope ye didna mind us lookin' at the books."

"No, no, of course not."

I took from the sack an old wooden sword, a small portrait of Cousin Bran and his family, and a tiny alabaster box with blue flowers on its lid, filled with red rose petals. I handed the other items back to them.

"My mother meant for you to keep these," I said. "The gold coins are, of course, payment for your months of care while she was sick. And the Scriptures are God's Word to us. Treasure them well, for they show the way to Eternal Life."

"My favorite story is about baby Jesus in the manger," Lyneta said.

"I like to read how the Lord Jesus died on the cross and rose again," Hywel added.

"Please teach us more about Him," Fiona said.

Five pairs of eyes stared at me expectantly. I gazed at the little company gathered around the table, at the golden-haired brother and sister, and thought how my mother must surely have resembled them as a child. It had been my great privilege to be raised in a Christian home, and I knew many of the Scriptures by memory. Yet had I sometimes taken them for granted? My parents had gone on to Glory. Now it was my turn to stand for Christ. I took a deep breath, and opened the Book of John.

As I read, the elderly granddad fell to his knees on the dirt floor, his weathered cheeks wet with tears. "I want to accept Jesus Christ," he said simply. "If only I could find peace in my heart! Could He forgive a wicked old sinner like me?"

"John 3:16 says, 'God so loved the world, that He gave His only begotten Son, that whosoever believeth in Him should not perish, but have everlasting life,'" I said.

The man looked Heavenward and clasped his hands in front of him. "Lord Jesus, I didna' know before that it was *my* wretched sins Ye was a' dyin' for, and it was me Y' came to save. I believe it now, and trust Ye as my Saviour!"

Picen Rodrigo and I knelt beside him to pray. My heart thrilled with the joy of the angels as one more sinner was brought to repentence! And at that moment I knew that, Lord willing, I would return again someday to Britain.

The Emperor Domitian was assassinated later that year, in a plot initiated by his wife Domitia, after she learned she was to be his next victim. The kindly old Nerva was proclaimed Emperor, and he restored the property and lands to the bereaved families of Domitian's martyrs. Trajan, who had shared the Consulship with

Acilius Glabrio in the year 91, succeeded Nerva as Emperor in A.D. 98.

Claudia and Pudens' four children lived well into the next century, and continued to use their family fortune to do the work of the Lord, "supporting many of the Christians with alms."* Timotheus is believed to have preached the Gospel in Britain, and possibly in Gaul. He may have been martyred in Rome during the reign of Marcus Aurelius, when he was more than 90 years old.

After leading many souls to Christ, Apelles Aristobulus was probably martyred in Montgomeryshire, on the Severn.† After the death of Bran "the Blessed," his son Caradoc assumed the throne of Siluria (South Wales). Caradoc's son Cyllin later became king. "Many of the Welsh were converted to Christ through the teaching of the saints, and many godly men from Greece and Rome preached in Britain. Cyllin was baptized by his cousin Timotheus." Cyllin produced no son, but his daughter Claudia Glwadus married her cousin, Llin's son Lucius Mawr.†† Their kingdom of Siluria was the first in the world to proclaim itself Christian, before the close of the second century. Dumnonia (Devon, Cornwall and west Somerset) soon followed. The Christians "continued in peace and tranquillity until the persecution of the Emperor Diocletian in 303 A.D."§

---

* St. Ado

† Achau St. Prydain

†† From family records of Justin ap Gwrgant, Prince of Glamorgan.

§ Venerable Bede